Shedding
Light on
Murder

Patricia Driscoll

Shedding Light on Murder

Formatting: Hale Author Services

This book is for Nick Klimenko, my incredible husband, who has supported me every step of this adventure.

L.U.M.T.A.

Author's Note

I've had a love affair with all things Cape Cod since I was a child. It was a pleasure to set my novel in charming and historic Barnstable Village. I've endeavored to be true to the village, but out of literary necessity, I've made a few changes to the landscape of the town.

If Pearl's lamp shop seems familiar to locals, that's because I have been inspired by Barfield's in Yarmouthport. My mother, Fran Driscoll, worked there for twenty-seven years and loved every minute of it.

Chapter One

GRACE TOLLIVER INSERTED her key in the lock and with a little push, the door gave, a bell jingled and she stepped into a small hallway. She reached up and tugged on a faded red ribbon. The bell came loose at once and she shoved it into the pocket of her leather jacket.

Kicking off her boots, she stepped into a pair of black clogs, hung her coat in a closet and ran upstairs to her shop, Pearl's Antique Lamps and Shades. Ducking into her small office, she placed her purse in the bottom drawer of a battered metal filing cabinet, reached behind a ruby tinted shade and fumbled for the thermostat. Last night's storm dumped almost twenty inches of snow on Cape Cod, and temperatures were in the high teens. Grace rubbed her hands together and blew on her cold fingers. At least the power was on. She hadn't been so lucky at her own house, which sat on the edge of a great marsh a short distance from the harbor, and about a half mile from the town center. Around midnight, gusty winds felled an old ice-laden maple, sending it crashing into a power line, and cutting off electricity to the aptly named Freezer Road.

As she circled around the shop, turning on lamps, she heard the door downstairs slam shut followed by thudding, slapping noises on the stairs. "Life sucks," muttered Duane Kerbey as he leaped over the top three steps and sped by her, his wet hair plastered under his wool ski cap. A blue jacket was zipped up to his chin and he carried a Dunkin Donuts bag. His tennis shoes dripped water on the wood floors as he headed for the kitchen area, mumbling something that sounded like "Gotta help mink."

Grace decided to ignore whatever it was he said, for the time being at least. Knowing Duane, his foul mood might reflect a major life crisis or simply the lack of jelly donuts at the nearby coffee shop. It was difficult to imagine her new employee worried about the mink population, but she would talk to him later, after he had a few minutes to chill out.

The phone rang. "Pearl's," she said.

"Grace, it's Danielle Whitney," a voice purred in what, Grace thought, was an appealing French accent. "I wonder if you could send someone over to pick up a lamp I want to have cleaned and rewired. Would it be a bother?"

"Of course not, Danielle. I'll send Duane right over." Matt and Milo, the former owners of Pearl's, introduced her to the attractive woman not long before they retired, when Danielle came into the shop to get a new liner for a shade.

"An excellent customer," Matt had said.

"But picky," Milo added.

"I also want you to make a new shade. I'm sure when you see the lamp and finial, you will come up with something special and unique. It's going to be a Christmas present, so I must have it back by next week. Wonderful storm, isn't it? I'm afraid my front walkway is deep in snow. The young boys who shovel it haven't come by yet."

"That's okay," Grace assured her, at the same time wondering how she was going to complete all of her special orders by Christmas, which was only two weeks away. "Duane can walk through the snow if he needs to. And we'll get that lamp ready in plenty of time for the holidays."

As she hung up the phone, Grace felt a ripple of unease. The annual Barnstable Village Stroll was Saturday. There was a stack of orders of hand-painted shades to finish. She had to figure out what kinds of refreshments she would serve and spruce up the shop for the crowds that would descend on the one-block town. This would be the first time that Grace participated in the event and she wanted everything to be perfect. More than perfect. She wanted to make a killing. After all, there were bills piling up, and the kinds of renovations she was planning would not come cheap.

"Duane, I need you to go over to Mrs. Whitney's house and pick up a lamp for repair. It's down the street. A big brick house with black shutters. Finish your coffee, then go. Okay?"

"Yup."

Duane took a few gulps of coffee, shoved half a donut in his mouth, and headed down the stairs, trailed by a cloud of powdery sugar.

Chapter Two

"MY GOODNESS! HAVE you ever seen such a gorgeous snowstorm?" Michael Shipworth said as he arrived at the shop a few minutes after Duane's departure. Holding a pair of shiny leather loafers in his hand, and dripping wet boots in his other, he squinted at Grace through wire-rimmed glasses. "And what's happened to our bell?" he asked.

"Hey Michael, I'm sorry about the bell, it's charming but annoying, clanging every time someone opens the door. I thought we'd see if we could get along without it for a while," Grace said as she crawled halfway under a table to plug in a yellow tea caddy lamp with a black toile shade. "Thanks for coming out in this snowstorm, and on a Sunday morning too. I'm feeling a bit guilty taking you away from Edith and church."

"Not to worry," he told her as he threaded his way between two long tables cluttered with old lamps of all shapes and sizes. "I went to church last night. But I am concerned about Edith. She was still in bed when I left the house and, as you know, she's getting on in years. I turned on the heating pad so she would be nice and toasty. I don't think she likes snow. She turned up her nose at her dish of Fancy Feast. I even gave her the Ocean Whitefish with Gravy but she wasn't interested."

Tiptoeing to the wood ladder-back chair in the corner, Michael, a man of elfin proportions, disappeared behind a large empire lampshade as Grace came out from under the table and brushed some dust off her jeans. Spotting him in the corner, she watched as he used his sterling silver shoehorn to push his small feet into his tasseled loafers. He was bending over in such a way that Grace had a bird's-eye view of a large bald spot, with a nest of fine mouse brown hair combed over it.

Michael patted his hair and straightened his bow tie. "My front door was frozen and there was a waist-high drift on the front porch. I was lucky to get the slider to work and get over here. I had to take several detours because there were road closures and abandoned vehicles in the way. This is a big storm for Cape Cod, and the road crews are not equipped to handle it. Missing California?" he teased. Like many people who had never lived anywhere but their hometown, Michael delighted in making fun of places he had never been to and knew little about. Anything to do with California in particular seemed to amuse him no end.

"Not really," Grace replied, walking to the bay window and looking out at the almost white-out conditions. "I enjoyed my years in San Francisco but don't forget, I grew up on the Cape. Believe it or not, I missed snow."

Michael nodded in agreement. "Oh, by the way, I saw Bella last night at church. She was rehearsing for the annual Christmas concert. It's a benefit for our daycare center and . . ."

"Wait a minute. Bella sings?" Grace asked incredulously. Bella, the shop's electrician and lamp restorer, had a voice that reminded Grace of family camping trips to Maine during moose mating season.

"Oh yes! She sings in our choir. Been there for years. Of course it's not the Mormon Tabernacle Choir or anything. But Bella is very enthusiastic."

Picking up a purple feather duster, Michael started to dust the lamps in the bay window. "Look, here comes Bella now. A little snow is not going to stop her."

Grace watched Bella Benson making her way down the middle of the roadway, the only place that had so far been plowed. She walked briskly, her head covered by a felt waterproof hat pulled low over her face. Dressed in a dark gray overcoat and black galoshes, she carried a cane but hardly used it.

"Did you know that Bella is a veteran?" Michael asked Grace.

"No kidding?"

Yes. U. S. Army Corps of Nurses. She landed with MacArthur in Korea. She has the most amazing stories."

The stairs were difficult for Bella, but she never complained. Waving her hat at them, she went directly to her work area in what Grace had come to recognize was her way of hiding the fact that she was out of breath. Giving her a minute to get settled, she waited while Bella switched on the fluorescent light above her workbench, hung her coat on an old wooden coat rack, and sat her bulky, eighty-one-year-old body down heavily on a low stool to replace her boots with a pair of worn flannel slippers. Grace thought that Bella and Julia Child might have been twins separated at birth. There was a striking resemblance.

"Coffee will be ready in a minute," Michael said.

"Thanks," Bella said, pulling a worn red sweater over her green shirtwaist dress. "I'll help myself in a minute. Just let me get organized a bit."

"Speaking of charming and annoying, I see that Duane's been here," Michael said, staring at the sticky sugar-covered floor. He shook his head. Clearly, this was not the kind of thing he had encountered during his employment at The Pilgrim House, purveyors of fine furniture since 1909. He worked at the venerable store for many years, and lost his job when it went out of business. When he stopped by Pearl's a couple of months ago to commiserate, Grace hired him on the spot. "No wonder we have a mouse problem," he grumbled as he swept up some crumbs.

Grace took the broom out of his hands. "Here, I'll sweep and you scoop," she said. "I know, Duane drives me crazy too. But, when I was a probation officer, I used to get frustrated when no one would give my probationers a job. When Sean came by from Pinewood, the halfway house, and asked me to take on a Christmas helper, I wanted to give Duane a chance. He's doing well in rehab. However, I'll admit, he's a work in progress for sure."

Michael frowned. "I haven't seen much work or progress yet, but I trust you know what you're doing."

"Let's give him a little time," Grace said, putting the broom and dustpan away. "Duane's had a tough time, and his life hasn't been easy. How much trouble can he get into in a lamp shop anyway?"

"Well, for starters ..." Michael began, as he straightened a lampshade, turning the seam so it faced the wall.

"I hope it's quiet here today." Grace interrupted him. "I can't wait to decorate this gloomy old place. Let's start by hauling the Christmas tree inside. It was delivered yesterday. It's out on the back porch. Then we can drape white lights around the windows and hang a wreath on the front door."

"Okay," Michael replied as he followed her down the hall, past the chandelier room and the fairy lamp alcove to the back door.

Grace unhooked the small bolt-style locks from the top and bottom of the glass-paned door, and with a sharp tug, pulled the door open to find the tree leaning against the side of the shop covered with layers of snow and ice.

"Uh-oh," Michael said. "I think this is going to take a bit of work. The tree is frozen to the siding. I'll go get some tools from Bella and chop it loose. It's going to take some defrosting before we can put lights on it."

Michael stepped back inside as a gust of wind blew snow across the oak floor. Grace slammed the door shut and waited impatiently as Michael went to get the tools. Now she'd have to rearrange her day. They could string up the lights but it was going to take hours for the tree to warm up. She should have realized, when she woke up this morning without electricity, that today was not going to go as planned. She took a deep breath, counted to ten and reminded herself that her blood pressure was a bit on the high side when she had it checked last month. No use getting worked up. After all, there was nothing she could do about it.

Michael returned a few minutes later followed by Bella, who was carrying a large handsaw and a hair dryer. He rolled his eyes at Grace and shrugged as Bella pushed forward saying, "I can handle this in no time."

After plugging in the dryer, Bella stepped onto the second-story porch where, planting her feet squarely against the wind, she sawed and blew-dried the tree, all the while humming a chorus of "Jingle Bells."

Michael and Grace tried to help by picking up the sawed-off branches but Bella kicked the pine scraps off the side of the porch and down the wooden steps with her slipper-shod foot.

"I'll go get some newspapers, and we can put them under the tree so it can drip dry." Michael said helpfully. "And, since Duane seems to be taking a long donut break or whatever, I'll move those delivery boxes away from the top of the stairs before someone falls and breaks their neck."

Grace checked her watch as she returned to her office. She had forgotten all about Duane and his errand. What could be keeping him? He was so darned flaky. It was just like him to take thirty minutes to run a five-minute errand, particularly when she needed him back at the shop now, unloading boxes and packaging up mail orders. Matt and Milo had said that there might be some holiday decorations up in the attic, and she wanted him to look for some old drawings and shade templates. She wasn't too keen on going up there herself. The lighting wasn't the best and there were mice or rats, or, at the very least, spiders and God knows what else up there.

Her thoughts were interrupted by the sound of the door slamming downstairs, followed by the rapid steps of someone running up the stairs, and finally by Duane bursting into the shop, a mask of sheer terror on his face.

"I think that lady you sent me to see is dead!"

Chapter Three

GRACE RACED UP the walk to Danielle's house with Duane close behind her. She brushed past a wreath that hung on the half-opened door. As she hesitated in the front hall, Duane came up behind her and pointed into the living room.

"Oh, God!" Grace gasped. She ran to the body of Danielle Whitney. Lying on her right side, her arm was crumpled beneath her.

Grace saw a deep gash in the back of Danielle's head. She reached down for Danielle's wrist. There was no pulse. She looked at Duane who was still standing in the hall.

"I've got to call 911. Do you have a cell phone?"

"Nope, the rehab doesn't let us have them."

Grace spun around. There was a phone on an end table a few feet from where Danielle lay. She grabbed a paper cocktail napkin from the coffee table and used it to pick up the receiver and place the call.

"Go out on the porch and wait for the police," she told Duane. Although she wanted to look away, Grace forced herself to look at the body, feeling that she ought to be doing something, but realizing that Danielle was beyond help. Dressed in dark gray slacks and a pearl gray cashmere sweater, her feet in expensive-looking black pumps, she appeared elegant, even in death.

A massive walnut desk in the corner appeared to have been ransacked, tea from an overturned cup staining the leather top. Papers were strewn around the floor below it. A candle with the essence of cinnamon and honey sat on a stack of books on the glass coffee table, its dying flame a speck of amber. The doors of a large mirrored armoire were open, exposing a collection of vases, linens, note cards and correspondence. On the bottom shelf a small light glowed on the CD player, Frank Sinatra was crooning "Have Yourself a Merry Little Christmas."

Grace looked down at Danielle Whitney again. A bronze candlestick lamp was resting on the carpet a few feet from her head. There was no shade, but the harp was still attached and a smear of blood was congealing on the lamp's marble base. She stayed there for a moment, not wanting to leave Danielle alone.

But, after a minute or two, feeling lightheaded, she stepped into the front hall. It wasn't enough; she knew she needed to breathe some fresh air.

On her way out the front door, she almost ran into the first of three emergency medical technicians. Dressed in bulky coats, boots, and carrying heavy equipment, they filled the doorway and towered over her.

"Hey! Slow down, lady!" one of them said. "What's the problem?"

It was now Grace's turn to point to the living room. She stepped aside as each man wiped his feet on Danielle's front door-mat before entering the house. As they surrounded Danielle's body, Grace joined Duane on the porch.

"Gosh!" Duane said. "I've never seen a dead body."

"Listen, Duane, what happened?" Grace demanded. "What took you so long to get back to the shop?"

Duane took a deep breath. "It's like this, Ms. Tolliver. I came over here like you told me to and ..."

He broke off as a uniformed officer, who appeared to be not much older than twenty, came up the stairs. His name tag identified him as Officer Gelb. "Are you the one who made the call?" he asked Grace.

"Yes, I'm Grace Tolliver and this is Duane Kerbey, my employee. We found Mrs. Whitney."

One of the emergency crew came out of the house. "We've got a body here," he said to Gelb. "Better come and take a look."

"I'll be there in a minute," Gelb said. He fumbled for his radio, and then called for backup. He stared at Grace and Duane as he gave information to the dispatcher. It was clear that he wasn't going to leave them alone until backup arrived.

Grace gripped the porch railing, feeling faint again. She took a deep breath and counted to ten for the second time this morning. "This can't be happening," she mumbled under her breath.

They waited in silence until another car pulled up and Grace saw State Police Detectives Andre Cruz and his partner Emma Rice, both of whom she recognized from her years of working at the nearby courthouse, step out and proceed up the front walkway. On Cape Cod, the State Police usually handled homicides with the local cops providing assistance. Officer Gelb hurried down the porch steps to meet them, and Rice pulled out a notebook and began taking notes. Cruz continued up the walk, his black hair blown upward by the strong wind. His eyes darted from left to right, but he seemed to Grace to be watching her at the same time. She noticed a dimple in his cheek, although he wasn't smiling.

He glanced at Grace, nodded and went into the house. Detective Rice instructed Gelb to secure the scene. "We need a thirty-foot perimeter around the entire house, and don't let anyone, even another officer, inside the tape. Call the Crime Services Unit and the M.E.," she said.

A few minutes later, Cruz came back outside. "Aren't you a probation officer?" he asked Grace.

"I was," Grace replied. "I quit a few months ago and took over Pearl's lamp shop, down the street. Over the bookstore. This is Duane Kerbey, my employee. I sent him here earlier this morning to pick up a lamp for repair from Mrs. Whitney. And he ..."

Cruz held up his hand, cutting her off. He turned to Rice and said, "Take Mr. Kerbey to the car and get a statement." Grace looked at Duane, who was now slumping his shoulders and wiping his nose with the back of his hand. Rice gestured for Duane to go down the walk. As Duane sidled toward the street, casting Grace a baleful look, he pushed his hands deep into the pockets of his jacket.

Cruz stared silently at Grace for a minute. "You were married to Jack Tolliver, weren't you? I remember you from the funeral."

"Yes," Grace said as she reached up to brush a stray lock of chestnut hair out of her face. She felt a familiar rush of emotion as she thought about Jack, a drug enforcement officer for the Barnstable Police Department, whom she met in court while waiting to testify at a probation revocation hearing. Four years after their marriage, Jack, who had gone for a swim at Craigville Beach, suffered a heart attack halfway out to the mooring he used as a turnaround point, and drowned. Cruz was silent for a long second or two, staring at her with eyes the color of dark limes. "Okay," he said, "tell me what happened this morning."

As Grace was finishing up recounting the morning's events, Detective Rice came over to Cruz. "I think we should bring Kerbey in for more questioning. He's on probation. One month left. He's got a record for narcotics and theft. Gelb can transport him for us."

Cruz handed his card to Grace. "I'll be contacting you soon. In the meantime, call me if you remember anything else."

The two detectives went into the house, leaving Grace standing alone on the porch. An officer was interviewing two young boys who were leaning on snow shovels, their cheeks rosy and their eyes bright with excitement. Grace recognized them as Jose and his older brother Rafael. The boys were a familiar sight in the neighborhood, always eager to shovel snow, rake leaves or wash windows.

It was still snowing hard and she was suddenly aware of how cold she was. Hugging herself for warmth, she hurried out to the street. There was a knot of neighbors standing around Danielle's front gate. Most of them were there long enough to accumulate a dusting of snow on their heads and shoulders. Their murmuring quieted as she walked firmly through the small group, staring straight ahead so as not to make eye contact with anyone. The last thing she wanted now was to answer a bunch of questions. All she could think of was getting back to the sanctuary of the shop and Bella and Michael.

She was just in time to see the patrol car pull away with Duane in the back seat. As he looked out of the back window at Grace, he mouthed the words, "Help me."

Chapter Four

BACK IN THE shop, breathless from having run all the way and shivering with cold, Grace threw herself down on a Martha Washington chair with a blue and white striped fabric that had seen better days, and looked up at Bella and Michael who were now standing expectantly in front of her.

Bella spoke first. "We saw the police and the ambulance go down the street to Danielle's house. What's going on?"

"Oh, God! It's so unbelievable," Grace gasped. "It's Danielle Whitney. She's dead! It looks like she might have been murdered! Oh God!" Grace said again. "And the cops came and they've taken Duane in for questioning."

"You don't suppose he might ..." Michael began but was interrupted by Bella.

"Don't even say it," she said, scowling at him. "It's routine. Isn't it? Questioning him, I mean."

"I guess," Grace said. "I didn't get a chance to talk to him so I don't know exactly what happened. As we were running over there, he told me he went into the house to get the lamp, and there she was on the floor. He said he ran back here immediately."

"But, where was he before that? What took him so long?" Michael insisted. "It couldn't have taken him more than a few minutes to get there. He was gone for more than half an hour."

"I don't know. I can't imagine where he would have gone. I can't believe any of this," Grace said. "I guess I better call Pinewood and let Sean know what's happened."

She went into her office and closed the door, her heart still pounding. She began to think about what Michael had been saying.

Could she have been so wrong about Duane? She tried to calm herself. She knew Duane's prior criminal history. He had a record of drug offenses, trespassing and theft. But he had no record of violence. She never would have hired him if he did. Besides, he seemed to be turning his life around, and he was doing well at Pinewood.

Grace picked up the phone to call Sean Anderson, the director of the rehabilitation program. She had met Sean on numerous occasions during her years as a probation officer and referred many defendants to his program, which was highly respected by most people in the criminal justice system. But not all. There were assistant district attorneys, judges and cops who objected to any kind of intervention other than jail.

Sean's assistant, Terry Struthers, answered the phone. "Sean's away from his office. Is it important?" he asked.

"Yes. I need to talk to him right away. It's urgent. Is there any way you could locate him for me?"

There was a pause as Terry spoke to someone nearby. Grace tapped her pen on her desk and twirled it around her fingers. Terry was a former resident of the program who graduated and stayed on to become Sean's right-hand man. He wasn't the most efficient assistant but he had been there a long time and everyone who needed anything relating to the program had to deal with him.

"It's an emergency," she said when he came back on the line. "Sean's got my number here at Pearl's. Please have him call me right away."

Grace went to the mirror that hung behind her door. Drawing a brush through her disheveled hair, she put on some lipstick, relieved to be doing something ordinary, something familiar. Michael was talking to someone in the front room. She threw a sweater over her shoulders and went out to see who it was.

She found Clay Davenport, a local decorator, leaning over Michael, his buzzard-like face within inches of Michael's nose. "What on earth was she thinking?" he said in a stage whisper. "Sending a criminal to Danielle's house." When he saw Grace, he straightened and gave her a look of exaggerated concern.

"What a tragedy!" he said. "Poor Danielle! Such a special person. I decorated her entire house a couple of years ago. It was beautiful, if I do say so myself."

He held up a yellow moonstone vertique Aladdin lamp to the light from the bay window and ran his fingers up and down its ridges. Uranium had been used as a coloring agent, and it glowed like moonlight in the gray mid-morning light.

"Of course," Clay went on, putting the lamp down, "she had it redecorated a year ago by Sunset Interiors. I haven't seen it myself, but I hear it's ghastly. And you, Grace, poor thing. You found her. You and that young man of yours. I'm sure you must feel awful. After all, here you try to do a good deed by hiring him and this is how he repays you. I do hope you have a good lawyer, because you'll be needing one I'm sure." He turned back to Michael and said; "Show me that red Aladdin beehive oil lamp you've got over there. The color is gorgeous. And look what a lovely display you've made."

Michael took the old lamp from a shelf on which were also displayed several more beehive lamps arrayed like precious jewels. Amber, jade green, rose, and a very deep red.

"It's got original markings on it. I believe it dates to 1938 or '39. It's a very fine lamp indeed." Michael picked up the yellow moonstone Aladdin again for comparison and held it next to the red one. "I think that these lamps can be used in either a contemporary or traditional décor. The colors are outstanding."

Clay's sharp birdlike eyes sparkled. "Yes indeed, Michael. I see that. I do."

Grace was grateful for Michael's ability to distract Clay. She could feel the blood that had risen in her cheeks slowly subsiding. But what did he mean she would need a lawyer?

Chapter Five

STEPPING OVER CARDBOARD boxes full of lamp parts that were strewn around the floor of Bella's work area in flagrant violation of fire safety codes, Grace slid onto a wooden stool and watched as Bella painted a flowerpot a silky lilac and propped it up on a stack of newspaper to dry.

Bella pulled out her hand drill and prepared to make a hole in the center of a piece of wood that she had cut in a circular shape that would slide into the bottom of the pot. Glancing at Grace, she removed her protective glasses. "You okay?" she asked

"I guess," Grace answered. "I can't settle down and work. It's so disturbing, Danielle's death, Duane getting detained for questioning. He was gone a long time, wasn't he? Nothing was open around here at that hour. Even the general store was closed. At least it was when I came in a little after eight."

"It was still closed when I came in about eight-thirty," Bella said. "Goodness, I waved to Danielle as I went by her house last night. She came to the door and we exchanged a few pleasantries. What an attractive woman. She always looked so put together and refined, regardless of what she was doing. She was a top model in her day, as you no doubt have heard." Bella picked up a screwdriver and turned it over in her hand. "The truth is, she was a very complicated woman. She was involved in many local charities, and from what I've heard, gave generously to many of them. But, she could also be very hardheaded and arrogant."

Grace thought about all of the hardheaded and arrogant people she met when she was a probation officer. And not all of them were the criminals. Judges, lawyers, cops, and other assorted courthouse denizens often complicated her days. Sometimes it seemed as if her whole world was filled with difficult people. She had hoped to get away from all of that when she bought Pearl's five months ago.

"Michael can tell you how difficult she could be at the Historical Society meetings," Bella continued thoughtfully. "Everyone around here is interested in preserving the historical integrity of the town, but Danielle carried things to extremes. If someone wanted to make even a slight change to a historic property, she would oppose it. Even Matt and Milo clashed with her a few years back when they wanted to put a skylight in the attic. It wouldn't have been visible from the street, but she vetoed it anyway. That's not to say I'm not saddened by her death. I've known her a long time, and she didn't deserve to be murdered. Not that anyone does, of course."

"She was French, wasn't she?"

"Oh, yes. She was born in Paris, into the cream of French society. At least that was the way she described it."

"What a shame that her life should end this way." Grace sighed.

"Hi, Mrs. Benson!" Grace and Bella both turned to face a chubby girl with peppermint cheeks peering at them over the edge of the counter. Grace guessed she was about nine years old, but she couldn't be sure. She never could guess anyone's age correctly. Take Michael, for instance; he could be almost Bella's age. He was very fastidious and took great care in how he dressed and presented himself. She certainly wasn't going to ask him. Now Bella was another story. She proudly announced her age to Grace the first time they met.

"Sophie!" Bella said with surprise. "I didn't hear you come in."

"I can be very quiet sometimes," the little girl replied, obviously pleased with herself. She was sharply outfitted in pink mittens and a pink jacket, her dark bangs pressed down under her pink knitted hat. "I was looking at the fairy lamps. I really like the green owl with the red eyes. I like the pink flowery one too. I'm saving my allowance to buy one."

"Those fairy lamps are expensive, Sophie," Bella said. "They're wonderful collectibles and were very popular during the Victorian era. People used them mostly as nightlights. Their domes cover a candle, and most of them are very small. They'd burn for a few hours as people drifted off to sleep."

"Did they keep the bad guys away?" Sophie asked.

"Of course. The Clarke Company in London even had one called 'Burglars Horror.' How's that for using scare tactics in advertising?" she chuckled. "But what on earth are you doing out on a day like this? Are you all by yourself?"

Sophie frowned. "I've lost Stanley. He's been out all night and I can't find him anywhere."

"And Stanley would be ...?" Bella inquired.

"He's my cat!" Sophie said in a voice almost as loud as Bella's.

"Oh, yes. Goodness! That is troubling. Grace, have you met Sophie Calabrese? Her parents are the new owners of the Beach Sparrow Inn and Tea Room."

Sophie extended a mitten and gave Grace a tight squeeze, leaving her with a wet hand. "Hi Sophie. It's nice to meet you," Grace said, glad of the distraction. "And I am sorry you can't find Stanley. What does he look like?"

"He's gray with white stripes and white feet," Sophie declared. "Can you call my mother and tell her where I am?"

"Right this way, young lady. I'll show you where the phone is and you can call her yourself." Grace led the way to her office, Sophie scraping along behind her in her white rubber boots.

Sophie grabbed the receiver, lifted it and then, smiling at Grace, said, "I can't remember my number. Oh wait. Yes, I do!" she added, pulling off her wet mittens and putting them down on an important invoice. As Grace rescued it, she noticed that Sophie's fingernails were painted a now fading mauve.

"Mom's not too happy that I'm over here," Sophie said, hanging up the phone. "I guess I better go home now."

"How about if I walk you home? We'll keep a look out for Stanley." Grace wasn't getting any work done, and if there was a murderer running around town, it wasn't a good idea to let the little girl walk home alone. She shuddered as she thought about walking home alone later herself.

Chapter Six

WHEN THEY GOT outside, Sophie slipped her hand into Grace's. The storm showed no sign of letting up as they made their way down the shoveled path to the street. They climbed over a three-foot pile of snow that had been deposited by the snowplows and walked along the edge of the road. Traffic was still very light, and only a few people were out and about. Except for a few cars parked where their owners abandoned them, the townscape was pretty much the way it was two hundred years ago. Fewer trees perhaps, and of course paved roads and overhead wires, but Grace had seen the old photos of the town that hung behind the register at the bookstore. She loved the fact that not a whole lot had changed. Most of the same houses still lined the winding streets, many of them with historic markers affixed to the front facades like badges, which seemed to boast, "I'm still here, after all these years!"

It was a short walk, and as they approached the stately white colonial home that had been converted to an inn, Sophie ran ahead, pulled open the front door and disappeared inside. As Grace waited in the front entryway that smelled of fresh pastry, she admired the deep yellow ochre walls, which were decorated with very modern abstract prints in dark frames. As she was examining a life-sized stone statue of a woman holding a basket, which was filled with fresh holly leaves and berries, she heard footsteps coming down the stairs at the end of the large hall.

Sophie was trailing a pretty woman with dark, short, curly hair and black eyes, who approached Grace with an outstretched hand and a warm smile.

"Hi, I'm Jill," she said. "Thanks so much for bringing Sophie home. I've been going crazy getting this place ready for the holidays and didn't realize she had gone out. She's been told a hundred times at least not to leave without telling either her father or me." Sophie was tugging on her sleeve. "I think Sophie wants me to invite you in for some tea. We've got some apricot scones, jam and clotted cream. It's on the house. The least I can do."

The tearoom was off the main lobby. Grace sat at a table next to the fireplace and gazed at the shelves full of teapots, tea cozies, teacups and loose tea wrapped in black bags with gold ribbons. Warming up, she stripped off her hat and jacket and placed her gloves in her pockets. A large wreath above the mantel twinkled with tiny red and white lights. Grace estimated that there were about eight tables in the room and despite the bad weather half of them were occupied. The peach-colored walls, the glow from the crackling fire and the light passing through the delicate hand-cut shades on the table lamps made Grace feel that she was encased in a pumpkin. A comforting sensation on such a dark morning, she thought.

"Do you have a favorite tea or should I bring you a menu?" Jill asked.

"Earl Grey!" Sophie said loudly. "That's the best!"

"Sounds great to me too," Grace told Jill.

After giving instructions to a young woman with a blond ponytail who was decorating a Christmas tree between waiting on tables, Jill glided into a chair opposite Grace. Sophie leaned against her mother, her cheeks still rosy from the walk. Jill gave her a squeeze. "How about we go out together right after lunch and look for Stanley?"

"Do you think he's okay? We haven't seen him all night and it's so cold," Sophie's dark eyes were wet.

"I lost my cat once, and it turned out, he found a nice cozy spot in my neighbor's garage. Cats are good at seeking out warm spots for themselves." Grace said.

"Stanley is very smart. I bet that's what he did." Sophie brightened.

"I've been hoping to meet you," Jill said. "Matt and Milo told me you were taking over the lamp store. We bought the inn about seven months ago and opened up in September after a major renovation. We still have more to do, if we can get permission from the Historical Society, that is." She let out a deep sigh.

"Have you had trouble with the society? I haven't had a chance to do anything around the shop yet, but I do have plans. Is there a problem getting things approved?"

"You might say that," Jill told her wryly. "The problem is Danielle Whitney. Do you know her? She opposed our plan to add a small addition to the back of the house. We wanted to expand our kitchen and dining room. We also wanted to add six more parking spaces in back of the inn where we tore down an old shed. But she said it wouldn't be good for the neighborhood, whatever that means. None of our neighbors could see it and, it was to be hidden by landscaping. In the end, she caused such a ruckus that the Historical Society has put our request on indefinite hold. Tony, my husband, was furious. Furious!" she repeated with emphasis.

Grace knew she had to tell Jill what had happened that morning. Luckily, at that moment Sophie decided to help with the tree trimming. The waitress arrived with a steaming pot of tea, a plate of scones and a basket filled with bowls of jams and cream.

"Danielle Whitney is dead. It looks like someone killed her," she said in a low voice. "I sent an employee over there earlier this morning and he found her. He brought me back to her house and I called the police."

Jill stopped pouring tea into Grace's cup in mid-pour. "She's dead? Murdered? That can't be. I can't believe it." She put down the teapot. "Do the police know who did it? Have they arrested anyone yet?"

"Unfortunately, they've taken my employee in for questioning," Grace told her. "I hired a resident of Pinewood to work for the holidays. You know, to give him a chance at some legitimate employment. But I don't believe for a minute that he had anything to do with whatever happened over there."

"Gosh. It's going to be hard to tell Sophie about this. Strange, but despite her opposition to our plan, Danielle has been very kind to her. When Sophie went around selling cookies for a school fund-raiser Danielle bought thirty boxes. She told Sophie that she would save a few for herself and donate the rest to the Regency senior center and to Pinewood. She was an odd one, though. Sometimes I'd see her on the street and she wouldn't even acknowledge me. Other times she'd wave and ask after Sophie."

A short, muscular man appeared in the doorway. His dark hair was combed back over a high forehead, and he had a white apron over his shirt and jeans. He waved at Jill to come over to him.

"That's Tony," Jill explained. "Along with being my husband, he's the head chef around here. I'd better tell him about Danielle." Jill got up, took the man by his muscled arm, and steered him away from the busy tearoom.

Sophie, who had been energetically throwing tinsel at the tree, came running to join Grace and sat in the chair vacated by her mother. Cupping her chin in her hands, elbows on the table, she proceeded to tell Grace about the desserts, recommending several favorites. She seemed to get more and more excited talking about them. She was just winding up, when Jill appeared and gave Sophie a look that said "Enough," and Sophie reluctantly slid away from the table and went back to her tinsel tossing.

"I told Tony what you told me. He was totally shocked. I guess everyone will be when they find out about it," she said, looking around at the customers enjoying their tea. "I suppose I'd better tell Sophie now, before she hears it from someone else. I feel bad that I haven't been able to spend as much time with her as I'd like to. I think she's a bit bored and lonely. Especially now that Stanley has gone missing."

Chapter Seven

IT WAS A strange thing, Grace thought as she left the inn. Apparently, Danielle Whitney was adept at making enemies. But surely, the mere fact that she rubbed some people the wrong way was not enough to explain why someone had seen fit to murder her.

Halfway back to her shop her cell phone rang. It was Irene Papadopolous, her father's next-door neighbor.

"Hello, Grace? I thought you would like to know that at this very moment, your father is shoveling snow off of the roof of his studio," she announced.

Grace sighed. Last year her father fell off the roof doing the exact same thing. Although semi-retired now, he kept a studio cottage with a dark room badly in need of repair, in the back yard. The roof was weak, and he was afraid a heavy load of snow might collapse it.

"Thanks, Irene," she said. "I'll try to get there as soon as I can. I've got to run home and get my car. The roads are pretty bad, so it might take me a while. Yell at him for me, will you?"

"A lot of good that will do!" Irene replied. "You know your father!"

A short time later, she drove past Danielle's house, the yellow police tape flapping in the wind, law enforcement still busy with the scene. Coming down the front stairs was Margot Banks, the new Cape and Islands District Attorney. A steel-haired woman in her late forties, she was engaged in a walking conference with two assistant D.A.s. Banks, who had recently moved down from Boston, had narrowly won office in the recent election.

In a matter of minutes, Grace was outside of town and heading south. The main roads were plowed, but the secondary roads were fouled up with fender-benders and spinouts, and she had to stop, back up and turn around on more than one occasion, with the result that it took her about fifty-five minutes to get to Cotuit, a village on the south side of the Cape. As she pulled up in front of her family's weather-beaten white house, the roar of a snowblower greeted her. She spotted Irene's teenage grandson clearing her father's driveway. She waved to him as she parked and climbed the back steps. Her father was in the kitchen pouring coffee into a chipped mug. His thick white hair was askew, and there was white stubble on his chin. He raised his black eyebrows at her as she came in the back door.

"Why, hello, Gracie," Thomas De Pace said serenely, pulling out a chair and sitting at the table. "Irene told me you were coming by for a visit." The cuffs of his plaid flannel shirt were unbuttoned and flapped loosely over his thin wrists. "Would you like some coffee? I just made it."

"Dad, Irene told me you were up on the roof again," she said, not bothering to hide her exasperation. "You're almost eighty-four. You can afford to hire someone to take care of these things. Besides, it's time you got that roof fixed. You've got to be sensible."

"Irene should mind her own damned business," he muttered into his cup. "I wasn't on the roof. I was on a ladder, very steady, and I was dispersing snow, not shoveling." He looked up at Grace who was standing with her hands on her hips. "Now sit down and have some coffee with me."

"You're hopeless." Grace said, pulling out a chair and taking a stale cookie from a plate offered her. "But I'm relieved I don't have to drag you out of a snow bank. I've had quite a day already."

And with that, she proceeded to tell her father about the day's events while finishing off the plate of cookies. As he listened raptly, he shook his head in disbelief.

"I'm really sorry to hear about Danielle," he said when she was finished. "She was in my studio a month or so ago. I took a series of photos of her to update her portfolio. She said she was starting to get work again now that the fashion industry had figured out that mature women actually continue to buy clothes. She was quite excited about getting back to work.

"What did you think of her?" Grace asked.

"Well," he said, dabbing cookie crumbs with his finger, "she was really stunning. Perhaps you've heard she was a very successful model in the 1960s. She lived in New York and apparently had quite a great career appearing in the leading fashion magazines. From some of the stories she told me, she had quite a wild time. No specifics, mind you. She wasn't the tell-all type. Then, as she got older, her career declined. She met George Whitney, and moved to his family home here on the Cape in the late 1970s. He was some kind of financial analyst, I think. They weren't hurting for money, that's for sure. Anyway, she threw herself into all sorts of charitable and social activities. She seemed to be everywhere at once, appearing often in the society pages. She became a big fish in a small pond, I guess you could say."

"Did you like her?" Grace wanted to know.

"I did," he said. "But that doesn't mean that she couldn't be a complete pain in the neck at times. She was a perfectionist, I suppose. Which makes sense, given how important a portfolio could be to a model's career. She always wanted me to make her look thinner and younger. If she didn't look like an absolute stick, she was fit to be tied."

When Grace got up with their cups, she noticed the sink was loaded with unwashed dishes and the white linen curtains that her mother had sewn years ago were faded and in need of washing. Grace remembered her mother, who had passed away a few years ago, bustling about the house cleaning, cooking and sewing. Her mother's absence was obvious everywhere in the kitchen. The counters weren't quite clean, there was dust on the shelves in the cupboard and her father was eating store-bought instead of the home-baked ginger snaps that he loved. Grace missed her mother keenly, and she knew her father did too.

Thomas was staring out the window with a faraway look in his eyes. "Do you really think someone killed her?" he asked.

"It looks that way," Grace said as she plunged her hands into the warm, soapy water and started to wash the dishes. "I'm sorry to bring you such sad news. I knew you'd worked with her a while back, but I didn't know you had seen her recently. It's awful to think about what has happened to her. But I'm sure Duane had nothing to do with her murder. Why on earth would he do such a thing? It doesn't make any sense."

"Murder seldom does."

Grace glanced at him as she turned off the water and fished around for the plug. "I hope the detectives have finished questioning Duane and let him go. There's so much work for him to do. It's a busy time. I've got a lot of custom shades to paint before Christmas, and I'd like to have some new ones completed to put on display for Saturday. Bella was telling me that the Stroll brings in lots of folks who might not have been in the shop before. I could use a successful event to jump-start my business." Grace dried her hands on a towel hanging from a cabinet near the oven.

"Danielle's death certainly casts a pall on the whole season though," she continued. "It's hard now to think about cheery things like Village Strolls." Grace looked through the storm door at a lopsided pile of firewood. "I see you've already started stacking your wood on the porch. You should have called me. I could have done that for you."

"I'm fine, really I am. Don't worry about me so much." Thomas put his hand on her shoulder and gently steered her out the door. "But a piece of advice, if I may. Maybe you should tell Duane to look for another job."

"Duane is innocent," she replied, irritation creeping into her voice. "I know what I'm doing. I'm a good judge of people, and Duane's no murderer. I can't believe you don't have more faith in me."

"I do have faith in you, honey, but you may have gotten yourself into a serious situation. I want you to be happy and enjoy your lamp shop. That's all. You've had plenty of your own troubles the last few years."

Grace's phone rang. She gratefully answered it.

"Hey, Grace, it's Michael. Sean Anderson from Pinewood called. He's going to stop at the store around five. That okay with you?"

"That's fine. I was just leaving here." She put her phone back in her purse and zipped up the top. "I've really got to go, Dad. I know what you're saying, but I know what I'm doing. I really do." Grace gave him a little kiss on the cheek and headed out the door to her car.

The snowfall had let up, but it was dark for mid-afternoon and she turned on her windshield wipers against a fine mist. Low patches of thick fog were settling here and there, making it necessary for her to drive slowly and cautiously. As she peered through the windshield at the murky streets, she thought about what her father had said. Maybe he had a point, but there was no way she was going to desert Duane now.

Chapter Eight

Back in the shop, Michael was busy showing a middle-aged woman who was leaning heavily on the counter a series of shades for a brass desk lamp. Grace immediately went to assist another customer, a woman with a young child in tow, who wanted to order a hand-painted shade for a Christmas present for her mother.

"I want you to paint a picture of my mother's house on a shade. Can you do that? I've got a photograph here."

Grace looked at the picture of a charming cottage with a picket fence. "It's wonderful. It will come out beautifully." Grace helped the woman pick out a square drum shade. She proposed adding the owner's cat and dog to the painting, and the customer loved the idea.

When she returned from seeing the woman out, Michael was wrapping his customer's purchase and placing it in a large sea green shopping bag with gold letters that said Pearl's Antique Lamps & Shades. The beautiful bags were one of his innovations. Matt and Milo had, much to his disapproval, sent customers home with their purchases wrapped in plastic grocery sacks.

"A customer spotted one of the new finials," he said. "The dragonfly. She found it enchanting. I showed her a dragonfly lampshade and a Chinese canister lamp, and she bought the whole thing. It all started with the finial. A finial on a lamp is like jewelry on a fashionably dressed woman. It's essential to a polished appearance."

"Absolutely, I agree," Grace said, keeping a straight face, although Michael's old-fashioned comparison amused her.

"I unpacked those boxes that were delivered yesterday. You

picked out a lovely selection."

She looked at the finials he lined up on a table in parade formation. Matt and Milo had taught her the importance of crowning a lamp with a carefully chosen finial, but when they retired, they had left only a sparse collection in a small display case. She went online a week ago and splurged on a large order.

"Santas and reindeer. Just in time for Christmas," Michael said.

"I know I can move these. And the lighthouses are nice. Very Cape Cod. And a pink flamingo? What do you have in mind for this?"

"Don't know yet. I thought it was cute. Something will come to me, I'm sure."

Looking out of her office window at the darkening afternoon, Grace placed a call to Florida. Milo answered the phone and after exchanging weather reports (it was sunny and eighty-two degrees in Jacksonville) and other pleasantries, Grace told him about Danielle Whitney's death. Matt got on another extension and Grace found herself explaining the day's events again.

"I thought you'd both want to know," she said. "Bella told me about her opposition to your skylight, but I know Danielle was also a longtime customer."

"Indeed she was," Matt said. "How shocking."

"Unbelievable!" Milo exclaimed. "Are you sure? I mean that it was murder?"

"Yes, I'm afraid so. Did you know her well?"

"Yes," Matt replied. "She spent a lot of money at Pearl's and she referred scores of people to us. She'd become very difficult and demanding recently, and of course there was the skylight issue, but who in God's name would want to kill her?"

There was silence for a moment and then Milo spoke. "I'm not saying murder, of course, but Matt, do you remember Valerie Elkins? She was definitely upset with Danielle, to say the least."

"Of course I remember, Milo. I don't forget everything! But, Grace doesn't know what we're talking about." Matt sighed audibly and then continued. "Valerie is the real estate agent who sold our house in Yarmouthport for us. She'd recently been commissioned by Danielle to sell her property because at the time, Danielle had this idea about downsizing to a condominium. Apparently, Valerie brought an offer to Danielle that was more than the asking price, but Danielle changed her mind and said she didn't want to sell after all. Although Valerie had held a couple of open houses and advertised, Danielle didn't think she deserved any commission at all. Valerie said she was going to have to sue Danielle to get her money, and that was going to cost her time and more money. She seemed kind of panicky about the whole thing."

"But she wouldn't kill Danielle. That's preposterous," Milo exclaimed.

"I didn't say she did, Milo, for Pete's sake. I'm trying to tell Grace what we heard," Matt protested.

Grace thought it was a good time to change the conversation. "So, how's retirement? You guys enjoying your free time?"

Silence. "Sure we are." Matt finally said. "We've joined a lawn bowling group, and Milo is active in the homeowners association. We're both signed up for water aerobics too. It takes a while, Grace, to meet new people and get established. Honestly, we moved here for the weather, but we didn't realize how difficult it is to change your whole life and make a new home somewhere."

"Give it time," Grace replied. "You've only been there a few months. Think of the cold and snow up here, and you'll feel better."

They both heartily agreed and Grace promised to keep them informed about the startling events. She hung up without telling them anything about Duane. They didn't even know that she hired him, and she didn't feel like telling them now. Besides, she was feeling guilty enough, even though she knew that was absurd. Still, the sooner this murder was cleared up, the better for everyone.

Bella was sitting at her workbench, her large, strong hands wrapped around a tuna on rye. She had a pot of steaming tea beside her and a delicate china cup that was filled to the brim. A colorful real estate brochure was spread out in front of her and she was flipping through the pages.

"Bella, are you thinking about moving?"

"I might," Bella said, crossing her slipper-shod feet at the ankles. "When I retire next month, I was thinking that maybe I should move somewhere warm and sunny. Like Matt and Milo did. Can't you picture me sitting on a beach somewhere, sipping a margarita or gin fizz? Enjoying my golden years?"

"I'm having a hard time imagining you anywhere but here at Pearl's, but I'm being selfish. You deserve a wonderful retirement. I just don't know how I will get along without you."

"I'll teach you a few things before I go," Bella promised. "But eventually you're going to have to get someone to do the repairs. The hand-painted shades are a huge part of the business, but often it's the repair work that brings customers in the door. I'll start asking around, but you're probably going to have to place an ad in the paper. In the meantime, you and Michael will be able to hold down the fort. And hopefully Duane will be back at work soon." Bella held up her plate and offered some of her sandwich and tea to Grace, but she declined. She was starting to feel the effects of having had nothing but caffeine and sugar all day. The energy high was over, and now she was feeling just plain tired. She plopped down on a stool across from Bella and asked her if she knew that Danielle's house had been for sale.

"Of course," she replied, washing down some tuna with some tea. "About six months ago, a "For Sale" sign appeared on her front lawn, and about a month later down it went. I didn't see Danielle during that time, so I don't know much about it. The property is worth a bundle though. There are several acres, and it backs up to marshes that are part of a protected conservation area. The house is very old, probably built around 1800 or so, and Danielle has maintained every inch of it. It's a real showplace and I'm sure worth a few million. Are you sure you won't have a chocolate chip cookie?"

"Oh, I guess so. Why not? My diet's been shot today anyway,"

Grace said as she accepted a cookie from Bella. "Do you know her realtor, Valerie Elkins?"

"I don't know her personally. I think she has her own real estate company. I mean she's not part of one of the big outfits. I did hear that there was some kind of dispute between her and Danielle, but I don't know the whole story. I bet Matt and Milo would know."

Grace recounted her conversation with M and M, her own personal nickname for the pair. "I hope the police catch whoever did this soon. It's disturbing to think that a murderer might still be around. A while back, I wrote pre-sentence reports on a couple of guys who preyed on elderly people. They'd show up at the door and say that the electric company or the water company sent them out to check on a problem and convince the homeowner to let them in. Then, while one of them would create a distraction, the other would go into bedrooms and steal jewelry and cash. The poor victims usually didn't even know they had been robbed until hours later. Maybe these guys are back or someone like them is operating around here."

"Could be."

Grace got up from the stool, having finished off the rest of the cookies. "Why don't you go home? It's been a long day and you look tired. I'm going to tell Michael the same thing. It's getting late, and I doubt we'll have any more customers. I'll stay here and wait for Sean Anderson from Pinewood, and I think I'll try to get a shade painted. I didn't get anything done today, and here I thought I'd have a whole day of peace and quiet to catch up."

The offer was genuine enough, but she was surprised when Bella immediately took her up on it.

Chapter Nine

BELLA AND MICHAEL had left when Sean Anderson arrived. Dressed in a dark blue sweatshirt and sweatpants, his only concessions to the weather were his gloves and the scarf he had wound around his neck. Silver loop earrings decorated both ears, and his long gray hair was tied in a ponytail.

"Hi, Sean. You look like you've been jogging. Are you crazy? It's freezing out there."

"Hey, Grace," Sean said as he stepped into the shop. "I don't have a lot of spare time, so I try to exercise when I can." He took a deep breath and gazed around the room full of lamps. "Wow. This sure looks different from the probation department. Are you happy with your new career?"

"I was until this morning," Grace replied. "Have you seen Duane?"

"I went to the jail, but the cops were still questioning him. I know about the murder, of course, but how was Duane involved?"

Grace filled him in with what she knew. "I didn't hesitate to send Duane to Danielle's house. When I agreed to hire him for the holidays, you told me that he has been doing well in the program."

"Duane has been doing great in the program," Sean assured her. "He's been with us for more than a year now. We drug-test frequently. He had the usual adjustment problems in the first few months, but I wouldn't have let him be part of the community employment program if I didn't think he was ready. I thought this would be a perfect placement for him, you being an ex-P.O. and all."

Grace was feeling more confident hearing Sean saying what

she herself thought just a day ago.

"I guess we'll have to see what happens," Sean continued. "We have our biggest fundraiser of the year on Saturday night after the Village Stroll, and this is already having an impact. We're starting to get calls from donors wanting to drop out. The press is all over us. Anyway, I've got to go now and try to do some damage control. Hopefully Duane will be released tomorrow and everything will settle down."

"Was Danielle Whitney a big contributor to Pinewood?" Grace asked.

Sean nodded. "Yes. She once told me that she liked being able to make a difference in a young person's life. She gave a good deal to her favorite charities."

"I wish I'd gotten to know her," Grace told him. "She sounds like she was a very interesting woman."

"Absolutely. Very interesting. Well, I better get going. It's getting late, and I've got a bunch of stuff to do at my office. Let's keep each other up to date on Duane's situation." He pressed his palms together, bowed and sprinted down the stairs.

♟

Grace's worktable was in a corner of the main room. She liked this arrangement because it put her in close proximity to her papers and trims, but also because it gave customers a chance to watch her construct and paint the shades. Next to the wide table was a shelf unit full of her shade-making supplies. Yesterday before she left the shop, she started constructing a round empire shade, which now rested upside down, balanced on a nest of clothespins. She touched it gingerly to make sure the glue was dry and the parchment paper hadn't warped.

As she overlapped the sides of the paper, making a seam and securing it with double-sided adhesive tape, she thought about Sean. Now that she had spoken with him, she felt better about her decision to hire Duane. Sean was in serious trouble himself years ago, and he had even done time in prison, but that experience and a strong desire to change made him a good example for the residents of his program. He had heard all of the stories and excuses of addicts. If he perceived any risk in allowing Duane to work in the community, he would not have permitted it.

Turning the shade over, she secured the bottom wire to the edge of the shade with glue. But there was something about Sean's New Age Zen affectations that irritated her. She wondered if they were real or a put-on. On the other hand, if that was how he managed to stay straight, so be it. Using the clothespins again, she clipped them along the edge to prevent any gaps from forming. Next, she ran glue around the edges, top and bottom and down the seam, and attached handmade paper to the lining. She'd let it dry a little while. Her eyes were feeling tired.

Grace laid her head on the table and took a few deep breaths. As she drifted off to an unexpected sleep, she told herself that things would be better tomorrow. Duane would be back, and she would be able to catch up on her shades and decorate the Christmas tree that was now leaning against the back wall, looking forlorn and pathetic.

When she awoke, about forty-five minutes had passed and night had fallen. The streetlights were on. A few cars passed by silently, headlights glistening on the white stacks of snow by the road. Across the street, customers were coming out of the general store, their arms filled with paper bags. Grace imagined them buying candles, matches and lanterns. Another storm had been predicted for tonight.

She finished up her shade and decided to head for home. Turning off most of the lamps in the store, she left a few lit in the front window. Despite the musty air, a potpourri of dust, paint and glue, not to mention the colonies of dust mites that were camped out and hiding in the rolled-up fabrics, Grace was enthralled by the romance of the shop. All of the lamps intrigued her because each one of them contained an unknown history. She had her favorites, though, and when Michael sold one, she would feel a pang of sorrow and loss. She particularly admired the oil lamps. She imagined the people who depended on them for schoolwork, sewing and dining. Perhaps carrying a finger lamp to a bedside table to read a favorite book or to make love.

Although many of the oil lamps were converted to electric use, Bella never marred the original lamp or pottery piece in any way. If a customer wanted her to drill a hole in a vase or jar, she would only accommodate him if there was no other possible way of installing a socket. But Bella wouldn't ruin a nice antique. As far as she was concerned, they could take their business elsewhere.

Grace turned off the thermostat and checked Michael's Italian coffee espresso machine. Everything was all set for tomorrow morning. At the bottom of the stairs she pulled on her boots, coat, scarf, hat and gloves and locked the door behind her. She decided to leave her car at the shop. Perhaps a brisk walk in the snow would clear the ache that was making its way up the back of her spine and into her neck.

Chapter Ten

T HE WHITE CHRISTMAS lights that were strung up in the trees
along Main Street looked hazy and cheerless in the gloom,
and the few blocks of commercial businesses interspersed with
antique homes were empty now. As the chilly night air settled
into her bones, Grace saw an old man peering out of an upstairs
window of a gray shingle house next door to Danielle's place. He
drew back into the murky light when he saw Grace glance his way.

Grace thought about how much had changed since she walked
by the property early this morning. Now the house, cocooned in a
blue haze, appeared to sink into the snow that surrounded it. The
police tape still wrapped the property, but was torn, frayed and
twisted by the wind. Crushed and despondent, Grace thought, like
Cinderella after the ball. The evergreen wreath that had greeted
visitors cheerily only this morning now hung haphazardly on
the door, a victim of investigators brushing against it all day.
Christmas lights strung around the front porch remained unlit.
The house appeared diminished as the fog pressed and clung to
the surrounding trees.

As she walked along the sidewalk she thought she saw a light in
an upstairs window above a side entrance. But the glow vanished
as quickly as it had appeared. How odd, Grace thought. Looking
around, she searched for an outside cause of the light. But across
the street, the cemetery was as dark and peaceful as it had been
this morning. No cars were in sight and the nearby streetlight was
too dim to cast a reflection in the damp night. Looking back at
the house, she saw nothing but darkness. She must have imagined
the light, she thought to herself as she shuddered and pulled her

fleece hat tighter on her head.

Another few minutes and Grace was at Freezer Road. A mix of houses, reflecting architectural styles of the past centuries, were tucked here and there behind maples, oaks and evergreens. Like most of the streets on this, the north side of Main Street, it was nestled near Barnstable Harbor, which is protected by a barrier beach and three thousand acres of salt marshes.

Now the lane was dark, with only a few lamps burning in the houses she passed on her way to her own cottage. Walking as quickly as she could through the deep snow, she couldn't help looking over her shoulder every few minutes. She didn't see anyone, but it was deathly quiet. She plowed her way through pale drifts of snow and stamped her feet on the front porch before pulling off her boots. Soon she was inside, greeting Clambake, her black and white Maine Coon cat, who promptly headed off to the kitchen to sit forlornly on the floor, staring down at his empty food bowl.

Clambake was a shelter cat she and Jack adopted shortly after their marriage. Close to nineteen pounds, he was on a diet and not happy about it. "Poor kitty!" Grace said as she opened a can of the low-fat food and put it on the floor in front of him. "I understand, I really do."

Feeling guilty about her own lack of discipline, she rooted around in her refrigerator until she found enough odds and ends to make a decent salad. A half a head of lettuce, some radishes, celery, red onion and one pallid tomato later, Grace was in business. After eating, she washed up the dishes and put on some hot water for tea. Her salad leaving her unsatisfied, she opened cabinet doors searching for something to follow the light dinner. As she pushed cans of tomato sauce out of the way she thought about her answer to Michael's question this morning. The truth was, she did miss the San Francisco Bay area. How could she not think fondly of the fresh year-round produce, the fog rolling in, cooling everything off after a warm day, and the scent of lavender in the wine country in June? She traveled across the country with a friend after college and stayed in San Francisco, where she worked as a probation officer for about ten years. After her mother died, she moved back to the Cape and was hired by Barnstable County Probation. Her father needed her, and she was ready to return to the East Coast, where she had grown up. She loved New England. And Cape Cod was home. If she could find a way to live in two places at once, she would. For now, she would remember that though the fog might not roll in with any regularity on a hot day, she could stroll down the street and take a dip in Cape Cod Bay.

Gratified to find a package of crackers, she put two on a plate and poured her tea. Although it was late, Grace felt awake after her nap at the shop and the brisk walk home. She didn't want to get into bed and risk lying awake thinking about Danielle, brutally murdered, lying on her living room floor. And — she hated to admit it — but she wasn't in any hurry to turn off the lights. She was sure no one followed her, but she couldn't shake her feeling of uneasiness. Instead, she decided to hang a few Christmas lights and set out some ornaments and other decorations. The past two years without Jack were hard, the holidays in particular almost unbearable. Decorating was unthinkable. She spent every day of December longing for January and some relief from the painful memories of the holidays Jack and she spent together. But this year, despite some trepidation, she was looking forward to unpacking some favorite old holiday items and jazzing up her cottage a bit.

After Jack died, Grace sold the house they bought together and purchased the cottage. Like many of the houses in Barnstable Village, her cottage was more than a hundred and fifty years old. It consisted of a living room, dining room, kitchen and a study on the first floor that she used as a place to store the overflow from the lamp shop. A large pine worktable occupied the center of the room.

Upstairs were two bedrooms and a bath. All of the windows on the back of the house faced the marsh, with Barnstable Harbor and Sandy Neck in the distance. Grace bought the house for the view. It needed work, but she knew she would never tire of the expanse of sea, beach and sky.

Grace's decorating style was simple. The dark beaded boards that covered most of the interior walls had been cleaned and brightened with fresh white paint. The wide pumpkin pine floors were repaired, stained and polished. She covered them with an assortment of sea grass and natural jute rugs. Most of her furniture was encased in white slipcovers.

And there were books everywhere. Books she had read and books she planned to read. Books that were beautifully constructed and books with worn, dilapidated bindings had equal prominence in her collections. It was a bit of a problem at times, this addiction of hers. But, it was an addiction she was not likely to seek treatment for anytime soon.

Removing some cardboard boxes labeled "Xmas Ornaments" from a cupboard in the living room, she pulled out strands of white lights, which she proceeded to drape around the staircase and front windows until, too tired to continue, she sank into the overstuffed chair by the window and waited for the sense of exhilaration that preparing for the holidays had brought in the past. An exhilaration that, no doubt because of Danielle's murder, failed to come.

Chapter Eleven

THE NEXT MORNING, Grace peeked out from under her pile of blankets to find the air soft with dawn and cold and the windows in her old cottage rattling in the wind. Gently rearranging Clambake, who was curled up against her side, she reached for her clock on the bedside table. The luminescent display read 6:10 a.m. The storm had been blowing all night, it was still dark, and she was tempted to roll over and sleep another hour but she forced herself up and out from under the covers. Shivering, she grabbed her robe and padded down the stairs, her sock-covered feet sliding on the bare wood floor, the events of yesterday forcing themselves into her sleepy consciousness.

She gazed out the French doors at the marshlands lit by the falling snow. It was so bright, the bushes and trees cast dark shadows on the pale ground.

Clambake was meowing and giving her a look that seemed to say, "Feed me now, please!" Grace opened a can and dished out a chunk of salmon pate for the large cat. The meowing abruptly stopped and Grace filled the kettle and set out a handmade mug for her tea. Pushing back the kitchen curtain to let in the morning light, she marveled at her woodpile, which resembled neatly piled stacks of marshmallows.

Michael was right, she thought. Snow this deep was definitely unusual for the Cape, where the weather was usually milder than most of New England. Of course, snow fell on and off all winter, accumulating gracefully on the old towns and villages and then, because the ground was warmer from the proximity of the Gulf Stream, it melted into the sandy soil. But this storm, like the one before it, had blown in from Canada, bringing with it fierce winds and freezing temperatures. Grace watched as gusts of wind blew veils of snow off velvety tree branches, and her bird feeder twisted sharply as a congregation of chickadees dressed in their black berets clung fiercely to it.

Opening the back door to throw some crumbs out for the birds, she was surprised to see Jose and Rafael grinning up at her.

"Can we shovel your driveway and walkway for you?" asked Rafael, the elder of the two brothers, in his squeaky voice.

"School's closed. We're going to make a lot of money today," piped up Jose, who looked to be about ten.

"Okay, you two. When you get cold, come in for some hot chocolate."

Grace could hear their voices as she was drinking her third cup of tea and writing out some bills. She remembered the last time she had seen the boys, when they were being questioned outside of Danielle's house. Yes, the storm dropped a lot of snow, but Jose and Raphael had competently shoveled up any tracks a killer might have left. She looked out the window to see Jose hit Rafael with a snowball that exploded on the back of his cap. Rafael yelled, picked up a fistful of snow and went charging after Jose. Jose started running but was easily caught by the bigger boy, who grabbed him by the scarf and smashed the snow down his back.

Time for that hot chocolate, Grace decided, opening the door and calling out to them. Still full of energy, the boys picked up their shovels and ran toward her, clomping their boots on the steps, shaking the excess snow off of their jackets and piling in the back door.

The boys sat down at the kitchen table and Grace placed a plate of iced snowman cookies on the table along with the steaming mugs.

"The police talked to us," Rafael blurted out. "They wanted to know if we saw anyone at that lady's house yesterday. Besides the guy they took away. We didn't know that she was dead. We didn't even see her."

"That guy is going to be in jail for a long time!" Jose said.

"Just because the police are questioning him it doesn't mean he's guilty," Grace said. "Let me run upstairs and get my wallet. Drink up your chocolate and I'll be right back," Grace said, deciding to nip this conversation in the bud.

When she returned to the kitchen after a few minutes, she was surprised to find Sophie, making herself at home at the table with the boys.

"I guess I snuck up on you again, didn't I?" she said, looking very pleased.

"Yes, you sure did." Grace agreed. "Would you like some hot chocolate?"

"Of course she would!" Jose said, grinning. "That's why she's here!"

"Sophie can smell hot chocolate from miles away." Rafael announced as Grace poured her new guest a cup of chocolate.

Ignoring the boy's remark, Sophie tested the hot drink with her tongue. "I still can't find Stanley. Mom says he's sleeping somewhere. Do you think so?" she asked Grace.

"Yes, I do." Grace said. She didn't want to discourage Sophie. But she was worried. Two cold nights had passed, and there was no sign of him.

She placed a napkin on the table in front of Sophie and another plate of cookies squarely in the middle of the group. There was a rustle as small hands shot out quickly and nabbed the half dozen cookies like a school of guppies diving for bait.

Sophie splashed a cookie into her mug. "I know the lady that was killed. She was a friend of mine. She has a mean brother. I heard him yelling at her. He said, 'You better watch out, you'll be sorry!'"

As Grace was registering what Sophie had said, she heard a knock at her front door. "You kids stay here. I'll see who it is," she said. Pulling back the drapes on the living room window, she was startled to see Detective Cruz standing there, his collar turned up against the wind.

"Can I talk to you for a minute?" he said when she opened the door.

"Sure, come on in," Grace said. Jose and Rafael appeared in the kitchen doorway. Cruz glanced at them, clearly surprised by their presence. He said nothing, but nodded a greeting at them. "We're going now," Rafael said as he put an arm in his coat and headed for the door. Jose was trailing behind him, glancing curiously at the detective as he walked by.

Grace shut the door and turned as Sophie, with a chocolate mustache, stepped into the room with a squirming Clambake in her arms. She looked up at Cruz and said, "Are you here because of the murder?"

Detective Cruz looked at Sophie. "Does your mother know where you are?"

"Not exactly." Sophie said.

"Maybe you better go home before I get another missing person call. Okay?"

Sophie nodded ever so slightly.

"Sophie has a way of wandering off and not telling Jill and Tony, her parents, where's she's going," he continued. "They own the Beach Sparrow Inn and Tea Shop on Main Street."

"Yes, I met Jill yesterday when I brought Sophie home after the ..." Grace caught herself. "You know."

Grace picked up a pair of mittens off the table. "Sophie, why don't you take a couple of cookies with you and go check in with your mother before she gets worried. Rafael and Jose are still out front. I'll ask them to take you home. You can come back and visit me again. Just make sure your mom says it's all right. Understood?"

Dropping Clambake, who meowed and scooted out of the room, Sophie pulled two cookies out of her pocket. "I already helped myself!" she announced smugly.

Grace closed the front door after Sophie and motioned to Cruz to have a seat on the couch. "Can I get you some tea or coffee or ... snowman cookies?"

Cruz cut her off. "Thanks, but I can't stay long. I wanted to let you know that District Attorney Banks is going to charge your employee, Duane Kerbey, with homicide."

Grace caught her breath and sank into the soft pillows of her armchair opposite him, wrapping her arms around a chenille throw pillow. "That's impossible!" she cried. "Duane has nothing to do with this!"

"Actually, there's some evidence supporting the charge against him," Cruz said wearily, and it occurred to her that he might very well have been up all night. "We have a witness who saw him go into the house. His fingerprints are on the front door knob and on the murder weapon."

Grace shuddered. She hunched over and put her head in her hands. She didn't want to hear more, but she knew she had to.

"As you already know, he's got priors for drug use and theft," Cruz continued. "I'm sorry you've gotten yourself caught up here, but, frankly, I am surprised that you, a former P.O., would hire a guy like this."

"What do you mean, 'a guy like this'?" Grace demanded. "He's done very well at Pinewood. You can talk to Sean Anderson, the director. Everyone deserves a second chance. People change, you know." Grace's voice rose so loud it surprised her.

"People change, sure," said Cruz. "But Duane Kerbey didn't."

"You mean, you think he did it?" Grace demanded. "What possible motive could he have had? Aren't there any other suspects? What about those thugs who pretend to be with the utilities and prey on the elderly? Maybe they're out of prison and are operating around here. Maybe you should interview the boys again. Maybe they saw someone else."

"Calm down, Ms. Tolliver. We thoroughly interviewed both of the boys." He pulled a notebook out of his pocket and flipped a few pages. "Let's see. They saw Duane come out of Danielle's house. They saw you and Duane run into the house, Gavin Murrey, the retired priest, walking his dog, Christine Sinclair coming out of her barn, Tony Calabrese knocking icicles off of his roof, Claiborne Davenport strolling along Main Street, Ysenia Gonzales, their mother who brought them dry gloves, two unidentified old men, a cat and two dogs. That enough for you? Basically, they saw the whole damn town."

"No need to get testy," Grace told him. "It was a perfectly

logical question."

Detective Cruz shot her a hard stare. "We're looking into a couple of long-shot suspects of interest. But, I'm telling you, things look bad for your friend."

"He's not my friend," Grace said. "He's my employee and I know he's innocent. In the first place, he had no reason to kill Danielle Whitney. What about that?"

Cruz stood up. "I've got to go," he said, avoiding her question. "I just thought I'd come by as a courtesy and give you a heads-up on the situation before the press starts calling you."

Grace's eyes grew wide. "The press! What do they want with me?"

"You hired him. You sent him to the victim's house."

"Oh, God!" Grace said. "You're right. They are going to crucify me."

"My advice is not to talk to anyone about this. Except myself and Detective Rice, of course."

Picking up Clambake, who had returned to his favorite spot on the couch, and hugging him tight, she watched as Detective Cruz got into his car. She wondered if her life would ever be the same again.

Chapter Twelve

A N HOUR OR SO later, the snow had slowed down to a few flurries, and Grace was walking to the shop when Danielle's house came into view. The wind was bitter and the house appeared empty and barren. For a Monday morning, the streets were quiet, the past two days of heavy snow having paralyzed the town. As she came closer to the house, she saw an imposing fair-haired man in a tan overcoat pacing in front of Danielle's gate. As she passed by, he said; "I'm Howard Pittman, Danielle Whitney's brother. I drove in from Providence. What a shock, I can't believe it. Did you know my sister?"

Grace, startled by the man's outburst, introduced herself and shook Howard's hand. "I'm so sorry about your sister," Grace said. "Did you get in from Providence last night?" Grace was remembering the light she saw, or thought she saw, in the window of Danielle's house on her way home last night.

"No. Why do you ask?"

"Oh, I thought I saw a light on in the house. It must have been my imagination," Grace said, wishing she had kept her thoughts and imaginings to herself.

"I got to town this morning. I checked in at the Beach Sparrow Inn and came right here. The whole place was locked up tight and surrounded by yellow tape. The police are on their way over now to let me in." Howard looked down at the front walk covered in new snow. "No one's been through this way since last night's storm." Rubbing his gloved hand through his fair hair that was flecked with gray, he rambled on. "Anyway, I'm sure I'm the only one who has a key. Unless she gave a key to that creep she was seeing. A professional gigolo if you ask me. Where she picked up that piece of … First she's in love and going to marry the jerk. Next thing I hear, she's going to sell the house, marry him and together they would buy a condominium. I talked her out of selling, but I hadn't gotten her away from him. Vernon. Vernon Somebody or other. Not that it's a real name or anything. Danielle was going through some life changes or something. I don't know." Howard looked down at Grace with an expression of pain. "I was here a couple of days ago. We were clearing out some odds and ends she had set aside when she was thinking of downsizing." Howard gazed up at the house. "We got into a bit of an argument about the jerk. I feel bad that our last words were spoken in anger, but I was just looking out for her."

"I'm very sorry for your loss, Mr. Pittman. If there's anything I can do, let me know. I own the lamp shop down the block."

"Wait a minute, Miss!" Howard's look of pain had been replaced by one of outrage. "Lamp shop! You mean you're the idiot who sent that junkie to my sister's house? Were you out of your mind?" Not waiting for Grace to reply, he continued. "Did you think that was a good idea? Sending a criminal over here?" Howard was yelling now, his face turning red. He took a step toward Grace, poking his index finger close to her face. "I'm going to talk to my lawyer. I'll sue you for all you've got. And then some!"

Grace backed up and looked around her. An old lady carrying a tiny dog in her arms hurried across the street. A man shoveling snow a couple of doors down paused and stared.

"Don't be so quick to pass judgment," Grace replied. "My employee didn't murder your sister. In time, you'll see that I'm right."

And then, without another word, she walked away from Howard, who was standing with his hands on his hips, his fingers clenching and unclenching. Her heart pounded. As a probation officer, Grace was skilled at diffusing angry people. But her technique of listening carefully and lowering her voice didn't look like it was going to work on Howard Pittman, who seemed to be on the verge of losing control. Sometimes it was best to walk away.

Now she was beginning to understand why Clay had said she might need a lawyer.

Chapter Thirteen

TAKING A DEEP breath, Grace tried to calm herself by admiring the holiday decorations in the businesses that lined the brick sidewalks of the commercial center of the village. A couple of women were opening up the consignment shop and she waved to them as she crossed the street and headed toward one of her favorite stops for coffee and muffins. She stared at the pastries for a couple of minutes before deciding to pass up the extra calories. Coffee and a sweet were not going to help her jitters. The District Attorney's office, a short block away, housed in a white clapboard building, was quiet. Looking up at the courthouse she remembered the years she ascended the hill and entered through the back door, climbing the stairs to the second floor to her tiny office in the probation department.

Grace loved Barnstable Village, not only because she could walk to work, but because its charm was the result of an unusual mix of small businesses, old houses and civic buildings proclaiming its status as the county seat of Cape Cod and the Islands. The business district was crowned by the imposing courthouse, which was built in 1832. Her former office was a small space she had shared with her friend and co-worker, Audrey Lee. She had liked being a probation officer, but after Jack died, working at the courthouse and passing the courtroom where they had met was excruciatingly painful. She knew that she needed to move on. Maybe not romantically, despite the heroic efforts of Audrey, who insisted on fixing her up with various cousins and ex-boyfriends. No, Grace had needed a project. And Pearl's seemed perfect. Of course, she hadn't contemplated the situation she now found herself to be in. At least managed to walk away from Danielle's brother with her dignity intact. After all, a shop owner had to maintain some decorum.

Grace was so lost in her thoughts that she didn't notice the van from the local TV station parked in front of Pearl's until a familiar newscaster, holding a microphone and wearing a plaid beret, started running in her direction from across the street.

"Miss Tolliver!" she shouted. "Did you know Duane Kerbey's criminal record when you sent him to Danielle Whitney's house? Is it true the murder weapon was a lamp?"

Grace turned just as a man stuck a camera in her face. Instinctively, she put one hand in front of the lens and with the other she shoved the cameraman's arm as hard as she could. He took a small step backward but his camera kept on rolling, capturing her as she tried to grab his camera. He stepped back again, pulling away from her grip. He adjusted the lens and smirked at her as she lashed out at him with a kick to his shins that missed by a few inches.

The shocked expression on the face of the newscaster indicated that she had not expected a scuffle. Grace took the mike out of her hand and said: "I have no comment, other than to remind your viewers that, although there has been an arrest in this case, there has been no trial. We haven't heard all of the evidence yet." She pushed her way between the newscaster and the cameraman. "Excuse me. I've got to get to work!"

Grace trudged up the stairs to the shop. Michael and Bella were drinking coffee and waiting expectantly for her. "Life sucks!" she said as she went in to her office and slammed the door.

Chapter Fourteen

Y OU'VE REALLY PUT your foot in it now, Grace told herself as
she plopped down in her desk chair. She felt sick to her stomach as she pondered the trouble she was in. She had hired Duane,
a former probationer with a record for drug use and theft, sent
him to the house of a prominent member of the community who
had subsequently been found dead, Duane had been arrested, and
her own father, as well as Detective Cruz, were blaming her for
her poor judgment. Furthermore, not only was the press outside
her door, but also the victim's brother was threatening to sue her,
which, if he did, would most likely result in her losing Pearl's.

Grace's melancholy musings were interrupted by a soft, ten-
tative knock on her office door. She jumped up and pulled the
door open to find Bella and Michael standing there with a cup of
coffee and a brownie on a paper plate.

"Here, Grace," Michael whispered as he placed the cup on
her desk. He took the brownie from Bella and put it on the desk
next to the cup. Backing away, he managed to step on Bella's foot.

"Darn it, Michael!" she cried. "Watch where you're going!"

Grace looked at the two of them and started to laugh. "You
two are too much."

"We want to help," Michael said. "Is there anything we can do?
That lady from the TV station has been hanging around outside
for the last forty-five minutes. We're afraid she is going to chase
away our customers."

"That's only part of our problems, or rather, my problems."
Grace said, filling them in on Duane's situation and Howard
Pittman's threat to sue her. "I've got to get to the bottom of this.

I still don't believe Duane would be stupid enough to murder a customer. Or anyone, for that matter, of course. I've got to find out who did murder Danielle Whitney, clear Duane, restore my reputation and save Pearl's."

Michael ran his fingers along the top of Grace's desk. "Yes, although Duane might be stupid enough to ..."

"What he means to say," Bella interrupted, "is, we've talked it over and we'll help you any way we can. Just tell us what to do and we'll do it."

Grace stood up and hugged Michael then Bella, causing them both to look uncomfortable. They clearly weren't used to getting hugs from their employer. Grace remembered how people in San Francisco often hugged, but New Englanders tended to be more reserved. She figured this would go into Michael's mental file of strange things people from California are likely to do if you let your guard down.

"Thanks," she said. "I'll probably need you to cover the shop for me more than usual. I think I need to pay Duane a visit and then ..."

"In jail?" Michael said, his eyes wide. "Such an unpleasant place. But I suppose he's been there before and ..."

"Oh, hush up. Isn't there something important you should be doing? Like dusting finials or straightening shades?" Bella said.

"If there is one thing that needs dusting and straightening around here, it's that disaster area you call a workroom. I'd like to get in there and tidy that mess of yours up."

"It'll be war if you do, so keep your mitts out of there."

Grace closed her office door as Michael and Bella traipsed back to the customer area. Taking a gulp of the still hot coffee and grabbing a piece of brownie, Grace dialed her friend Audrey's work number.

"Barnstable Probation. Audrey Lee speaking," the familiar voice said.

"Hey, Audrey, it's Grace."

"Ohmigod!" Audrey exclaimed. "What on earth is going on? I saw you on the news. You need to practice up on your karate, but you did good, telling that snarky reporter a thing or two."

"Oh, God. I'm so embarrassed. That guy with the camera pushed my buttons."

"Yeah, I could see that. Do you want to get together and talk? We could meet at the Dolphin."

"You know I love the Dolphin, but I need to talk to you without interruption about this whole mess." The Dolphin was across the street from the courthouse and filled with attorneys, cops, judges, court reporters and even an occasional probation officer. "How about seven at that Italian place in West Yarmouth?"

"Okay." Audrey paused. "And by the way, I guess you know that Andre Cruz is assigned to the case? He's so attractive! Maybe you'll get to meet him and ..."

"Yeah, we've already met. Don't go imagining a love connection. It isn't going to happen."

"I think you two would make a cute couple." Audrey said, ignoring Grace. "We'll talk later. Gotta go give a probationer a pee test!"

Grace hung up the receiver. If she didn't clear up this whole situation, she'd be back at the probation department herself, giving pee tests to understandingly reluctant probationers. And that was just not going to happen!

Chapter Fifteen

GRACE ENTERED THE Barnstable County Correctional Facility, where a deputy nodded to her, but not, Grace thought, in a friendly way. He gestured for her to sit on one of the blue plastic chairs along the wall, with a collection of sad-looking relatives and friends of the incarcerated.

After a few minutes she was directed to an interview area where Duane was waiting behind a plexi-glass window. She sat down opposite him on a cold, round metal stool and reached for the phone that was hanging on a cinder-block wall.

"I didn't do it, Miss Tolliver. You've got to believe me. I didn't do anything to that lady, Mrs. Williams."

"Slow down Duane, and it's Mrs. Whitney, not Williams." Grace leaned forward toward the glass that separated them to better engage in eye contact with him. "You're in a load of trouble, and you better start by telling me what happened when you left the lamp shop. Everything, you hear me?"

"Yup." Duane took a deep breath and pushed up the sleeves of his orange jumpsuit. "I saw her on the floor and ran and got you."

"I know that already. Now think. Start with when you left the shop," she repeated.

"Okay. I left the shop and went to the brick house with the black shutters like you told me to. I rang the bell and knocked on the door, but nobody showed up. I figured she must be in the bathroom or something so I decided I'd come back in a few minutes. It was cold, so I went to my truck to wait."

"Where was your truck?"

"Up the street in front of the church."

"Could you see Mrs. Whitney's house from there?"

Duane ran his hands through his fair hair. "Maybe. I'm not too sure."

"Either you could or you couldn't. Which is it?" Grace was losing patience quickly.

"You want to know the truth, Ms. Tolliver? I got in the truck and I think I took a little nap. You know, just for a minute. They had us up late at the rehab last night cleaning and shit, and I was kind of tired." Duane leaned back in his chair and stared at her hopefully.

Grace decided to buy the story. Knowing him as she did, she supposed that was exactly the kind of lame-brained thing he would do. "All right, Duane, you fell asleep. For how long? Any idea?"

"How should I know? I was asleep."

It was all she could do not to scream. She closed her eyes and breathed deeply. When she opened them she saw Duane, leaning forward, his mouth open, his gaze anxious.

"All right. After you woke up, what did you do?" Grace asked.

"I went back to the lady's house. I went in again and . . ."

"Wait a minute. What do you mean again? You didn't say anything about going in the house before your nap."

"Ms. Tolliver, I can't remember everything!" he exclaimed." I'm upset. I've never been charged with murder before. This is my first time!"

Grace took a deep breath. "Let's slow down. Try to remember what you can. It's really, really important."

"Okay. The first time I went to the house and the lady was in the bathroom or whatever. I tried the door and it was open, so I looked in the hall. There was a bunch of stuff by the door. There were two lamps. I didn't know which one you wanted me to get, so that's when I decided to go to my truck and wait."

"Did you touch the lamps?"

"Yup, I think I did touch the lamps. You know, while I was thinking about what I should do. But I put them both back, right where I found them. On the floor by the door."

"I don't think you did this and I'm going to try to find out who did. But you better be telling me the truth."

"For sure. That's it. Everything."

Grace couldn't resist one more question. "When you came into work, you were talking to yourself about helping mink. What's that about?"

Duane squinted. "Mink? I don't know nothing about any mink."

"All right. I've got to go. Don't talk to anyone in here about this."

"What about Gink?"

"Who's Gink?" Grace asked, "Is that what you were talking about? Helping Gink?"

"She's my girl. She used to be at the rehab but she left. She was working as a waitress in Hyannis, but she got canned a few days ago. I'm really stressed about her. She's got no money or anything. Maybe you could go see her and tell her where I am? When I called her on my cell from the truck, she was crying and cold." Duane ran his hands through his hair again.

"What do you mean, you talked to her on your cell? I thought you said Pinewood wouldn't let you have one?" Grace asked.

"Oh. Miss Tolliver, please, I don't want to get in trouble."

"You're in jail! You're in big trouble. Just tell me."

"Okay." Duane slumped further down in his chair. "I had a cell in my truck. I'm not supposed to have it, and I'm not supposed to have any contact with Gink, because she left the program. I called her after I went to the lady's house. From the truck."

"So, the cops probably have the cell now and are checking it out." Grace pondered this new information. "They'll find out what time you called Gink and that could be helpful."

"Actually, the cops don't have it. You do. I mean, I threw it in that closet by the stairs when I came back to get you. I didn't want to get in trouble on account of the cell."

Grace sighed. "I'll try to get in touch with your probation officer. I have to go now. Take care of yourself."

"Please, please tell Gink where I am. Couldn't you go and see her? She's at the Sandman Apartments in Hyannis. Number twelve."

"Duane, I'm very busy. I can't . . ."

"I'm begging you!" Duane got down on his knees and struck a prayerful pose for emphasis. "You're my only friend!" he cried.

There was that word, *friend*, again. Sighing, Grace said, "Maybe. I've got to go now. Get off the floor. You're attracting the attention of the deputy."

Duane looked over his shoulder at the burly officer heading his way and quickly leapt to his feet.

"Does Gink have a last name?"

"Yup. Sorenson."

"Okay, Duane. I'll see."

Duane grinned and gave her a thumbs-up sign as he was escorted out of the interview area.

Chapter Sixteen

THE SUN WAS trying to squeeze between the clouds when Grace drove into Barnstable Village. A stiff, steady breeze was whipping the flags outside of the old courthouse. It was lunchtime, and wanting to avoid the general store where the possibility of running into another reporter or a nosy neighbor was too great, she had to pin her hopes on there being something in Pearl's refrigerator that could tide her over.

As she hurried by the front window of Beau's Books, she saw Beau Henderson peering at her from above a stack of Audubon bird books. His dark brown hair was almost covered by a knit cap, and a thick red and white striped scarf was tucked into a leather bomber jacket. He waved a gloved hand at her and nodded.

Beau Henderson was a man of few words. She supposed that a nod and a wave was quite an overture on his part. His shop was as dusty, rundown and cold as Pearl's. The big box stores impacted his small business even more than the lamp shop, but Grace had been in it countless times, purging the stacks for gems to add to her book collection. She'd even scored a couple of old books by Joseph C. Lincoln, one of the Cape's cherished writers of the early part of the last century. She was always on the lookout for the kind with the plastic jackets covering the clever drawings on the covers. Grace smiled at Beau and waved back.

Grace pushed open the door to Pearl's and headed straight for the closet. She rummaged around in the bottom until she found Duane's cell phone. She ran up the stairs and went to the back room to check out the refrigerator.

Michael stood at the kitchen table. "Oh, hello, Grace. I didn't hear you come in." He was finishing an egg salad on white bread, and was wiping crumbs from the corner of his mouth with a linen napkin. "Of course, I would have heard you if we had a bell."

"Okay, okay. I'll think about it." Grace told him as she squatted in front of the refrigerator looking for something, anything, to eat. "Ah, a yogurt! Blueberry, my favorite. How lucky am I?" She stood up and put the yogurt down on the table next to Michael. He wrinkled his nose.

"Have you checked the expiration date?"

Grace held the container up to the light. It was frustrating how the date was printed in the same color as the lid, making it almost impossible to read.

"Darn! It's about five days past." Grace pulled off the lid and smelled the blueberry-studded, creamy-style yogurt. "Not bad. Not bad at all, and I'm starving. Are any of those fabulous brownies left? I'll wash it down with one of those."

Michael frowned. "You're living dangerously. And yes, I saved you a couple of brownies. They're in your office."

"Thank you. You are fantastic!" Grace said as Michael blushed. "And how is Edith? Feeling better today?"

"Much better. She ate all of her breakfast and was sound asleep when I left this morning."

"I'm glad to hear that." Grace perched halfway on the stool across the table from Michael. "I want you to know that I am so grateful that you've joined us here at Pearl's. I know this is a step down from your previous employment at Pilgrim's, but you've done such a great job here cleaning up and organizing the shop. I certainly hope you will stay on with me after the holidays."

Michael folded his napkin and placed it into his metal lunch box. "I'd be delighted. Pearl's has so much potential. I know you've got lots of plans for the shop, and I'd be so happy if I could be a part of the restoration."

"Great! I was afraid you might want to retire like Bella and head off to a tropical beach somewhere."

Michael's eyes widened. "Oh, no, Grace. I would never do that. I've never left Cape Cod and I'm not about to do so now."

"Never left Cape Cod? Never? Surely you've traveled. Been to Boston, New York?"

"No."

"But Boston's only an hour away."

"I won't go over the bridges. I have taken the ferry to Nantucket and Martha's Vineyard, though. I guess my quiet lifestyle drove my wife nuts. It's okay, Grace. I'm happy in my small world. It would take more than a lifetime to learn all there is to know about the Cape, its history, its people. I have my church, my friends, my books and of course, my Edith. I watch television, I stay connected. I don't feel the need to go anywhere. I'm a happy fellow."

"I didn't know you had been married."

"It was a very, very long time ago." Michael blushed and dove under the table to pick up a coffee spoon.

Michael was referring to the Sagamore and the Bourne bridges. Miles Standish himself had first proposed creating a water route across the seven-mile stretch of land that connected Cape Cod to the mainland of Massachusetts, but it wasn't until 1914 that the inland water route was finally constructed, one of the many bits of Cape Cod history that Michael had conveyed to her over the past few weeks. But Grace knew what Michael meant. He was a homebody in the true sense. His world was small, but it was rich enough. He was content with what he had.

"A lot of people I know would envy you."

Restored by an ingestion of Michael's brownies, Grace dialed Detective Cruz. She hated calling him, but he said to let him know if she learned anything new, and Duane's cell phone was certainly a new development. She wasn't sure of the mechanics, but she thought maybe the police could verify that he had called Gink, the length of their conversation and even the time of the call. It might be enough to exonerate Duane.

She got his recording. She left a brief message and hung up. Phew! That was done. She could hear Bella's drill shutting down as Michael greeted a customer. She thought it would be a good time to finish up that shade she'd started last night, but first, a cup of coffee and another brownie.

As she was getting up, the phone rang and Grace grabbed it on the first ring.

"Gracie! I'm at Cape Cod Emergency!" her father's familiar voice said. "Can you come pick me up? I hate this place!"

Grace's heart sank. Anxiety, her old friend, arrived in the pit of her stomach like a freight train. "What's wrong? Why are you in the emergency room?"

"Oh. I had a little accident in the pickup. I'm okay, but come get me. I'll be waiting on the sidewalk in front of the hospital." With that he hung up.

Grace groaned. Two incidents with her father in two days. She'd have to try again to convince him it was time to get some help. She walked to Bella's workspace and filled her in on her father's phone call. "I'll be back as soon as I can. My car is low on gas, so I'll take the truck."

She headed down the slippery stairs that led to the back yard, side-stepping snow and ice to the truck. PEARL'S ANTIQUE LAMPS & SHADES was emblazoned on the sides of the green 1947 Ford parked up against a shed and covered with snow. Grace did a quick job of brushing the snow off the windshield and rear window and hopped in. The worn leather seat was freezing, even through her heavy coat.

Crossing her fingers, she turned the key in the ignition. Miracle of miracles! It hummed!

Her father was standing outside the hospital door like he said he would be. He was wearing his favorite blue Greek sailor's cap and stuck his arm in the air as she turned into the drive that led to the ER. When Grace coasted the truck to a stop, he opened the door and slid onto the seat beside her. He handed her a bunch of red carnations with a sheepish smile.

"Got these in the gift shop," he said.

It was like him to try to distract her with a little gift. "Are you all right? What happened?" Grace took the flowers.

"I was on my way to the grocery store when a bread truck came into my lane." He told her. "I had to turn quickly and I swerved and ended up in a ditch! Damned truck drivers! Don't look where they're going. Now I'm going to be without transportation until I get the pickup checked out. I got a couple of bumps and bruises, that's all. They took me in the ambulance. I guess they figured they'd better check the old guy out."

"I'm so relieved that you're okay," Grace said. "You really scared me. Shall we stop by the grocery store on the way home?"

"That's great. But do you think we could go by Monti's and get some fried clams? Hospitals make me hungry."

"I thought you weren't supposed to eat fried clams because of your cholesterol."

"Once in a while, Gracie. I'm almost eighty-four. I want to enjoy my life. God knows, at this age everyone wants to tell you what you can't do."

Grace reached over and patted his hand. She was tempted to remind him that if he watched his diet he might still be enjoying life at ninety-four. Instead, she said "Monti's it is!"

A few minutes later, they were seated at a Formica table and ordering fried clams for two, along with a beer for him and a cup of coffee for Grace. Her father smiled contentedly as he gazed around the restaurant. "I'm feeling better already, Gracie." he said. "You could say I'm happy as a clam!"

Monti's Clam Shack had been around for as long as Grace could remember. It had been a family tradition on Saturday nights to pile into the old station wagon and head for the pier. Rain or shine, winter or summer. Saturday night was Monti's.

The place hadn't changed a bit, Grace thought. Even the décor remained unchanged. The same counter with six stools, the dozen or so square tables topped with Clam Shack accouterments and, of course, the view of Hyannis Harbor and the ferries that criss-crossed Nantucket Sound. Grace felt a sweep of nostalgia as she looked at the few boats still in the water and thought about her own little sailboat she sailed in this same bay when she was twelve.

The waitress arrived with their orders and they dug in. "How's your friend doing? The young man you hired."

"He's not my friend. I hired him from Pinewood to give him some work experience. He's still in jail. I saw him today. It's depressing. He had nothing to do with Danielle's death. I'm sure he'd never seen or heard of her before yesterday."

"You're probably right about that," her father agreed. "Danielle hung around in pretty rarefied circles. She was beautiful, rich and had that lovely French accent. She was a New York sensation about forty years ago and ..."

"Yes, so you said yesterday. Successful model. Party girl and all that."

Thomas looked out the window at the bay. "Too bad she won't get to finish that autobiography she was writing," he said, reaching absent-mindedly for the check. "It would have been a fascinating story.

"No kidding? She was writing a book?" Grace said, nabbing the check out of his hand. "That's really interesting."

Thomas stood up and put on his jacket. "She had been working on it for years. When she'd come in for photos, she'd always talk about it. The last time I saw her about a month or so ago, she seemed pretty frazzled. But she said she was still keeping her journal and she'd finish it one of these days."

"Why don't you write an autobiography?" Grace suggested. "You've had an interesting life and career."

Thomas pulled his hat down on his head. "Maybe you're right. But if I told all, you might disown me," he said, grinning.

"Not a chance, Dad," she said, taking his arm and heading out into the sunshine.

Grace maneuvered the old truck into Thomas's driveway. "I know you don't want to hear this, but have you thought about getting someone to help you with shopping? And cleaning? And maybe you shouldn't be driving anymore."

Thomas gave Grace a sideways glance and promptly jumped out of the truck. "Why don't you move back here with me?"

"Well, I . . ."

"Didn't think so. Just you take care of your problems, and I'll take care of mine. Come on, let's unload these groceries. I've taken up enough of your day." Grace sighed and grabbed a couple of bags. Clearly, it was the end of the discussion.

Chapter Seventeen

Turning the truck back onto Route 28, Grace realized that she wasn't far from the Sandman Apartments. Stopping at a red light, she could see that the parking lot in front of the seedy structure was empty except for two or three battered vehicles. She didn't see anyone hanging around. Waiting for the light to turn green and the intersection to clear, she recalled Duane's pathetic pleading at the jail. Oh, well, she thought. I'm here. I guess I could find Gink and let her know about Duane. Besides, maybe I can convince Gink to talk to Detective Cruz and corroborate Duane's story about the phone call.

Grace turned around and manipulated the truck into a parking space not far from number twelve, which was on the end of the first floor under the stairs that led to the second level. 'I love Tina' was scrawled on the door in fading purple paint and a concrete planter box was stuffed with cigarette butts. The blinds on the window to the right of the door were closed, but she heard voices and movement coming from within.

Grace had a moment of unease. After all, she had always had Audrey with her when she went to places like this, and they always scheduled home visits in advance, the idea being that an unarmed probation officer didn't want to walk into a dicey situation. In Cape Cod at least, that theory had worked well. In San Francisco she had encountered some difficult situations despite advance warning. Her mind flashed back to the time she visited a female probationer who had a mutual stay-away order from her boyfriend. They often beat each other up, exchanging roles of perpetrator and victim. On this day, when the boyfriend had unexpectedly showed up drunk, and before Grace could do anything, her probationer grabbed a beer bottle (which, of course, was evidence of another kind of violation) and struck her boyfriend on the head. Grace had managed to wrestle the bottle out of the woman's hand and use her cell phone to call 911.

Grace was abruptly brought back to the present when the door opened and a tattooed arm reached out and pulled her, none to gently, into the room. She looked up into the angry eyes of a brawny man with orange hair who let go of her arm but stared menacingly down at her. He slammed the door. Across the room, two other men leaned against the edge of a table with their beefy arms crossed.

"Who are you?" Orange Hair said, skipping niceties.

"I'm looking for Gink Sorenson," Grace told him, her voice unfortunately coming out in a squeak. It occurred to her that she might have put herself, quite unintentionally, in real danger.

"There ain't no Gink here." He growled. "You guys know a Gink?"

"No." The other two replied in unison.

"Sorry to disturb you." Grace said, assuming a cheerfulness she was far from feeling. "I thought she lived in number twelve. I'll be on my way. Thanks." She turned toward the door, now blocked by Orange Hair.

"Not so fast," one of the men, who was wearing a red Martha's Vineyard T-shirt, said. "You look kind of familiar. Maybe you're a cop or something."

"No, no," Grace protested. "I own a lamp shop. If you look outside you can see my truck." Orange Hair peered out the window through the dirty blind.

The T-shirt guy stepped toward Grace. "I've seen you at the probation department. That's where. Your hair is different, but I remember you."

Grace's heart was pounding. She wondered if they could hear it. "Oh! Yes, of course. I used to work there. I retired. I own the lamp shop now." Remembering that flattery often worked wonders with probationers who weren't used to getting any, she said, "You have an excellent memory."

"Yeah. Yeah, I do have good memory at that." He stood up straighter. As he did so, Grace thought she saw a bunch of plastic baggies on the table behind him along with a scale and wrapped-up parcels of what looked like white powder.

Orange Hair grabbed her arm again, squeezing it tight. "Lady," he said. "Get yourself out of here. I don't know who you are, but you better remember that you haven't seen anything or anyone in this room. If anything unexpected should happen, I'll find you. At the probation department or the lamp shop or wherever. I'll find you. Do you understand me?"

"Yes, of course."

Orange Hair opened the door and shoved her through it, giving her arm an extra hard squeeze. He slammed the door behind her just as she collided with a young woman carrying a pink plastic basket of laundry. "Oof!" Grace and the woman shouted together.

"Watch where you're going!" the woman said.

"You wouldn't be Gink, by any chance?" Grace said, as she bent down to help her pick up the clothes.

"Who wants to know?" she said, giving Grace a critical glance.

"I know Duane. I have a message from him. Do you live here?"

"I live in number twenty-one. Upstairs. Who are you, anyway?"

Grace was sure Duane had said number twelve. It was, Grace thought, just like Duane to get the numbers reversed. "I need to talk to you. I'll follow you upstairs. I don't want to go into your room or anything. I just want to talk for a minute."

"Whatever," Gink said. She started up the stairs with Grace following behind her. When they got outside room number twenty-one, which was about halfway down the open balcony, Gink and Grace both stopped and faced each other.

"I'm Grace Tolliver. I hired Duane to work at my lamp shop. I don't know whether you know this or not, but he was arrested yesterday and is in jail." Grace waited to see if Gink showed any signs of prior knowledge of this.

Gink didn't move a muscle. "Go on."

Grace studied Gink for another moment. She appeared to

be about eighteen years old. She was quite attractive if you could see beyond the lank red and green hair and the multiple piercings and tattoos that covered her fair skin. Her demeanor was cool, her eyes intelligent.

Grace filled Gink in on the details of Duane's arrest for the murder of Danielle Whitney. "Duane told me that you spoke with him on the phone yesterday morning. The cops will want to talk to you and verify that. It might help Duane. Will you talk to them?"

"Yeah, sure. If it will help." Gink scowled. "Duane wouldn't kill anyone. He's got a good heart," she continued. "We met at Pinewood, but since I left and he's still in the program, we weren't supposed to have any contact."

Grace thought about the many rules and regulations at the rehab. Not having contact with someone who had quit the program was one that Pinewood was consistent about enforcing.

"I've been doing good on my own, but Pinewood doesn't care about that. They have so many rules," Gink continued. "Duane was worried because I lost my job. He said he'd help me financially any way he could. He said he'd give me money from his job. Poor Duane. He couldn't hurt anybody. He's the most authentic man I've ever met."

Grace was startled by Gink's frank assessment of Duane, let alone her vocabulary. She hadn't thought about him in such a personal way. He was a probationer, a recovering drug addict, and an employee. But clearly, to Gink he was so much more.

"What do you mean? If you don't mind telling me, that is."

"What you see is what you get with Duane," the girl said with conviction. "He's got problems, sure, but he's honest."

"Why did you leave Pinewood?" Grace asked.

Gink shrugged. "There's some weird stuff going on over there. Duane told me you used to be a P.O., so I don't want to go into any details. Let's just say I was being harassed, so I left." Gink put her key in the door to her apartment and pushed it open with the laundry basket. "I don't like talking to cops too much. But if it will help Duane, I will."

Grace reached in her purse and pulled out Cruz's card. "Call him," she said. "He's got the case." She handed the card to Gink.

"Do you know those guys down there in number twelve?"

"I don't know anyone here," Gink replied, "and I like it that way."

"Good. I'd steer clear of them if I were you. Not a friendly bunch. You can get hold of me if you need to, at Pearl's. You know where it is?"

"Yeah."

"Before I go, I need to ask you a favor. I'm going back downstairs and get in my truck. If anyone hassles me or follows me, call the police. Okay?"

Gink looked at Grace quizzically and started to say something, but Grace cut her off. "It's better if you don't know."

As she drove away, she saw Gink standing by the railing watching her. One floor below her, Orange Hair was doing the same.

Chapter Eighteen

AFTER SHE HAD driven about a block, Grace called 911 and reported what she'd seen at the Sandman. She hung up. From numerous training classes, and having read thousands of police reports, Grace knew the signs of a drug operation. Plastic baggies, scales, powder, and usually lots of cash. She couldn't tell if this had been a cocaine or methamphetamine or heroin operation, and she hadn't seen any cash, but there was enough evidence in her mind that more than warranted a call to the police. After all, a meth lab inside an apartment building would be a dangerous situation. She knew it wasn't necessary to leave her name. All she hoped was that Orange Hair and the rest would not connect her with their hopefully imminent bust.

It was past mid-day now, and Grace tried to unwind on the ride back to her shop but she had to be hyper-alert because she was driving northwest, and the rays of the sun were bouncing off the snow and nearly blinding her. It was a relief to reach the shadowy Village's main street where there were still quite a few people scurrying about, Christmas shopping, running errands or walking dogs. Tony, Sophie's father, was coming out of the general store carrying a bag of groceries and a newspaper. He hopped in the cab of his pickup and roared off in the direction of the Beach Sparrow Inn. Father Gavin Murrey, the retired priest, whom Grace recognized because she had often seen him helping young offenders navigate the halls of the courthouse, was peering in the window of a real estate office; and Howard Pittman, sipping out of a Styrofoam cup, was striding in the direction of Danielle's house.

As she came in the back door of Pearl's, Bella waved for her to come into the repair area. She was packing a lamp into a carton, a job that Duane had been hired to do.

"How's your father?" she asked. "Everything all right?"

"He had a minor accident," Grace said, taking off her coat. "He said he ran into a bread truck. I don't know if it was his fault or not, but he ended up in a ditch. He's okay though. But sometimes I wonder if he is creating problems because he's lonely and wants me to move back home."

"I'm sure you are worried about him," Bella said, wrapping the lamp in bubble wrap. "It's no fun getting old, Grace. Our independence is so important to us, but we do get plenty lonely ..." she drifted off, lost in her thoughts for a moment. "Incidentally, that cop Cruz came by while you were out. He certainly is a looker." She peered at Grace over the large cardboard box.

"Yes ... yes, I guess he is," Grace muttered.

"He had a lady cop with him too. Rice. I think that's what she said her name was. None too friendly, that one."

Grace helped Bella stuff some old newspaper around the lamp that she had set in the box.

"Is he single, Grace? Or perhaps I should ask if he's available?"

Grace felt herself blushing. "I don't know. I don't know anything about him."

Bella pulled out a large roll of packing tape and deftly wound it around the box and then slapped an address label on it. "He seemed nice. Intelligent. Very polite."

"Really? He seemed cold and judgmental to me," Grace replied. "I'm going to finish up a shade I started last night. Do you need any help in here first?"

Bella threw her a curious glance. "No. I'm about to take a breather and have some tea. All of the packages are wrapped for shipping. I'm missing Duane already. His wrapping wasn't very pretty, but he got the job done."

Out in the main room, Grace found Clay Davenport pawing through a stack of empire shades. "I'm quite sure I saw a creamy silk one in this stack a few days ago," he grumbled. Michael was busy showing an elderly man an unusual pair of bird lamps.

The two pottery lamps, about a foot or so high each, had a red bird perched on the green trunk of a tree. The original red and orange shades were in great condition. Grace bought them from an antique picker a couple of weeks ago. There were plenty of bird watchers on Cape Cod and she was betting that she would sell them quickly.

Michael arranged the two lamps on a table and plugged them in. The shades gave off a tangerine glow. "These lamps probably date to the early nineteen hundreds, Mr. Begley," Michael explained to his customer. "Van Briggle Pottery was established in Colorado Springs in 1899. Bella has rewired both of them, changed the plugs, and put new felt pads on the bottom." Michael maneuvered the lamps so that the birds' beaks were touching each other. "Isn't that delightful?" Michael clasped his hands together. "A pair of love birds. A lovely gift for Christmas or Valentine's Day! I'm sure Mrs. Begley would be very pleased."

"Yes, I do believe you are quite right!" Mr. Begley enthused. "I'll take them, young man! My Maggie will be thrilled! Can you gift-wrap them? I'm not very good at that sort of thing."

Michael smiled, as delighted to have been called a young man as to have made a sale. "Absolutely, Mr. Begley. Here at Pearl's, gift-wrapping is complimentary. Come back here to our paper and ribbon section, and I'll help you pick out something very special."

"Oh, Grace. I need help, please," Clay called out to her in his whiney voice. He was up to his knees in empires, drums and round shades, having carelessly dismantled Michael's neatly stacked arrangement. Darn, she'd have to deal with him after all, Grace thought as she walked toward Clay, who was dressed in a natty chestnut tweed suit with a red paisley ascot. No one else on Cape Cod dressed like Clay. Grace supposed his flamboyant attire was his idea of how a successful interior designer should look. Gritting her teeth, she forced herself to smile.

"I do like these shades for this lamp, but I think I want one hand-made for one of my most important customers. Can you make me up one with some of your exquisite pressed flower paper? In soft pinks and greens, perhaps? My client wants something elegant for her boudoir."

No one talked like Clay either, Grace thought. She couldn't imagine that many folks, even the rich ones, on the Cape referred to their bedrooms as boudoirs. "Of course, Clay," she said politely, reminding herself that Clay was a good customer and that he knew more than a thing or two about lamps and how important they were to the décor of a room. Going to the wall covered with rolls of fabrics and papers, she settled on some pressed paper with pink and lavender flowers and pale green leaves.

"Yes, I like this." Clay said, fingering it. "Can I take a sample with me to show my client?"

"Of course. But can I make a design suggestion?" Grace asked. "What about something delicate and gauzy?" she continued, taking the glass lamp from the counter where Clay left it. "I could make a shade using a luxurious silk fabric. In lavender and pink with feathers around the rims. Or in any color you like. Very feminine and pretty. A fun shade. Would your client like something like that?"

Clay considered a smooth, delicate fabric that she spread out for him on her large worktable. "I like that idea, Grace. I do like it. Are you sure you could pull it off? This is a very important client."

"I can do it, Clay, but it will be time consuming. Do you want to talk to your client and get the go-ahead first?"

"I don't have to," he said. "She trusts me to make all of her design decisions. Yes, I do believe she will love this concept of yours. It's fun, playful. We're going for a tropical motif. I think the feathers are marvelous."

"If I use the best fabric, paper and real feathers, it will be expensive. There's quite a lot of work involved."

"Oh! Not to worry! She's got oodles of money. All of my clients are very well to do. Go ahead and make it. I absolutely know she will adore it."

After she finished up with Clay, Grace completed the empire

shade that she had started last night by trimming it with a black grosgrain ribbon, and overlapping the trim with a gold cord. Placing it on the black ginger jar base, she turned it around slowly, checking for any evidence of glue or pencil markings. Satisfied that the lamp was complete, she set it aside and cleared off the worktable and got out her paints. A week or so ago, a customer brought in a cherished toy boat. Bella worked her magic and the toy was now a polished lamp in need of a shade. Grace set about painting a Cape Cod scene of children playing on a beach, fish jumping out of water and white puffy clouds with smiling faces. The customer was giving it to a favorite grandchild for Christmas, and Grace was anxious to get it finished before she was inundated with even more last-minute orders.

Grace was hovering over the fish, using a large magnifying glass with a swing arm she had attached to her desk, when Michael said, "Here she is!" and handed her the phone.

It was M and M. They were both jabbering at once. Grace heard, "Valerie," "Open house," and "You should," before she interrupted them.

"Guys! Hey there! Slow down. What in the world are you talking about?"

"Matt, you tell her," Milo said. "I'll be quiet."

"Remember we told you yesterday that our real estate agent was mad as heck at Danielle?" Before Grace could reply, Matt continued at a rapid pace. "We spoke to the Claridges, Earl and Jamie. They moved down here from Yarmouthport a few weeks ago. It so happens that Valerie was their real estate agent too and she had an open house scheduled at their Yarmouthport residence yesterday morning. Well ..." Matt paused for effect, and Milo completed his sentence. "She didn't show up for the open house!"

Grace looked out the window as two seagulls flew by and landed on the roof across the street, ruffling their feathers and hunkering down against the wind.

"I guess I'm not following you. What's this got to do with ...?"

"She wasn't at the open house because she was busy murdering Danielle!" they both shouted at Grace as if sheer volume would help her understand the obvious.

Grace was too startled to answer, so Matt went on. "Valerie told the Claridges that the open house was a success and that several interested buyers had come by. But when the Claridges called their old neighbors, they told them that there hadn't been an open house. The driveway and walkway are still not shoveled. What do you think, Grace? We think she did it."

The gulls had moved farther apart and were both facing into the setting sun. Grace rubbed her eyes and said; "Matt, Milo, listen. Just because she didn't have an open house and lied about it doesn't mean she is a coldblooded murderer. She probably was snowed in like everyone else around here."

"She's got financial troubles. Danielle didn't intend to give her a commission without a fight. And did you know that she lives in one of those pricey condos on the way to the beach? That's right up the street from Danielle's," Milo said. "She could have run right down there, whacked Danielle and been back home in a matter of a few minutes."

"And Lord knows, we've watched enough *Law and Order* to know that when you've got motive, means and opportunity, you've got your murderer." Matt said. "The handy lamp being the means, of course. Maybe you should go talk to her. Michael tells us that you're investigating the murder."

Thanks Michael, Grace thought. "I'm not exactly investigating, but I'll pass the information on to the police."

There was a long pause. "We can't tell you what to do" Matt said, clearly disappointed, "but if you could meet her yourself, you might come around to our way of thinking. The police probably won't even bother to look into it. Valerie used to date a cop. They'll protect her."

"That's ridiculous. The police want to solve this as much as anyone." Grace replied, keeping her doubts about the investigation to herself. "But if it makes you feel better, I'll try to talk to Valerie."

"Oh, that's good, Grace," Milo exclaimed. "This is so exciting! What if we're right and we've solved the case? We'll be heroes!"

"If only Aunt Pearl was alive. How she would love this

intrigue," Matt said.

"Aunt Pearl?" Grace asked.

"Didn't we ever tell you that my aunt Pearl was the original owner of the shop? She owned it for almost thirty years before we took it over. She knew everything that went on in the village. I think she fancied herself a bit of a detective. She'd be so proud of us," Matt said.

"Guys. I'd love to learn more about Pearl, but I've gotta go. I'm way behind here. You remember how busy the holidays are."

"Do we ever." Milo said. "Not that we miss it, of course. Oh, Matt. We're late for water aerobics. Bye, Grace." With that they hung up.

Chapter Nineteen

G RACE LOOKED AT the Seth Thomas clock that hung crookedly on the wall above her desk. She made a mental note to get a ladder and straighten it. "It's five-thirty. Let's call it a day," she said to Bella and Michael. "I'm going to go home, relax, have dinner and come back later to work on some more shades. You two have had a busy day. You must be tired."

Bella leaned her elbows on the counter that separated her space from the sales area. "I think maybe I'll come back later too. Remember, we can sleep in January."

"Me too." Michael said. "After I have dinner and feed Edith, I'll be back. I'll have a chance to clean up and put some stuff away, so I can start fresh tomorrow. I'll drop that restored lamp with the South of France–style shade you painted off at Christine Sinclair's on my way home.

"Christine Sinclair? Where does she live?"

"Past Danielle's house. It's a traditional Cape Cod style with a large barn. White, with black shutters, wrought iron fence, big trees."

"I know the place." Grace said. "I'll take it."

"Christine was a very close friend of Danielle's," Bella spoke up. "She was in the modeling business too. Not nearly as success- ful as Danielle, but I do believe she had a solid career of her own. Poor thing. I expect she's in a state of shock."

Grace considered this information for a minute. "She'll prob- ably be upset with me too. Just like Danielle's brother Howard. But I can't hide from the whole town. I've got a business to run. Anyway, I'd like to meet her."

Michael picked up a carton and nestled it inside one of Pearl's green bags. After tying a red velvet ribbon through the handles, he handed it to Grace.

"That looks great, very seasonal. Perfect for Saturday's Stroll." Grace said. "I've been thinking. Maybe we could bring in a musician to add to the festivities. My friend Audrey plays the flute. I could ask her if she'd be willing to play for us. And I sure hope I can convince you to make more of those incredible brownies."

"Oh!" Michael clasped his hands together. "A musician. That would be lovely. And I'm so glad you like my brownies. They're from a recipe my mother passed down. I've upgraded it a bit with some imported chocolate from Belgium. It adds to the expense, but it's worth it in my opinion. Here, I have some extra bars, if you'd like one."

"Actually, this chocolate is made in California. It says so right here on the label." Grace said as she handed the chocolate back to him.

A look of shock passed over Michael's impish face. "California. You must be joking."

Grace laughed. "Berkeley, California, to be exact. Care to revise some of your opinions about the Golden State?"

"I don't know. But, I'll give it some consideration."

"You should get off of Cape Cod and travel a bit," Bella told him. "Might do you some good."

"I'll consider that too." Michael said without enthusiasm.

"I'll make some lemon bars and we'll have tea and coffee." Grace said. "I suspect that lots of other businesses will have hot cider. By the way, does Beau do anything for the event? He looked kind of down when I walked by the bookstore earlier today."

"He always looks down. That's Beau. It's who he is," Bella replied.

Grace knew that Bella was wise, and that accepting people as they were and not as one wanted them to be, was an enlightened idea. True change had to come from within. Take, Duane, for instance. He seemed to be trying to turn his life around. But what, Grace reluctantly thought, if desire and motivation weren't enough? What if Duane had not been strong in the face of temptation? She shuddered.

Michael wrapped his blue scarf around his neck before heading downstairs. "Maybe we could do something for Beau. You're right, Grace. He looks even sadder than usual lately. He called me earlier to tell me that he's found an antique lamp reference book that I should take a look at. I'll pop in and see what I can find out." Michael disappeared down the stairs. "See you later, ladies!"

Grace and Bella followed Michael out the door a few minutes later. Grace locked up the shop, said good-bye to Bella and headed down Main Street.

Chapter Twenty

THE EVENING WAS clear but so cold that Grace pulled her hat down over her ears. It was still busy on the street. People were returning home in what constituted rush hour on Cape Cod. Several cars were waiting in each direction at the traffic light at the intersection of Millway and Main. When she heard complaints about the traffic on the Cape, Grace would often tell people to visit the San Francisco Bay Area. Now that was congestion, and she was glad to be out of it.

Despite the low temperature, she enjoyed the walk to Christine Sinclair's house. Which was just as Michael had described. Candle lamps had been placed in every window of the large house, but they weren't lit tonight. Grace rang the doorbell.

When a few minutes passed without a response, she was about to leave the bag on the porch and head home when the cherry red door swung open and a slender figure silhouetted in the foyer light whispered, "Yes?"

"Christine Sinclair? Hi, I'm Grace Tolliver from Pearl's Lamp Store. I've got your repaired lamp."

"Yes, thank you." A skeletal hand reached out and grasped the bag.

Grace noticed the woman's ashen color and her pink-rimmed eyes. She looked like she had been crying for a week.

"I'm so sorry about your friend Danielle. I understand that you and Danielle were ..."

"You understand nothing." She spoke in such a manner that Grace was unsure if her emotion was anger or despair. "Can you come in a minute? I would like to speak with you." She opened the door wider.

Telling herself that she might as well take her licks and get it over with, Grace stepped in and closed the door behind her. Christine turned and, without another word, walked down the shadowy hallway toward the back of the house. Grace followed in her wake inhaling L'Air du Temps perfume until they arrived in a cozy library. Grace noted a Louis XIV console, elegant and light, and several antique display cases filled with bric-a-brac. The curtains were open on the double French doors, affording Grace a view of a back yard with many pine trees encircling a wide expanse of lawn covered in snow. A flagstone patio that had been swept clean was crowned with a stone fountain with gargoyles peering out from under hats of creamy snow and ice. A great barn with a rooster weather vane was visible behind a hedge.

"You can sit there," Christine said, indicating a chair slip-covered in powder blue velvet.

Grace sat on the edge of the soft wing chair. For the first time, she got a good look at the woman. She was tall and slender, mid-fifties, with pale hair. Her skin was flushed and raw, as if she was using too much wrinkle remover cream.

Christine wrung her hands together. She didn't sit down with Grace, but paced up and down the room while a mantel clock ticked away seconds, which turned into minutes. There was, Grace noted, a crystal glass half filled with something that looked like straight scotch on an end table near the fireplace.

"I'm aware that you sent that young man to Danielle's house," Christine said at last. "I think it was incredibly poor judgment on your part. I've been in touch with District Attorney Banks, and I want you to know that the community will not tolerate drug addicts and thieves in our midst. I couldn't stop Pinewood when they decided to locate near here, but I certainly intend to have some say in who is working in our town. Barnstable is a respectable old village with a long tradition of peaceful streets, and I intend to keep it that way." She hesitated for a moment, but then continued her pacing. "You might want to consider relocating your shop. Although Pearl's has been here a long time, it has obviously taken a turn for the worse under your ownership."

Grace looked up at Christine as she walked by again. She noticed that there were stains on her tailored blouse. "I know you've suffered a terrible loss," Grace said. "But please consider that Duane did not murder Danielle. I never would have sent him to her house if I believed for a minute that he was capable of violence. I know the D.A. has brought charges against Duane, but it's still early. There may be other suspects to consider."

"Like who?" Christine hissed. "Do you really think that someone from our community would do such a terrible thing? And what would be their motive? Danielle was a lovely, generous woman. Yes, she might have rubbed a few people the wrong way here and there, but that's because she had such high standards."

"The murderer might have been someone from outside of this community," Grace responded. "Do you know if she had anyone in her life who was a threat to her? After all, from what I hear, you were her best friend. She might have confided in you."

"I'm sure I don't," Christine snapped. She continued to pace the room, rubbing her hands together as if she were cold, although, thanks to the blazing fire, the room was as hot as a midsummer day.

"What infuriates me is that the young murderer came from Pinewood. One of Danielle's favorite charities," Christine continued. "If that drug addict murdered her and she left money in her estate to Pinewood, will it still go to them?"

Grace didn't think that Christine was expecting an answer to her question, so she was silent.

"I'm going to talk to D.A. Banks about that tomorrow. I'll make damned sure they don't get a dime of Danielle's money."

"I'm sure we'll hear all about the particulars of the estate before long," Grace said. "I suppose her brother Howard will inherit the bulk of it. From what I understand, he's her closest relative. Do you know if they were on good terms?"

"Of course they were. Why do you ask?"

Grace proceeded cautiously. "I heard somewhere that maybe they had been arguing lately."

"All brothers and sisters have their spats. I can say that he was as concerned as I about her recent involvement with a man named Vernon," Christine said bitterly. "That man is a gigolo, if you ask me. Danielle was displeased with both Howard and me for interfering in her personal life. We wanted to protect her. The thing is, I think she was finally starting to listen to us. In fact, she told me she was going to break it off with him this weekend."

"Do you think he might have hurt her?" Grace asked. "A lot of murders are domestic violence related. Someone not getting his or her way. Someone who might be angry at being rejected. Was Danielle strong enough to say no to this Vernon?"

"Danielle was a very strong woman. When she set her mind to something, there was no changing it. When she said no, she meant no." Turning her back on Grace, she said, "I think you better go now."

Grace knew that asking Christine any further questions would be fruitless. She was far too emotional. "Once again, I'm sorry for your loss. And I'm going to try my hardest to find out who's responsible."

Christine turned around. "What can you do? Haven't you done enough?" she said angrily. "Just stay out of it and let the D.A. do her job." She strode down the hall toward the front door. Halfway down, she stopped in front of a beautiful French console. On top of the table were two burgundy, French classic porcelain column lamps.

Christine picked up one of the lamps and reached down and unplugged it from the wall. "I spoke to Bella about this lamp a while ago." She shoved the lamp at Grace. "Maybe she can repair it before you go out of business."

Chapter Twenty-One

A FEW TENSE moments later, and Grace was out in the cold. Christine seemed to be quite a passionate woman. Grace couldn't help feeling shaken up from the encounter. As she recalled from her run-in yesterday with Howard, it wasn't fun to be on the other side of someone's grief and anger. Especially when they blamed you for it.

As Grace reached her cottage, a car pulled alongside of her.

"Hey," Andre Cruz called.

"Hi," Grace responded, stopping in front of the walkway to her front door. The light from a nearby street lamp shone on Cruz. He turned off the engine and stepped out. "Thanks for Duane's cell phone. I want to talk to you some more about that. We could go down to the Dolphin and grab a burger or something."

When Grace frowned, thinking of the people they'd encounter there, Cruz must have picked up on her body language because he said, "Sorry, I don't have time to go too far, and besides, I'm craving one of their cheeseburgers. I'll make sure no one bothers us. How about it?"

Her refrigerator was pretty empty since she hadn't had a minute to go shopping in the last couple of days, and she was kind of hungry — and curious, too. What harm could there be in having a quick meal with the detective?

"Okay, sure. Let me run in, put this lamp away and feed my cat," she said. "Do you want to come in for a minute?"

"I sure as hell don't want to stand out here in the cold," Cruz said, following her into the house. He scooped up Clambake who was sitting in one of his favorite spots on the back of the sofa in front of the living room window.

He scratched the cat's ears as Grace set the lamp on a table and got out a can of cat food. Clambake leapt out of Cruz's arms and landed with a thud when Grace placed the bowl on the floor.

"That's one big cat you have. How much does he weigh?"

"About nineteen pounds. He's part Maine Coon. They tend to be large. Especially the boys."

"He's a nice-looking animal. Doesn't look like he'd be afraid of my two dogs."

"Clambake can hold his own." Grace agreed. "He doesn't get rattled easily. As long as he's getting regular meals, that is."

"Nice place you've got." Andre said. "White. Pretty."

Grace cringed inwardly. She didn't want her place to be "pretty." Clean, fresh, stylish. Neutral even, but not pretty.

"Thanks, I'm still working on it," she said a bit defensively. "I'm going to go upstairs for a second. I'll be down in a minute."

Grace ran up the stairs to her bedroom, where she brushed her hair and put on fresh lipstick. She was not at all sure what Andre Cruz was up to, but it wouldn't hurt to freshen up.

Andre parked behind the Dolphin, and they went in the back door. The bar was about three-quarters full and the restaurant about the same. Grace noticed a cluster of lawyers had taken over a round table near the door and were engaged in a heated discussion. Over in the center of the room near the brick fireplace, Grace noticed Howard, deep in conversation with a tall, auburn-haired woman dressed in a green pantsuit. The woman was waving her hands around, and Grace wished she could catch their conversation. Two off-duty cops were at the bar, and Andre nodded to them as he steered her toward the end of the bar where there were a couple of empty stools.

The Dolphin looked nice tonight, Grace thought. The lights were low, casting soft shadows on the knotty pine walls and the blue carpet dotted with a design of tiny stars. The bar sparkled under a string of white lights, and red bows had been hung on lanterns, giving the casual neighborhood place an air of elegance. Cruz introduced her to the bartender, a retired police officer. He gave Grace a quick glance and a nod, took their orders, a cheeseburger with fries for Andre, and a shrimp salad for Grace. Andre ordered a dark beer, Grace a glass of chardonnay.

"Aren't you on duty?" Grace asked.

"What? Are you my mother?" Andre said, his eyes twinkling.

"Sorry," Grace said, feeling the color rise in her cheeks. She always seemed to say the dumbest things when she was around this attractive man. "It's none of my business."

Andre nodded in agreement. "So, how did you happen to have Duane's cell phone?" he asked.

He certainly doesn't beat around the bush, Grace thought. "I went to see him at the jail today," she told him. "When he was telling me about Gink, he mentioned the phone call he made to her as he sat in his truck up the street from Danielle's."

Their drinks were placed on the bar in front of them and Andre took a quick swallow of his beer. "Who's Gink? Duane didn't mention anyone by that name when we interviewed him."

"That's because most probationers don't tell the police everything they tell probation officers," she said. "We have a different relationship. We see them over a period of time and we get to know them better. Cops usually only see them at the time of arrest or for an interview after. There I go saying 'we,'" she added. "I sometimes sound like I'm still a probation officer."

"How did you get into law enforcement, anyway?" Cruz asked.

Grace wiped a drip of wine from the stem of her glass with her finger. "I was an art major. After a couple of semesters, I had to face the fact that I was never going to be able to support myself by painting landscapes. About the same time, a friend of mine got into some minor trouble with the law. I met his probation officer and was impressed with how he handled things. So I dropped out of art school, transferred to UMASS and majored in criminology. And, as they say, the rest is history."

"So, now you're painting lampshades. And making a living

at it."

"I haven't turned a profit yet. The previous owners taught me a lot, but I've still got so much more to learn about running a business." Grace felt Andre's sleeve brush against her arm in the tight space of the bar. "What made you decide to be a cop?"

Cruz stared into the well of the bar. "I needed a job that would pay decent wages and give me good benefits. I was married at the time and we were planning a family. It wasn't like I always dreamed of being a cop. I came around to it out of necessity."

"Do you like it?"

"Yeah, it's okay. I get to meet lots of interesting people," he glanced at Grace. "It was harder when I was married. My wife didn't like the hours I had to put in, and she couldn't relate to my job. So, after a few years, she went her way and I went mine." Andre looked at her with a somber gaze. "You were married to a cop. You know how it is."

"I do."

"Sorry, I didn't mean to, you know … bring up Jack. But now that I have, I have to tell you I thought he was a heck of a guy. Everyone did."

"Sure. Thanks." Grace looked across the crowd at the bar and through the front window out to the quiet street. The door opened and a young couple holding hands walked in. They grabbed the last two seats at the bar.

The bartender approached them with their orders. He reached under the bar and pulled out two napkins rolled and stuffed with silverware.

"Want another beer, Andre?" he asked.

Andre shook his head. He turned to Grace. "Another glass of wine?"

Grace shook her head. The bartender slid a wire basket containing catsup, mustard and relish in front of Andre. He wiped his hands on his apron and turned back to the bar. Andre dumped catsup on his burger.

"Look, can you tell me where I might find Duane's friend? What did you say her name was? Gink?"

"I met her today at the Sandman. She's in apartment twenty-one. She said she'd talk to you, and I gave her your card. She hasn't called you yet?"

"No. But I'll try to track her down tonight," Andre said. "You shouldn't be going around the Sandman. Lots of creeps hang out there, and there was a drug bust there today. It's not safe for a lamp shop owner. I should probably ask you why you went to talk to Gink in the first place."

"Duane asked me to find her. And I wanted to talk to her too. Find out more about the phone call Duane said he made to her. I know you believe Duane murdered Danielle, but I believe he's innocent. Everyone around here seems to have already made up their minds about his guilt," Grace answered wearily.

"Yes, you're right," he agreed. "I do believe Duane did it. But the investigation continues. If we get any leads, we follow them. Happy?"

Damn, Grace thought. He certainly can be irritable. They ate in silence for a few minutes. She decided to plunge in anyway and ask him about Danielle's boyfriend Vernon. "I was talking to Christine Sinclair, Danielle's friend. She said that Danielle was involved with a guy named Vernon, and that he might be a gigolo or something,"

"How come you were talking to Christine Sinclair?" Andre said, frowning. "I hope you're not trying to investigate the case yourself."

"I was delivering a lamp to her. In fact, that's where I was coming from when you came by my house tonight. She thinks I should be tarred and feathered and ridden out of town. Apparently, I'm bringing unsavory elements to her perfect village." Grace pushed her empty plate away from her so she could rest her elbows on the bar. "Anyway, before she practically threw me out of her house, she mentioned somebody named Vernon. She seemed to think that Vernon was bad news. She said Danielle was going to give him his walking papers last weekend. Have you looked into the possibility that this man might have something to do with her murder, or are you so sure that Duane did it that you're not investigating anyone else?"

"We are looking for him." Andre said, ignoring her sarcasm. "His name is Vernon Rugosa, but he has a lot of aliases. We identified him through some prints found at Danielle's. Anyway, he's on probation, and there is a warrant out for him. Apparently he hasn't been reporting in like he should. Missed a progress report in court about a month ago. Had a DWI a few months back. Rugosa's quite a ladies' man. He preys on older women. Sometimes he marries them. Other times he manipulates them into giving him vast sums of money. Then he disappears. He's able to change his appearance enough so that he doesn't get recognized. We've got mug shots of him with beards, mustaches, gray hair, black hair, you name it. The guy is a chameleon. A real sleaze bag."

Andre picked up the check from the bar. He threw down some bills and gave a wave to the bartender. They bundled up in their coats and went outside. The cold air was blowing steadily across Cape Cod Bay. Heavy with salt, it stung Grace's face until her eyes watered. She looked up at the dark sky, laced with stars. The moon was fuzzy, as if smeared with Vaseline.

"I always think a moon like that means snow is coming," Grace said hopefully, and then, seeing a light in the house where she had observed the old man staring at her the night before, she said, "Did you talk to the man who lives in that house over there?"

"Morris Bidlake? Yes, an officer interviewed him yesterday. He didn't have much to say, but he did see Duane going into the house. Apparently he's got a bird's-eye view of Danielle's front walkway. Come on." Andre pulled his collar up. "I'll take you home. I'm going to go check on this Gink lady."

"That's okay," Grace said. "I'm going back to the shop for a while. Thanks for the dinner."

Andre smiled at her as bright headlights illuminated them both. A car drove quickly toward them. When the driver pulled over and the headlights weren't blinding her, Grace could see that it was Emma Rice in a police cruiser. Giving Grace a cursory glance, she directed her attention to Cruz.

"What's up?" she said.

"Ready to take a ride over to the Sandman Apartments?" Andre asked her. "There's someone I think we should talk to. You can drop your car off, and we'll ride together."

"Sure I'm not interrupting anything?" Emma said.

"Nope." Andre said, stopping beside his car. "Let's go. I'll meet you at the lot. See you, Grace." With that, he got in his car as Grace stood alone in the cold parking lot watching the two cars pull swiftly away.

The sudden silence that enveloped her left her feeling empty inside. Andre Cruz was an enigma, but sitting next to him at the bar and sharing a meal had reminded her how pleasing having dinner with a smart, attractive man could be. It had, after all, been a long time.

On her way across the road to the shop, Grace looked over her shoulder at Morris Bidlake's window, the light she had seen a few minutes ago now extinguished. So that was the witness Andre had mentioned earlier. It didn't prove anything, Grace told herself. He might have been able to see Danielle's front walkway, but that didn't mean he knew who killed Danielle.

Chapter Twenty-Two

WHEN GRACE ARRIVED at the lamp shop, Michael was vacuuming the floor and Bella was humming as she polished a brass, urn-shaped lamp. The wintry scent of pine from the Christmas tree had replaced the familiar musty smell of the old building.

"Oh, that looks beautiful, Bella. I'm going to make a shade for that with some fabric that has a henna design."

"That sounds nice. The henna colors and the brass will work together nicely. What kind of a shade are you going to use?"

"I think a rectangular bell. Or a square."

"Those are both good choices." Bella said. "By the way, I spoke with Beau Henderson on my way in tonight. He's not sure if he's going to participate in the Village Stroll. He said business has been slower than usual, and he's thinking of giving up the store."

"Gosh, that would be sad," Grace, replied. "I think the town benefits from a bookstore. But I have to admit that his place needs a lot of work. I don't think he's very organized. There are stacks of books all over the place."

"Beau's all right." Bella said. "I can't say that I know him well, but I think maybe he's shy or reserved. He hasn't been in business too long, maybe a year or so. I believe he said he came from somewhere in Vermont. He seems very knowledgeable about books. And he's quite a handsome man." She glanced at Grace.

Grace, sensing what Bella was up to, let out a laugh.

Michael, having turned off the vacuum cleaner, had been listening in on Bella and Grace's conversation quietly until now. "I talked to him too. Maybe we can convince him to be open on Saturday for the Stroll if we donate some of our goodies to him.

I could make extra brownies. He seems so sad and depressed."

"Sounds good. If you can convince him, I'll help too," Grace said.

With that settled, they got down to work. Grace used the quiet of the evening to start a shade for a customer who brought in a silver teapot, a family heirloom. Bella finished the wiring that afternoon and shined the silver to such a degree that when Grace set the lamp on her worktable she saw her face reflected in the curved sides of the eight-inch pot. Bella used a soft brush to polish up a brass lamp she smeared with a paste floor polish, and Michael fussed around the shop straightening all the lampshades from their lopsided positions, turning the lamps so the switches were on the right. He also checked for smudges and fingerprints and restocked the towers of manufactured shades.

They worked another couple of hours in silence. Occasionally Bella would sing a few bars of a Christmas standard and Michael would sigh and *tsk-tsk* about the dust, the disorder or the scratching noises emanating from the attic, where a colony of mice had made a home. Outside, the wind had picked up and branches of a cherry tree scraped sharply against the windows.

Grace had done all she could for the moment on her shade, so she decided to do some paperwork. As she finished signing her name to the electric bill, the lights flickered. She reached up to the shelf above her desk and grabbed a glass finger lamp and lit the wick. A few more flickers, and the shop plunged into darkness.

"Oh, no!" Bella cried. "Power's out."

From across the room, Grace heard Michael fumbling around the bay window. "The whole street's dark," he told them. "Maybe a car skidded on the ice and hit a pole or something."

Bella emerged from her room with a lantern in one hand and a flashlight in another. She handed the flashlight to Michael. The lantern gave off a bluish glow that surrounded her as she traipsed around the shop. "Since it's not the usual faulty wiring problem, we might as well go home," she suggested.

"Right. Let's get out of here. Who knows how long it will take for the lights to come back on." Grace said.

"I'll take both of you home. My car is parked near the door," Bella said.

"Thanks, I'll take you up on that." Michael said. "I hope I have power at home. Edith's afraid of the dark, and her heating pad won't work."

"If that's the case, and I have power, you and Edith can bunk with me for the night," Bella said, putting on her overcoat.

Michael and Grace hurried to keep up with Bella as she headed down the stairs. Michael grabbed Grace's arm. "Isn't she incredible? My goodness. Nothing rattles Bella. I feel so safe with her. Don't you?"

Grace patted Michael's arm. "I do," she assured him. And it was true. What was she going to do when Bella retired? She followed him out the door. It was too awful to think about right now.

They piled in Bella's ancient Volvo, Michael in front and Grace in the back seat. Bella was grumbling as she tried to get the heater going, and Michael was gazing out the side window at the cemetery when they drove by Danielle's house.

"Wait! I see a light on in Danielle's." Grace said. Bella skidded to a stop.

"Perhaps it's her brother," Michael said.

"Maybe, but there aren't any cars around."

Bella pulled to the side of the road out of sight of the house and turned off the engine. "Let's go check it out," she said, opening her door and stepping out into the street. Michael turned and peered over the seat back at Grace, his eyes like saucers.

"Wait," Grace said, joining the older woman. "He's right. It might be Howard. The power probably went off when he was in the house." She looked down the dark, empty street. "Why don't you take Michael home? I'll hang around for a couple of minutes and see if someone comes out. We're just around the corner from my street. I can find my way home from here."

Bella appeared to mull this over for a moment and then, leaning into the car, told Michael to bring the flashlight. "I'm curious now," she said. "And I'm certainly not going to leave you here alone, what with a murderer on the loose."

Chapter Twenty-Three

"WHY DON'T I go have a look and you two wait for me here? It might be dangerous." Grace said.

"I think we should all go." Bella said. "We'll take a quick peek."

"I don't think Michael's up for this, Bella," Grace told her.

"Sure he is." Bella said as she walked around the car and opened Michael's door. "Come on, Michael. We need you."

"Maybe we should call the police?" Michael said as he got out of the car, his voice quavering.

"I don't think that would be a good idea," Grace said. "We don't have a reason to call them. Like you said, Howard could have been doing something in there when the power went off."

Michael didn't respond but followed Grace and Bella as they crossed the road and walked the half block back to Danielle's. When they got to the gate leading to the front walkway, Grace whispered, "We better turn our lights out. Be careful." The house loomed in front of them. Branches laden with ice crackled overhead and the cold wind shuddered through the hedges. "I'm going to go up to the front door and see if I can see in the window. You two wait here."

Grace tentatively moved up the front walk. With the power outage, the yard and porch were barely visible. She heard a noise behind her and turned around, her breath caught in her throat. It was Bella. She breathed easier.

"I'll go around the side. Michael's by the front gate." Bella said in a loud whisper, and before Grace could say anything, Bella disappeared around the side of the house.

This is so crazy, what if someone's in there? Grace told herself.

Howard could easily have come from the inn. It was, after all, only
a five-minute walk. And, if it *were* Howard, he'd have a fit when
he saw her poking around.

Reaching the front steps, Grace tiptoed up onto the porch and
peered in the window. Inside she could see the faint outlines of
Danielle's furniture, but that was all. Gaining courage, she went
to the door and turned the knob, recoiling momentarily when
it opened.

She left the door ajar and entered the foyer. A chill ran through
her as she remembered Danielle lying on the living room floor.
She stood for a minute or so getting her bearings.

A noise came from upstairs. A creak or a shuffle. And then,
silence. Had it, she wondered, simply been the sound of an old
house settling?

She started to shiver. Probably her nerves, she thought. She
stood there shaking for a few more moments before deciding that
the smartest thing she could do right now was to get the hell out
of Danielle's house.

As she turned back toward the front door, she heard a loud
crash from above, followed by what sounded like "Oof!" followed
by a loud expletive. She froze. Her heart beat faster. Someone
might be hurt. She should do something. She called outside to
Bella and Michael but there was no response.

"Howard! Is that you?" she called out. "It's Grace Tolliver.
Are you all right?" When her question was met with silence, she
began to inch her way up the stairs, testing each carpeted step
before putting her weight down, her heart pounding. "Howard!"
she called out again. "I was passing by and saw a light." She crept
forward, sliding her left hand against the wall of the hallway,
fighting the nearly overwhelming impulse to run back down the
stairs and out of the house. Her outstretched arm flailed in the air
as she reached a doorway opening. As her eyes adjusted to the
dark, she stepped into what appeared to be the master bedroom.
She hesitated as she took in the bed and bureau to her left. She
slowly let out a deep breath.

Suddenly she saw a tall, bulky shape silhouetted in the window.

It moved quickly toward her, pushing her hard out of the doorway. She fell back against the bed as the shadowy figure pounded down the stairs. She jumped up in pursuit and called out a warning to Bella. As she descended the stairs, she saw the intruder run through the still open front door. And then there was another crash. This time, she heard a couple of "Oofs!" and more expletives. Some, Grace realized, were coming from Bella.

"Bella! Michael!" Grace cried as she reached the door. "Oh, my God!" she said when she saw Bella sprawled on the porch, her lantern illuminating the snow bank from which Michael was trying to extricate himself. "Bella! Are you all right?" she knelt down next to her. "Michael?" she called out.

"I'm coming!"

"Just lie still for a moment." Grace instructed Bella.

"Whew!" Bella gasped. "I'm okay. Pull me up so I can get my breath." Grace reached out and grabbed Bella under her shoulder and arm. Michael, his glasses speckled with snow and his scarf askew, staggered up the few steps and grabbed Bella under her other shoulder.

"Oh, my!" Michael said. "Someone was in a big hurry!"

"Are you okay?" Grace asked him.

"Yes, I think so. I felt like a tumbleweed for a minute, but the snow cushioned my fall."

Bella rubbed the back of her head. Then she rolled her shoulders and waggled her arms and fingers in front of her. "I'm going to roll over onto my knees. I think it will be easier for me to get up. Then if you can give me a little boost."

Grace and Michael followed Bella's instructions and pulled her to a standing position. She held on to the porch railing and caught her breath. "I'm all right. Everything seems to be working," she told them. "I guess I had the wind knocked out of me. I suspect I'll have more than a few bruises tomorrow."

"Let's go to my house. I want to make sure you're both okay." Grace said. Michael steadied Bella as they made their way back to her Volvo. Bella got in the back seat followed by Michael, who wanted to keep a close eye on her, and Grace drove the short distance to her cottage, her fingers trembling on the steering wheel.

Chapter Twenty-Four

THE ELECTRICITY BACK on, Grace checked out Bella and Michael under the bright kitchen lights. Amazingly, they hadn't been seriously injured. Thanks to the snow bank that cushioned his fall, Michael seemed all right, not even a scratch. Bella was in good shape too. Nothing appeared to be broken or even sprained. Grace put on a pot of tea and settled Bella and Michael down in front of the fireplace. She threw a match on some newspapers and kindling, and when that was going she added a thick log.

Bella leaned back on the down cushions of an armchair and put her feet up on the ottoman. "Grace, tea sounds lovely, but do you by any chance have anything a wee bit stronger? I think we all need something to calm our nerves."

"You mean like whiskey?"

"That's exactly what I mean. How about you, Michael?"

"Yes, that would be lovely."

Grace brought out a black lacquered tray with three antique glass tumblers and placed it on the coffee table. She opened her pine armoire, selected a bottle and poured them all a shot. "Bottoms up!" Bella said and they downed their drinks.

Michael made a face. "I think I'll have some of that tea now, if you don't mind."

Grace poured tea into yellow ceramic mugs and passed them to her two friends. Michael pulled the tan chenille blanket over his knees and Clambake jumped on his lap and curled himself into a tight ball. Before long Michael was sound asleep, lightly snoring, comfy as a bear cub in his den. Bella and Grace stared into the fire watching the dancing flames and drinking their tea.

Grace broke the silence. "Whoever was in Danielle's house must have had a key, because the door was unlocked. I'm pretty sure it wasn't Howard. He's not as tall as this guy was. Have you any idea who it could be?"

"Actually," Bella said, continuing to gaze into the fire, "I know who it was." She reached forward and placed her mug on the coffee table. "But, I just can't believe it."

Grace blew the steam on her tea and inhaled the essence of bergamot as she waited for Bella to continue.

"It was Father Murrey," she said.

"Father Murrey?" Grace sputtered. "The retired priest? *That* Father Murrey?"

"Yes, that Father Murrey," Bella assured her. "I'm having a hard time believing it myself. He was our pastor for years. I recognized the smell of his tobacco."

Grace considered this. "There could be others who use the same tobacco. I mean, I don't think that's enough . . ."

Bella cut her off. "The man fell on top of me. It's been a long time, but when a man is on top of you, even for a few seconds, you know who that man is."

Michael stirred in his chair. He looked at the women and said. "Gosh, I couldn't help myself. I got so sleepy." When there was no immediate response, he said, "Did I miss something?"

"Bella thinks that our mystery man was Father Murrey."

"No!" Michael exclaimed.

"Remember that tobacco that he always used in his pipe?" Bella asked him. "It had the aroma of ripe peaches."

"Yes, I guess I do, now that you mention it. I only remember because I drove him to that little pipe and tobacco store that used to be in Dennisport, a few times so he could purchase some. I can't say I smelled it tonight, but then, I was nose-down in a snow bank."

"But why would he be poking around in the dark at Danielle Whitney's house?" Grace asked.

Michael sat up straight in his chair. "And the man swore. Father Murrey would never do that. He's a man of the cloth."

"Don't act so innocent," Bella sputtered. "After all, they're human beings."

"But would he have a key to Danielle's house?" Grace asked.

"Certainly," Bella said. "He has keys to half the houses in the village. Since he retired, he often takes care of pets when their owners are away. Anyway, it's late. Let's not worry about this anymore tonight. We'll sleep on it and talk about it in the morning. Are you ready to go home now, Michael?"

Grace was uncomfortable about Bella driving after her fall and the evening's excitement, but Bella assured her that she felt fine. "I think I'll take a dunk in my bathtub and see if I can warm up my muscles before going to bed. I better get Michael home, Edith must be mighty hungry by now."

"And Edith is going to be so jealous when she gets a whiff of Clambake!" Michael said as he tenderly picked up the large cat, kissed him on top of his head and gently lowered him to the floor.

Chapter Twenty-Five

GRACE FED CLAMBAKE, checked her doors and then turned off the lights and headed up the stairs to her bedroom and bath. She peeled off the day's clothes and stepped into a hot, steamy shower. As she rubbed shampoo into her hair she thought about how crazy the last couple of days had been. Danielle's murder. Duane's arrest. Gink. Orange Hair. Christine and Father Murrey. Was it possible Bella was right about him? Whoever it was hadn't acted in a very priestly way, but then maybe she, like Michael, was being naïve. And if he did have a key, it would explain the front door being unlocked tonight. Danielle didn't have any pets that she was aware of, but she might have given him a key at some time or other. And if it was Father Murrey, what had he been doing there, fumbling around in the dark? She'd have to figure out a way to talk to him without accusing him of anything.

And Christine. Another friend of Danielle's, who was a real piece of work. She did seem a bit unhinged to Grace, but that didn't mean that she couldn't still try to make life difficult for her and the shop.

Bella had told her that Danielle was a complicated woman. It appeared that some of the stands she had taken on preservation issues might have made her some enemies in the community. Even Jill, Sophie's mother, had said that her husband, Tony, had been pretty worked up when she protested his request to add an addition to the inn. And then there was the mysterious Vernon Rugosa. Maybe he'd been sent packing by Danielle and hadn't liked it. It sounded like he had plans for Danielle. Trying to get her to sell her large house and move to a condo, pocketing a bundle in the process. According to Cruz, he preyed on older women of means.

She pictured Danielle lying on the floor with a large gash in the back of her head. The lamp had been easily within the murderer's reach. Grace thought it might have been a crime of passion, unplanned, brought on by rage. Vernon could have been angry that he was not getting his way, creating a fairly classic domestic violence situation. There had been no sign of a forced entry, and Duane had said that when he got to Danielle's the front door was unlocked. Danielle might have been waiting for someone she knew. Vernon Rugosa was becoming a viable suspect in Grace's mind the longer she thought about the whole sorry tragedy. She hoped the cops caught up with him soon, but in the meantime she had an idea. She'd call Audrey first thing in the morning.

Grace wrapped herself in her fluffy terry cloth robe and climbed on top of her white down comforter. She picked up a tattered copy of a book of poetry that she had purchased at Beau's Books. She opened the book, removed a bookmark and scanned a few sentences. But her eyes were heavy, and after only a few pages she set the book aside and climbed under the covers.

Pulling the comforter up to her chin, she turned off the light above her bed and closed her eyes. She was exhausted, but her head was still spinning. How was she going to figure out who killed Danielle? And what was Andre Cruz up to? He certainly was attractive, but she didn't flatter herself that he was interested in her. The dinner had been more or less friendly, but she felt that his real motivation had been to get information about Duane. He had said he believed that Duane was guilty. And she wasn't sure she believed that he was seriously checking out other leads. And what if Duane *was* guilty? What if she was responsible for Danielle's death? Indirectly, of course, but nevertheless responsible. It was too horrible to think about.

After about an hour of tossing and turning, she got up and went downstairs and fixed herself some hot chocolate. The house had already chilled off, but she was warm in her robe and wool cowgirl slippers. She leaned on the counter under a glass oil lamp with an off-white shade on which she had painted a design of herbs and flowers. It had been a practice shade, and some of the flowers were blotches where she had added too much water to her paints. Instead of a sunny, bright image, it had a rainy, moody atmosphere. She turned the shade in a circle and smiled at her mistakes. She sipped her chocolate and reminded herself that it had only been about four months since she had started her new career. She had learned a lot about the lamp business and how to paint lampshades. She had worked long hours and had never been happier at work in her life. Howard could sue her, Christine could try to marshal support to close her down and Andre Cruz might question her judgment, but she was not about to let anyone take it all away from her. If the D.A. and the cops were unwilling to find out who really killed Danielle, she would have to do it herself.

Chapter Twenty-Six

G RACE ARRIVED AT Pearl's early Tuesday morning, munching on a croissant she picked up on her way to work. The coffee shop was full of customers getting their caffeine fixes before facing another day of snow and clogged streets, but unless she was mistaken, a quiet had settled over the hubbub of the usually friendly morning crowd when she walked in, and there was no question that people were staring at her as she waited to pay for her pastry. The attention was infuriating. People were so judgmental. In time, they'd see how narrow minded they had been.

"Grace! I'm fine, but how are you holding up?" was Audrey's first question when Grace phoned her. "You're the talk of the probation department."

"I bet I am." Grace replied. "Not that I want to be. The whole town seems to be whispering behind my back. It's so frustrating. But enough of all that. I need you to look up something for me. Can you get an address for me for a Vernon Rugosa from the Clerk's office? Hopefully there is only one person with that name in the system, because I don't have any other particulars about him except that he's probably fifty. Maybe sixty."

"What are you up to?"

"Mr. Rugosa is someone I'd very much like to have a conversation with," Grace told her. "There's a warrant out for his arrest, and the cops will be checking out last known addresses from police reports and things like that, but maybe we could find him first."

"'We?'" Audrey said. "What do you mean, 'we'?"

"I don't want to get you in any trouble, but believe me, I wouldn't be asking if this wasn't important."

"I'll see what I can find out. I'm not sure I like the sound of this. Does this have something to do with Danielle Whitney's murder?"

Grace picked up a gel pen and began drawing doodles of houses and trees. "I'd better not say anymore until we get together tonight. Dinner at seven."

Grace was grateful that Bella and Michael had both shown up at work this morning like nothing out of the ordinary had transpired the night before. Michael was busy with customers, and Bella was finishing up a repair of an old lamp for a young decorator who had recently discovered the shop, and was introducing the whole concept of appropriate lighting to her customers. She had just left the shop with her repaired lamp, when Bella came into Grace's office.

"Got a minute? I've been thinking about Father Murrey all morning. And half the night too. I don't think I got but two hours of sleep."

"Sit down," Grace said, pulling up a chair. "You don't look so good. Maybe you should go home and we'll talk about this another time."

"No. I've got to talk this through with someone. I won't be able to sleep until I do."

"Go on, I'm listening."

"I've known Gavin Murrey for many, many years." Bella said, looking down at her hands that she had folded in her lap. "We grew up in this town and went to the same high school, though I'm a few years older. My younger sister was in his class, and he used to come by our house. I think he had a crush on her. He was quite the ladies' man, quite the young rascal. So it came as a surprise to me when he joined the Catholic priesthood."

Grace had some difficulty picturing the Father Murrey she recalled from the courthouse, as a ladies' man or as a rascal, but Bella appeared to be relishing her memories as she briefly closed her eyes.

"I went into the Army Nursing Corps and I didn't see him for many years," Bella continued reflectively. "But he eventually managed to get assigned to a nearby parish, oh, maybe twenty-five years ago, and I've seen him on a regular basis since then. Although he's retired now, he often comes by to listen to our choir in the evenings. Did you know that Michael and I sing in the church choir?"

Grace couldn't help thinking about the moose in Maine, but she smiled at Bella. "Michael told me you sing. I'm jealous of anyone who can sing. I'm tone deaf myself."

Bella looked pleased, but within seconds her brow was furrowing. "I didn't tell you about something else last night. When Gavin ran into me, or over me," Bella corrected herself, "he dropped something. A letter, to be exact. It's addressed to Danielle. The return address is his. I struggled all night over whether or not I should read what was inside but I couldn't do it." She sighed deeply. "It's just not right to look at someone else's mail."

Grace couldn't agree more, but she'd sure love to know what was inside that letter.

"But I have to speak with him," Bella continued. "I'm going to his house now. I need to confront him about his behavior last night. I want to know what was so darned important that he had to run roughshod over us and not even stop to see if we were all right. It better be something very, very important, because I've got a pretty stiff back today. And the truth is, I'd feel more comfortable if you would come with me."

"Of course I'll come with you. I've got a few questions for him myself. But I think you should have stayed home today. You and Michael push yourselves so hard." Grace reached out and patted Bella's hand. "I don't want you to feel that you always have to come in. I can hire some more help for the holidays."

Bella shook her head. "I've been through a lot worse than this. I admit that my age slows me down some, but I don't let a whole lot stop me. So I'm going to get up every day and get dressed and brush my teeth and come to work. I've made a commitment to you to see you through the new year, and I plan to keep it."

"Michael told me you were an army nurse in Korea. I can't imagine. That must have been such a difficult time."

"Difficult is too nice a word. Hell is more like it," she said. "It was 1950, and there were thirteen of us nurses in the landing party with MacArthur. We were young and ill prepared for what was to come. After we landed, we traveled with our supplies on narrow roads over some pretty rough terrain. We took cover in muddy ditches when the enemy attacked. It rained a lot and was bitter cold. We were overwhelmed with the wounded and dying." Bella stopped and took a deep breath. "I saw terrible things. It was when I first became acquainted with death. Up close and brutal."

"Oh, Bella, I'm sorry," Grace told her. This conversation, she saw now, was leading them from one painful topic to another. "I didn't mean to bring up the past."

"That's all right," Bella assured her. "The memories are never very far away. But you've had a taste of violent death yourself this week, and I know it's been hard on you, but remember, I'm here to help any way I can." She stood up a little more slowly than yesterday. She took a quick stretch. "How about we go visit Father Gavin?"

Michael agreed to watch the shop. "If it gets too busy, put up the 'closed for lunch' sign," Grace told him. "We'll be back soon."

"Are you sure it's safe for you to go over there? You won't have me to protect you," Michael said, looking sharp today in a striped three-piece suit, white starched shirt and red tie.

"Don't worry about us," Grace and Bella said in unison as they hustled down the stairs.

Chapter Twenty-Seven

"JUST A MOMENT please," a voice squeaked from behind the front door at Father Murrey's mid-twentieth century, brown-shingled house. A tiny wizened face peered out from behind a lace-curtained window. Grace smiled, and a second later the door opened and an elderly woman stood before them. "Oh, here you are. I've been waiting for you all day," she said cheerfully.

She ushered them into the entryway cluttered with coat racks, umbrella holders, piles of coats and an aluminum walker. "Come in. Come in," the old lady said and gestured toward the living room.

"Did I hear the bell, Mother?" Gavin Murrey said as he came rumbling down a hallway that Grace could see led to the kitchen. His white hair looked uncombed, and his cheeks were rosy. Grace noticed how tall and broad he was. It had been very dark last night, but he could be the intruder they encountered at Danielle's.

"Bella Benson! What a nice surprise," he said, taking his old friend's hands. "I don't know if you've met my mother, Daphne. Mother, do you remember Bella from church? She sings in the choir."

The old woman looked confused. "Yes, I know you," she said to Bella. "You've come to give me my bath today."

Smiling indulgently, the priest steered his mother to a pink and gray paisley couch in front of the television. The walls were papered with blue and lavender begonias.

"Look, that newscaster you like is on. I'm going to chat for a minute with these nice ladies, and then we can have lunch."

Bella introduced Grace and they followed him down the hall. Before they got to the kitchen, he stopped, opened a door on his left and invited them to step in.

They found themselves in a crowded office with a large desk that faced into the room and toward the one window that looked out on the back yard. The desk was piled high with all manner of papers, pens and coffee cups as well as a carved wooden stand that held a collection of pipes. A chessboard with a game in progress was on a side table. Gavin pulled up a couple of chairs and gestured for them to sit down. He gathered up some notebooks and papers and placed them in the center drawer of his desk, locking the drawer with a metal key. He sat down heavily and rested his folded hands in the newly cleared spot. "What can I do for you, Bella? Is there a problem with the choir?"

"No, Gavin, I've not come about the choir," she said, sitting up as straight as possible. "I suspect you know why I've come to see you today."

"Why, what is it? How can I be of service to you and Ms. Tolliver?"

"You can be of service, if that's what you want to call it, by telling us why you were in Danielle Whitney's house last night and why you left in such a hurry that you knocked me flat on my back and pushed my dear friend, Michael Shipworth, into a snow bank!"

"What on earth are you talking about? Danielle's house last night?"

"Excuse me, but don't try to pull the wool over my eyes," Bella scolded him. "We've known each other a very long time. When you knocked me over and then fell on top of me, I recognized the distinct smell of peach-scented tobacco!"

Gavin leaned back in his chair and stared defiantly first at Bella and then at Grace, who matched his stare with one of her own.

"You assaulted all three of us last night," Grace said. "There's no doubt in any of our minds that it was you who ran out of Danielle's at about nine-thirty. I first encountered you in an upstairs bedroom before you pushed me and ran down the stairs and knocked Bella and Michael over. So why don't you tell us what you were up to?"

The priest was now looking very unfriendly, Grace thought, alert to the possibility that he could be dangerous if pushed too hard. She wished she had some pepper spray with her. She glanced around the room, hoping to find something to use in defense, if need be.

"Yes, you're right," he suddenly confessed, taking her by surprise. "I was in Danielle's house last night. And I am very sorry if I hurt any of you. Truly sorry. And I know it looks particularly strange that I was there right after the poor woman's murder, but I was searching for something, and frankly it is none of your business what." He adjusted his glasses. "I can assure you that my mission last night has nothing whatsoever to do with her murder, if that's what you're thinking."

Bella fumbled around in her large brown leather purse, pulled out an envelope and threw it across the desk to him. "When you collided with me, you must have dropped this letter."

"What's this?" he said as he picked up the envelope, turning it over so that he could read the front inscription. His hands shook.

He opened the unsealed letter and gave it a cursory glance. "I suppose you read this?"

Bella nodded.

"Then you know."

She nodded again.

Bella folded her arms across her ample chest. Grace sat still, marveling at Bella's ability to bluff. She must remember to invite her on a trip to a casino down in Connecticut sometime.

Gavin stood up. His face was flushed, contrasting sharply with his snowy hair. "Would you ladies like some tea?" They both shook their heads in reply. "Then if you'll excuse me, I'll get myself a cup and be right back." He stood up, walked around the desk and headed for the kitchen.

"Do you have any idea what he is talking about?" Grace whispered.

"Not a clue." She raised her eyebrows and shrugged. "Let's string him along and see if he tells us some more." Grace got up and wandered over to a shelf where a number of boxing trophies were displayed. They were from the priest's youth, but Father Murrey looked to still be in pretty good shape for a man of his age. As she returned to her seat next to Bella, who was sniffing the pipes and nodding, Father Murrey, carrying a mug of steaming tea, returned to the room and heaved himself back into his chair.

"Of course, it was a long time ago," he said.

"Yes, I figured that," Bella said. "But really, could it have mattered so much that you had to sneak into Danielle's house the night after she was murdered? It does seem very suspicious."

The priest coughed but didn't respond to Bella's question. He looked miserable now. Grace leaned forward and lowered her voice an octave. "Why don't you tell us the whole story? I'm sure that would help us understand."

Murrey shifted in his armchair. "Do you mind if I smoke?" he asked, reaching for a pipe and lighting it without waiting for an answer. Grace and Bella watched while he stoked his pipe. The scent of peaches filled the room. Finally, he leaned back and looked at them with what Grace thought was a measure of defiance.

"It was more than twenty years ago," he began. "I'd been a priest for a very long time, and I'd adhered to all of the rules of my vocation. I settled in near my mother and was enjoying being back in my hometown."

He paused and cupped one hand around a tarnished silver chalice filled with red and white striped peppermints. "Then one day, this beautiful woman came into my church. She and her husband had recently moved to the area, and they both became very involved in the parish. Of course, I'm talking about Danielle and George Whitney. There was something about her that swept me off my feet. I knew that I had been lonely in the priesthood, but I didn't realize the extent of the emptiness in my heart. The yearning for a greater experience of life, I suppose."

He let out a deep breath and combed back his hair with a trembling hand. "We had an affair. There, I've said it," he said bluntly, and Grace heard Bella gasp. "It went on for more than a year, and I loved her very much. I knew that it was wrong. She was married and I was a priest, but I couldn't help myself. I prayed endlessly for strength to end it, and finally I prayed for understanding. She was the one who broke it off. I think she loved me too, but maintaining the affair was becoming too difficult. The sneaking around, the guilt."

Grace thought about Father Murrey sneaking around Danielle's house the previous night. Of course, she was there too, but she wouldn't have been if she hadn't seen his light.

"We'd written some letters to each other," he continued. "Yes, I know, a dangerous thing to do under the circumstances, but we did," he went on. "She told me she had hidden them in a place where George would never find them. I thought he destroyed them years ago, but a few weeks ago she told me that she was writing her memoirs and that she still had the letters to refer to. I admit this threw me into a panic. I begged her to give them to me, but she refused."

"What did you do?" Grace asked, seeing that Bella had apparently been thunderstruck into silence.

"What could I do?" he shrugged his shoulders and lifted his hands, palms up. "Danielle and I remained friendly through the years, but she'd changed quite a lot in recent months. She was always strong willed, of course, something I admired in her, but she had recently become very difficult. She was quarrelsome and impatient." He folded his hands again and gazed past Grace and Bella toward the window behind them.

It was odd, Grace thought, how the priest's revelations caused her to look at him with completely different eyes. He was, she had to admit, becoming more sympathetic. But of course, she reminded herself, that didn't mean that he couldn't be Danielle's murderer.

"Last night I went to her house," he said. "Danielle gave me a key after George died. I started to look for the letters. She once told me about a ceramic elephant with a false bottom that she brought back from India. I searched around until I found it in her bedroom closet. Sure enough, it was crammed with papers. That's when I heard you arrive." He looked at Grace. "I stuffed them in my pocket and left." Grace noticed that he skipped over the part of the story where he had trampled Bella and Michael. "I have them now. I hope I have all of them."

"I see," Grace said. "Did you find a diary, by any chance?"

"A diary! No, nothing like that. Just letters. They're letters that I wrote to Danielle. They belong to me."

"Hmmm." Grace wondered about the legality of this assumption on his part. She was certain that they belonged to the estate. But deciding not to pursue that problem now, she asked, "Do you have any idea what else might have been stressing Danielle out lately?"

"She was trying to resurrect her modeling career, and she had a good chance of making a go of it because, of course, she was still a beauty. Maybe that was causing her some stress. I don't really know. I tried to talk to her. I wanted to help her, but I also wanted her to destroy all of our correspondence. I was hoping that with some success in the modeling business, she might forget about the whole idea of writing her memoirs. I don't know all the details of her private life, but I know she had been seeing a man named Vernon for the last year or so. She brought him around to a couple of church functions, and I have to say I didn't like the guy at all. I thought he was using her. She wouldn't talk to me about him. In fact, when I asked about him, she accused me of being jealous. You're not going to tell anyone about this?" he asked warily.

"We may have to," Grace said. "After all, you were in Danielle's house, and you removed something from a murder scene. The police will want to talk to you."

"It's no one's business but mine!" he said, angry now. "If my relationship with Danielle becomes public knowledge, the church may try to take away my pension. It barely supports my mother and me," he said with a groan.

"We'll let you tell them in your own way about you and Danielle. And we won't mention what you told us to anyone else. I'm sure the authorities will be discreet under the circumstances." Grace said, although she had her doubts about the discreet part. The courthouse was chock full of gossipers and busybodies.

"I guess I knew that someday this all might come out." He looked toward the door. "I'm sure you noticed that my mother has Alzheimer's."

"Yes we did, and we're sorry about that," Bella said. "I don't know what to think about all of this. I never suspected a thing about you and Danielle."

"One last question before we go," Grace said. Hoping to find out the answer to something that had been nagging at her, she risked angering him further. "Were you at Danielle's house on Sunday night too?"

"No. I thought about it, but I was too distraught over her death. I had a few too many drinks to ease the pain and I fell asleep early. Why do you ask?"

"I thought I saw a light on in her house on Sunday night. That's all." Grace told him. She stood up.

"I accept your apology, Gavin," Bella said, rising. "And I do have some compassion for you, as well. But I'm quite certain that you will fully cooperate with the police, because right now the wrong person is in jail for Danielle's murder."

It was, Grace thought, typical of Bella to assume that everyone would do the right thing. But from the look in Father Murrey's eyes, she wasn't at all certain that he would.

"I didn't have anything to do with Danielle's murder," he said dryly, gazing at Grace. "And from what I've heard around town, you've got nothing to be smug about yourself. Weren't your employee's fingerprints found on the murder weapon?"

"Don't believe everything you hear," Grace said. "Duane's not a bad kid. He would never do something like that. It's only a matter of time before the real killer is found. Come on, Bella. Let's get back to the shop."

From the front hall, she noticed that the priest's mother was asleep on the paisley couch. A beagle was curled next to her. One eye opened as Bella and Grace passed by.

Chapter Twenty-Eight

GRACE AND BELLA wrapped themselves up in their wool scarves. The wind was blowing squalls of snowflakes around them as they walked back to the shop that was around the corner and down a block or so.

"Goodness! I'm so surprised by Father Gavin's confession," Bella said. "It's rather disturbing, yet understandable I suppose. A priest's life is a lonely one. Always taking care of others, and then retiring to an empty rectory at night. I can understand now why he wanted to get those letters back."

"I can understand too, Bella," Grace agreed, "but it also gives him a motive for murder. He told us himself that Danielle wasn't going to give him the letters and that she was writing a memoir. Her revelation might have scared him enough to do something to stop her. They might have argued, and in the heat of the moment, he might have lashed out in frustration and anger."

"I suppose so. And yet ..." Bella paused. "It's hard for me to believe, even if Gavin weren't a priest, that he'd be capable of murder."

"He is capable of a certain level of violence when under stress, as we know from last night," Grace said "He may be your trusted priest, but he's also a man with something to hide. I'm sure the church authorities wouldn't be too happy to know about his transgression. And his standing in the community would be affected too. I didn't get the sense that his apology was heartfelt, either. He struck me as someone who, when confronted, will do what is necessary to get what he wants. And did you notice that he didn't seem surprised when I mentioned a diary? You'd think that the news of that diary would have alarmed him."

"How did you hear about a diary? Or did you make that up to see his reaction?"

"My dad told me. He saw Danielle recently to update her modeling portfolio. She mentioned the memoir and diary."

"All of this is so upsetting, Grace. I'll have to mull it all over a bit." Bella said as they climbed the stairs to the shop.

It seemed to Grace that as time passed, things were getting far more upsetting and complicated than she ever could have imagined.

Chapter Twenty-Nine

MICHAEL WAS SITTING at a table trimming a hexagon-shaped shade with a luxurious double ruffle in lavender silk. Across from him sat Sophie, still in mittens and earmuffs. They look like two children at a tea party, thought Grace. Michael was telling her an amusing story about a wedding that took place at the Beach Sparrow Inn back in 1955. Michael had been an usher, and he was describing how guests from California dressed and behaved, in what he considered to be an outlandish way.

Michael set down his glue gun. "How did everything go?"

"Okay, although I think we have more questions than answers," Grace said in a low voice as Sophie proceeded to help herself to a box of Christmas cookies that were sitting on a table by the stairs. "I'll fill you in later on the details."

"Would you like a cookie?" Sophie brought the box over to Grace.

"Why, yes, thank you. Where did these lovely cookies come from?"

"My mom said I should bring them to you," Sophie replied. "Daddy baked them this morning and I helped."

"They're delicious. The best Christmas cookie I've ever had," Grace said, as she savored the buttery, powdered sugar confection. "I guess your mother knows where you are then? We don't have to call her?"

"Nope. She told me I should stay here until one. The police came to talk to Daddy. That pretty lady and her friend."

"You mean Inspectors Rice and Cruz?" Grace asked.

Sophie nodded. "I guess. Is it one o'clock yet?"

Grace looked at her watch. "It's about five after," she said, just as the phone rang. Jill was on the other end of the line, and she was clearly upset.

"Hey, Jill," Grace said. "Yes, I guess they have to talk to everyone. I wouldn't worry about it. I'll tell Sophie that you'll be by to pick her up in about five minutes."

Trundling over to Michael's table, Sophie picked up a stack of wrinkled papers with her sugar-coated fingers. In large letters on the top of the papers was the word "Lost." A black and white photograph of a cat sitting on a bed was underneath the headline. "I haven't put up all of my flyers yet. Stanley will never come home if I don't put them up."

"Leave them with me, dear," Michael said. "I would be very happy if you'd let me hang them up for you. I can't do it until after work, but I promise I'll get them up today. We must do everything we can to find Stanley. I know if my Edith was missing, I'd want someone to help me."

"I'll take some too," Grace said, stuffing them in her purse. "Come on, Sophie, let's go down and meet your mother."

A few minutes later, Jill pulled up in front of the store. "Do you think I'm fat?" Sophie asked Grace as they emerged onto the sidewalk.

"Of course not. I think you're beautiful," Grace said, opening the car door for her.

"Oh. There's something else I want to tell you." Jill said, leaning her head out of the window. "You know that Danielle Whitney's brother, Howard, is staying at the inn? He's been telling everyone that he's suing you for wrongful death. He met with a lawyer in the tea shop this morning. I thought you should know. They had an early reading of the will, and Danielle left more than three-quarters of her estate to Howard and his three children. You'd think that might be enough for him, but apparently not."

Grace felt a sinking pain in her stomach. "He's angry and wants to blame someone," she said.

"Thank goodness Tony was in the kitchen surrounded by employees on Sunday morning," Jill said. "Everyone knew that he was upset with Danielle for turning down our request for an addition to the inn. Well, I guess this is going to sound crude," she continued, "but now that Danielle isn't around, I think we can get our project approved."

It *was* a crude sentiment but the truth was that Danielle was dead, and others would benefit from her demise. Grace wondered who else might profit from the woman's death. Or did they silence her out of rage or jealousy or thwarted desires that might have had nothing do with profit? And would they get away with it?"

"I know it's not fun to be interviewed by the police, but personally, I'm glad to see that they're continuing to investigate," Grace told her, brushing snowflakes out of her hair. "There's no way that Duane killed Danielle, but D.A. Banks is out to make a name for herself. I'm sure she'd like to wrap this up as soon as she can, and unless I'm wrong, she'll do whatever she needs to make it happen."

Grace spent the rest of the afternoon painting a shade with oversized flowers for the president of the garden club. This is going to be a nice gift, Grace thought as she placed the shade on top of the lilac flowerpot base that Bella had finished wiring. She was turning it around, checking it for any flaws, when Michael came to take a closer look.

"That's lovely!" he exclaimed. "You've been a quick study with these lampshades. Milo and Matt would be so proud of you. Well, I suppose I'd better call it a day, if I'm going to hang Sophie's flyers around town. I do hope she finds her Stanley soon."

"Me too." Grace said. "Poor girl. She seems kind of lonely to me. She asked me if I thought she was fat when we went out to the car. I wonder if she has any friends her own age."

"I don't know. She's always wandering around the town by herself. She seems like one of those kids who like to hang out with adults more than their own peers. I was like that myself, and I was chubby too. It's hard to be an oversized kid," Michael said knowingly.

Grace looked at Michael's compact frame. "It's hard to believe you were ever fat, Michael."

Michael's head twitched ever so slightly as he patted down his tie. "I work at keeping in shape. Fifty sit-ups every day and thirty minutes on my treadmill. One must exercise discipline. But if I shared my house with a baker like Sophie does, I'd be in big trouble."

Bella emerged from her work area, pulling on her gloves. "I'm on my way out too. I think I need another soak in my tub. I'll see you both tomorrow."

Grace put away her paints and checked the back door. The Christmas tree, now beginning to dry out, had slid to the floor, untrimmed and forlorn. Tomorrow decorating would be her first priority. After all, there were only a few days left until the Village Stroll, and the shop wasn't ready. She'd have to bring some decorations from home or find the time to go buy some new ones. Scrounging around in the attic for any M and M might have left behind was not something that she wanted to contemplate.

As if on cue, she heard scratching noises above her head. Michael stared up at the ceiling too, but stayed quiet. The shop needed so much attention, Grace thought. It was strange how something that happened to Danielle Whitney, a woman she scarcely knew, could affect everything she did or had to do.

Chapter Thirty

"WHAT'S THE SMALLEST dinner salad you have?" Grace asked the hovering waiter after he had finished reciting the day's specials.

Audrey Lee looked up from behind her oversized menu. Tonight her shoulder-length black hair was tied back in a ponytail. Her bright pink lipstick perfectly matched the pink hoodie she wore over a white turtleneck. "This is an Italian restaurant, Grace. You're supposed to order pasta."

"I saw Emma Rice at the gym," Grace said grimly, remembering the awkward moment when she and Rice had been working out on adjacent treadmills, and she had to face the fact that the attractive officer was not only younger than her by a few years, but in tip-top shape as well.

"Oh. I see."

"I'll have the smoked chicken salad," Grace said, "and water." Audrey ordered a dinner salad, spaghettini with littleneck clams and a glass of red wine. Grace settled back in her comfortable steel chair and admired the coffee ice cream–colored wainscoting and the dazzling white walls. Soft music was playing and the crisp linen and candles created a warm and soothing atmosphere. She closed her eyes and listened to the clinking of glasses and took in the aroma of rosemary, oregano, garlic and tomatoes. Her stomach rumbled.

Audrey interrupted Grace's brief meditation. "Are Andre Cruz and Emma Rice a couple? I mean a romantic couple. I know they're partners and all."

"I have no idea," Grace answered. But, for the first time, she found herself caring about the answer to that question.

Audrey shrugged and pulled a piece of paper out of her purse. "I've got an address for Vernon Rugosa for you. It's on Route 28."

"How about we swing by there after dinner and see what we can find out about him? If he's there, we'll call the cops." Grace said. Audrey took a sip out of the glass of cabernet the waiter had placed in front of her. "Yummy! So, are you going to tell me who this guy is and why you want to talk to him?"

Grace stabbed at her greens as Audrey dug in to her main course. After a few minutes, Audrey reached down in her purse again, pulled out a set of chopsticks and commenced eating her pasta with them. A middle-aged couple at the next table, mouths half open, stared at her. "Works great! You should try it some-time," Audrey said to them as she snagged a piece of spaghettini and held it in the air.

Audrey was a true original. Grace wasn't sure herself if she was having fun at the other diners' expense or if she really enjoyed eating her pasta with chopsticks. With Audrey, either explanation was possible.

She was about three years younger than Grace, single and living at home with her parents. She had recently become inter-ested in genealogy and traced her family history back almost two hundred years, when her great-great-great-grandfather, a renowned chef, boarded a ship in Canton, China, that was bound for Nantucket Island.

While Audrey finished up her wine, Grace filled her in on Vernon Rugosa and his connection to Danielle Whitney. "I know the cops are looking for him," she explained, "but I want to talk to him before they take him into custody on his warrant. Christine Sinclair, a friend of Danielle's, told me that Danielle was going to break off her relationship with him this weekend. If he was count-ing on getting access to her money, that could have set him off."

"Sounds like a classic motive to me," Audrey said.

"Uh-oh! Look who's coming in the door," Grace exclaimed. "It's Banks and her entourage of Assistant D.A.s. What are they doing here? Isn't anywhere safe, for God's sake?"

"So it is," Audrey replied, swiveling around in her chair to have a look. The hostess led the group, who were streaming behind Banks in her turgid wake, to a round table in the center of the room.

"Anyway," Audrey continued, taking a last sip of wine, "I was getting around to telling you that Banks held a press conference a couple of hours ago in front of the courthouse." Grace pictured the pillars of the granite nineteenth-century building. Sitting on a slight rise above the harbor, historic, stately and dramatic, it was a perfect backdrop for the press conference.

"You can catch it on the late news." Audrey deftly applied pink lipstick without the aid of a mirror. "She basically reiterated what she said before. Duane Kerbey murdered Danielle Whitney, and she was going to make sure he went away to the Big House for a long time. She didn't mention you directly, but she did say something to the effect that the community has to use common sense when hiring people with criminal backgrounds."

"Let's finish up and get our check and get out of here before she figures out who I am and rounds up her posse to hang me from the nearest tree," Grace said, wincing.

Chapter Thirty-One

AUDREY PULLED HER jeep in front of a weathered, ramshackle bar on Route 28 in Yarmouth. A faded red neon sign blinked 'Shifty's.'

"Well, well. This doesn't look like it could be Vernon Rugosa's house, now does it?" she said.

"Not at all," Grace replied without surprise. It wasn't uncommon for probationers to provide incorrect information, especially about where they were living. "Let's go inside and see if anyone knows him."

Grace pushed open a heavy door covered with fake leather and metal studs. Even though state law had banned smoking in bars, the place still smelled like cigarettes. A few men in plaid shirts sat on stools, talking and glancing at the TV that hung above the bar. A couple played pool in the back of the room behind a half dozen empty tables.

A short, burly bartender slapped paper napkins down in front of them. "What's it gonna be, ladies?" he growled.

"Ginger ale," said Audrey.

"Make that two," echoed Grace.

The bartender scowled but wandered to the other end of the bar to get the sodas.

When he returned a few minutes later, Audrey gave him a flirtatious smile and asked, "Do you by any chance know Vernon Rugosa?

"Who wants to know?" he muttered.

"Oh, we're old friends of his daughter," Audrey said sweetly. "We've lost track of her and we were hoping we could find Mr.

Rugosa so he could put us in touch with her."

"Funny. I didn't know Vernon had a daughter."

"So you do know him then?" Grace asked.

The bartender stroked the gray stubble on his chin, his eyes lingering on Audrey. "I guess I can tell you. You two don't look like cops. Fact is you just missed him. He left about an hour or so ago."

The bartender smirked at Audrey, folded his hairy arms on the bar and leaned toward her. "He's seeing a lady who owns an antique shop on Route 6A . Very classy lady too, from what he tells me. I don't know the name of her shop. It's up Brewster way, I think. My wife dragged me into the place once. But, I couldn't tell you the name. Sorry." His glance lingered on Audrey again.

"Thanks anyway, Mr ...?" Grace asked.

"Bruce." Ignoring Grace, he reached out his hand to Audrey, who gingerly took his hand in hers.

"Bye, Bruce. We really must be on our way. Thanks ever so much. Please give our regards to Vernon."

"You didn't finish your drinks!" Bruce said.

"It's getting late. But we'll be back again soon, now that we've discovered your terrific bar," Audrey replied.

"Yuck!" she said when they were back in the jeep. "Pass me that container of hand sanitizer, will you?"

Grace handed her the plastic bottle from the console. "I think old Bruce took a fancy to you," Grace said.

"Ha! Just my type," Audrey said as she rubbed the liquid into her hands and passed the bottle to Grace. "There's a bunch of antique shops in Brewster. What do we do now?" she asked.

"I've got an idea. Wait here." Grace slipped out of the jeep and ran back into the bar. She returned a few minutes later and was greeted by a skeptical glance from Audrey.

"I gave him my cell number. I told him that if he could get the name of the shop from his wife, I'd put in a good word with you."

"Great. Just what I need in my life, a married old bartender with bad breath."

"Really? His breath was bad?"

Audrey laughed. "I'm taking you home now. Enough

matchmaking for one night!"

Grace's phone rang as Audrey swung into the driveway of her cottage. "Yes, could you hold on for a minute?" Grace turned to Audrey. "It's Andre Cruz. Thanks for everything. I'll call you tomorrow."

Audrey grinned. "A little late for a business call, no?" Grace grabbed her purse and waved to Audrey as she shut the door of the jeep.

"Grace. Hey. I've been trying to call you. Where've you been?"

Grace listened to the deep voice. Who does he think he is, asking me where I've been? After all, it's not as if I were a suspect, she thought.

"I had my phone turned off for a while," she answered

"Oh." He paused before continuing. "Looks like your friend Gink has taken off for parts unknown. Checked out of the Sandman. Any idea where she might go?"

"How should I know?"

"You told me probation officers know things the cops don't. I thought maybe she might have mentioned something to you about her plans."

"No. I have no idea where she is. I don't know anything more about Gink than you do. But she did say that she would call you. I gave her your card."

"Yeah. I'm not going to hold my breath. If you see your buddy Duane again, maybe you could ask him. He's got nothing more to say to us."

"I wasn't planning on talking to Duane any time soon," Grace assured him. "But I do have some other information that might interest you. Do you know Father Gavin Murrey? Lives with his mother on Millway? Used to be the pastor at St. Anselm's."

"I know him, sure. Why?"

"He was in Danielle's house last night."

"Probably helping her brother Howard with the funeral arrangements."

"No, I don't think so." Grace hesitated.

"How do you know he was in Danielle's house?"

"Murrey and Danielle had a special relationship," Grace blurted out, ignoring the question. "I think you should talk to him, that's all."

Andre's sigh was audible over the phone. "Okay. I'll check into it. You got any other information I should have? Suspects I should check out?"

"No. But I heard you talked to Tony Calabrese from the Beach Sparrow Inn."

"We're talking to a lot of people. We're not sitting on our hands, though I sometimes think that the D.A. wishes we would. But for the record, Tony appears to have an airtight alibi for Sunday morning."

"Yes, I knew that."

"Of course you did," he said dryly.

"So what about all of the other people she clashed with over historical preservation issues?"

"We're about through running them all down," Andre said. "You wouldn't believe how many people that was. She made more than a few enemies in this town. She had a lot of friends too. No one stands out as a murderer though. At least not yet."

"Not that you would tell me if they did."

"Exactly."

"Okay then." Grace paused. "I'm tired and I've got some lamp shop stuff to do tonight. So I guess I'll see you around."

"And another thing," Andre continued. "Narcotics picked up a couple of drug dealers over at the Sandman."

"And?"

"And, they traced the 911 call to your cell."

"Hey, you guys are good."

"Just be careful. I don't know how you happened to know about the drug dealers, but I suspect it has something to do with when you were visiting Gink. And I don't know how you know that Gavin Murrey was in Danielle's house last night, but you should leave the investigating to the police."

"Of course," Grace said, hoping that she sounded sincere.

"One other thing."

"Yes?"

"Have lunch with me tomorrow?"

Chapter Thirty-Two

WEDNESDAY MORNING ARRIVED with more record-breaking low temperatures. The cold, dank fog that followed another six inches of snow the previous night hung around until nine and then was blown out to sea by a strong westerly wind. There was no sun, but the sky was brightening as Grace pulled her car off the road and parallel-parked between a Ford SUV and a Chevy van. She peered out of her side window at the clusters of bundled-up mourners walking up the hill to what would be Danielle's final resting place.

Grace got out of her warm car and looked around for Bella and Michael. She wasn't comfortable coming to the service and was hoping to find someone she knew to stand with. She hadn't known Danielle, but she wanted to pay her respects with the other people from town. Not seeing anyone she knew immediately, she started walking up the hill where a large crowd was gathering. As she got closer, she spotted Howard standing with a portly woman whom she presumed was Mrs. Pittman, and three teenage children. Christine Sinclair and Father Murrey were huddled together, deep in conversation, a few steps from the gravesite. Wanting to avoid them all, she walked around to the back of the crowd and stood alone among the graves.

To pass the time she started reading the names on the worn headstones. Pettit, DeMarche, Vayonne, Ladier. This was the French section of the cemetery. The French had a long history on Cape Cod. Samuel de Champlain, the renowned explorer, having visited the outer edges of the Cape in 1605, had drawn the first map with a comprehensive outline of New England. It seemed a fitting burial spot for Danielle.

Shoving her hands deeper into the pockets of her black over-coat, Grace watched as Rafael and Jose worked feverishly to shovel the walkways that were covered with the latest snowfall. Jill and a subdued Sophie were standing under a barren maple tree. Behind them a substantial contingent of black-clad mourners were arriving in several cars with New York license plates. Grace assumed they were from the fashion world Danielle had once been a star of and had hoped to rejoin. Andre Cruz and Emma Rice were standing at a respectable distance surveying the crowd. Grace was wondering if Vernon Rugosa would have the nerve to show up, not that she knew what he looked like. Given the fact that he had a penchant for wearing disguises, he would be hard to spot anyway. And then she saw Bella and Michael walking up the hill toward her, followed by her father and his neighbor, Irene Papadopolous.

She had offered to pick up her father, his truck was still getting repaired after his accident, but he told her that Irene, who rarely missed a funeral even if she didn't know the deceased, would be coming so he would ride with her.

Michael, resplendent in a charcoal wool suit with a tie emblazoned with the French flag, tapped her on the shoulder. "That's Valerie Elkins. The woman with the red hair, in the tan coat with the earmuffs."

"Valerie Elkins?" Grace, puzzled, looked at the woman. "Oh yes, Valerie Elkins. M and M's real estate agent." Grace watched the woman striding among the headstones in pointy-toed boots and talking on her cell phone. "Interesting."

Michael nodded.

"I saw her at the Dolphin on Monday night. She was with Howard Pittman, Danielle's brother." She supposed that Howard was hoping to sell Danielle's property after the estate was settled. If that was the case, he certainly hadn't wasted any time contacting a realtor, which was, as far as she was concerned, pretty distasteful.

"Does she look like a murderer to you?" Michael asked. "Matt and Milo are convinced she's guilty."

"Murderers don't necessarily look like murderers," Grace said.

"They come in all shapes and sizes, all walks of life and all colors. So the answer to your question is yes and no."

Michael nodded again. When the graveside service began, Father Murrey surprised Grace by speaking fluent French in his final remarks. "*Au revoir* Danielle," he said, his voice breaking. She heard several voices echo his final good-bye. Bereaved lover or prime suspect? Grace couldn't help but wonder. Of course, it was possible that he was both.

"Hey! What are you doing here?" The angry voice drew Grace's attention back to the knot of people who were now separating and milling about the gravestones, greeting one another and murmuring condolences. "Hey!" Howard was fast approaching where she and her father were standing. "You have no business being here. This is a private ceremony."

Hardly, Grace thought to herself even as Howard came toward her with clenched fists.

"You're not welcome here. We wouldn't be here today if you hadn't sent a dangerous criminal to my poor sister's house. I want you to leave immediately!"

Her father took a step toward Howard but Grace grabbed his arm and pulled him back next to her.

"Dad, let's go," she said. "It's okay. Maybe I shouldn't have come."

Howard stood in front of them, now breathing hard. "Get out!" he yelled.

"Now just a minute," Thomas said, pushing Grace away. "Who do you think you are? I'm an old friend of Danielle's and this is my daughter. We have every right to be here. Her employee didn't kill Danielle. In fact, my daughter is investigating the circumstances of this awful crime, and I have no doubt she will get to the bottom of it soon."

The already quiet crowd had now become silent, the mourners turning in their direction, shocked by the outburst.

"Yeah, I don't know who you are and I don't care, but I want this woman away from here immediately!" Howard bellowed, his face crimson.

To Grace's astonishment her father put his fists in a boxing position and invited Howard to try to remove him.

"I guess stupidity and insolence must run in your family, old man!" Howard said as he reached out to grab Thomas.

"Hey! Stop it!" Andre Cruz stepped between Thomas and Howard. Grace could see out of the corner of her eye that Emma Rice was standing several feet away, a wry smile on her face. "Everyone, calm down. Mr. Pittman, please go back to your family," Cruz commanded.

Howard's eyes narrowed, but he stepped back, turned around and walked back to his wife, who was standing with her arms wrapped protectively around her children.

"I wish I could have popped him one!" Thomas said as Grace steered him down the hill toward Irene's car.

As she was settling her father in the front seat, Michael appeared behind her. "Good job, Mr. DePace. I had your back!" Grace rolled her eyes at Bella. All she needed now was to have her father engaged in a fistfight with a man who was about to sue her, and who might have reasons of his own to murder his sister.

Chapter Thirty-Three

THE RESTAURANT NEAR the wharf was filled with a noisy party of office workers having their holiday lunch, as well as clusters of small groups enjoying the view of the snow-covered boats. Omnipresent sea gulls sat on pilings and stared back at the customers. Grace spotted Andre Cruz seated in a table by a window writing furiously in a notebook.

"The great American novel?" Grace asked by way of a greeting.

He laughed. "You're right. I should be taking copious notes on all of the strange and bizarre things I encounter on a typical day so that when I retire I can pursue the leisurely life of a crime writer. But, actually I'm catching up on some very basic, boring paperwork."

A young woman, her hair in a neat bun, came by to take their orders. Crab cakes and a sauvignon blanc for Grace, and fish and chips and coffee for Andre.

"Your dad is quite a guy," he said, his dark eyes dancing with amusement. "I thought I might have an assault and battery on my hands at the funeral this morning."

Grace sighed. "My dad will be eighty-four years old in March. He's been living alone since my mom died a few years ago. He's very independent and stubborn as a bull. He's got an Italian soul, but an Irish temper."

"And what about you? Italian soul? Irish temper?" Andre asked, staring into Grace's dark eyes.

"Um, well, I guess." She fumbled with her napkin and placed it in her lap. "If you hadn't intervened, I have no doubt that he would have tried to clobber Howard Pittman."

"Defending his daughter against a big bully. I don't think even D.A. Banks would want to prosecute that kind of case."

"Howard Pittman would probably try to sue Dad too."

"Too?"

"Supposedly he's planning on suing me because I sent Duane to Danielle's house. It makes me sick to think about it." Grace looked out the window at the parking lot full of cars, the roadway beyond them. "Like everyone else around here, he's convinced that Duane is guilty."

Cruz raised an eyebrow. "Howard Pittman inherited a lot of money from the estate."

"That's what I heard."

"Of course you did."

Grace tried not to smile, but failed. "I heard he got eighty percent. Who gets the rest?"

"She left about ten percent to the Historical Society, five percent to the food bank and five percent to Pinewood. Pittman told me that he would challenge that, given the circumstances of her death."

"I bet he will. Do you know what her connection to Pinewood was? I know that she was a big contributor, but I wonder what prompted her interest in a drug and alcohol rehab program," Grace said.

"I was hoping you might know," Andre said, putting down his fork. "Would you like some of my fries?"

Grace looked longingly at his garlic French fries but shook her head. No to his reference to Pinewood, and no to the fries.

"Have you located Vernon Rugosa?" she asked.

"Not yet. But we will. Guys like him usually turn up in a few days. He has a lady friend up in Boston and we're checking into that."

"Another lady friend?"

Andre nodded. "It's hard to believe how gullible some of these elderly people are. He never seems to run out of new victims. It appears that he gets involved with more than one at a time so that if something falls through he's got a backup plan. Sort of like insurance."

"It's not just elderly people who get conned," Grace said, taking a sip of wine. "If he thought he was getting close to her fortune and she snapped it away from him, it would make him a strong suspect in her death. Why isn't D.A. Banks slowing down her speedy prosecution of Duane until all of the facts are in?"

"Politics, mainly. Banks wants to keep her name out there. Show that she's doing something tangible. And Duane is still the most obvious candidate. And speaking of Duane, we located Gink early this morning. She's staying at a motel. The Rusty Anchor."

"I've been there a couple of times on field visits."

"Nice place, huh?" he said. "Anyway, she told us about the phone call from Duane. It doesn't appear that they talked long enough to give him an alibi. She also told us that Duane promised to find money to help her. Maybe Duane tried to rob Danielle and things got out of control. It's something we have to consider." Cruz looked at her now with cop eyes. "You didn't think that was important enough to mention?"

Grace tried not to squirm in her seat. So this was what it felt like to be interrogated. "I thought it best if Gink told you herself."

"You knew that Gink could provide the motive for Duane to kill Danielle." Grace could see frustration and disapproval on his face. "Look, Grace, stay out of this investigation. You may think that you're helping Duane, but remember, if it isn't him, then there's someone else out there who won't like you stirring up trouble for them."

"Right." Grace looked out the window again just as Emma Rice pulled into the parking lot and gracefully exited her patrol car.

"Emma and I are going to see the priest now. Is there anything else you want to tell me about him?"

"You haven't got the time," she replied as Emma, radiant in black parka and red cashmere scarf, strode up to their table and slid into the seat next to Andre. He smiled warmly at her. Grace noticed that Andre didn't move over so that Emma sat close to him, her elbow touching his. Emma smiled back at Andre and then shifted her gaze to Grace. She nodded at her without speaking, her smile fading.

"Ready to go see Murrey?" she said, turning back to Andre.

"Yeah, we're done here. Grace and I were discussing her friends Gink and Duane. Anything new on Rugosa?"

"Not yet. Boston P.D. is going to check an address for us. I've been doing some credit card checks on him too. He was in Boston on Sunday night and used an ATM on State Street. But his most recent charge was at a bar called Shifty's on Route 28 in West Yarmouth. He was there last night."

Grace slid out of her chair as nonchalantly as she could and pulled on her jacket and scarf. If Cruz discovered that she had been to Shifty's Bar last night, he'd be more than mad.

"Boston is a little over an hour away," Andre said to Emma. "He could easily go back and forth. Let's check out Shifty's after we talk to Murrey," he said, watching Grace as she pulled on her gloves. "Nice seeing you again, Grace. I'll be in touch. If you hear anything that could help your friend Duane, let me know. Okay?"

"Sure. Thanks for lunch." She turned and walked toward the door, self-consciously aware that now both Andre and Emma were watching her.

Grace headed back to town, the car heater on high. What was it with Andre Cruz that was so tantalizingly confusing? He was obviously smitten with Emma. His smile gave him away. But who wouldn't be? She was gorgeous. And yet, Grace had to admit that she had looked forward to lunch with more than casual interest. Was she letting herself be influenced by his good looks and unmistakable charm? Charm when he chose to use it, that is. He wanted to get information from her. She must remember that the next time she saw him. She couldn't afford to become emotionally involved with a man who was so obviously interested in someone else. And a cop, no less. She knew all about the long hours, the worry and the stress of being a cop's wife. She had to be more careful. Jack's absence created a hollow wound that permeated her life. A wound that was slowly healing. She didn't want it ripped open again.

Grace was still trying to sort through her own feelings about Andre Cruz as she hung her coat in the coat closet and changed into her clogs. Another better part of a day had passed, and she had made no progress on her piles of shades to be painted and trimmed. She clumped up the stairs, where Bella and Michael greeted her.

"We're glad you're back," Michael said. "A very strange man came in here looking for you."

"How strange was he?" Grace asked teasingly.

"No. It's not a joke. He was very rough looking. He had piercings all over and tattoos. He was wearing sunglasses, even though we haven't seen the sun for days. And bright orange hair. The minute I saw him, I knew he hadn't come to buy a lamp," Michael said

Grace felt a sudden chill. So Orange Hair had tracked her down at Pearl's. "Did he say what he wanted?" she asked.

"He left this," Bella said as she handed Grace a piece of crumpled paper. Grace spread it on her desk and read the note that had been written with a soft pencil that had been pushed hard into the paper. It read: *I warned you, Lamp Shop Lady! Don't get involved in my business. You better watch your back*!

"Is he someone you know from California?" Michael asked.

Grace wanted to laugh, but her heart was pounding. "No, I met him right here on old Cape Cod."

"What are you going to do?" he asked.

"I'm going to watch my back, that's what."

Chapter Thirty-Four

BEFORE GETTING DOWN to work, Grace called her father. "You okay?"

"Gracie! Sure, I'm fine. That was the most fun I've had at a funeral in long time. I wish that police fellow hadn't intervened. I could have gotten at least one good shot at that blowhard. Thinks he owns the cemetery, does he? And accusing you of having something to do with Danielle's murder. Preposterous. Even if that young man did kill her, that doesn't mean that you had anything to do with it," he exclaimed.

"Oh, Dad. I appreciate your wanting to protect me, but getting into a fistfight with Howard Pittman wouldn't help at all. And frankly, I wish you hadn't told everyone that I was investigating the murder. What are they going to think? That I'm some kind of Nancy Drew or Miss Marple?"

"Really now, Gracie. Let's not get too upset. No harm done, and I had a little excitement. Better than hanging around all day taking naps."

Grace laughed. "I have an idea. The Village Stroll is on Saturday. Why don't you come help us at the shop? You could bring your camera and record the day for posterity. And you could greet customers and help Michael. What do you think?"

"You sure I wouldn't be in the way?"

"Not at all. We've got plenty of things you can help us out with. So get your photography stuff together, and we'll see you on Saturday morning around nine."

"Sounds good. I'll be there," he said.

"Do you have enough food in the house? With all of these

storms rolling in this week you should be prepared. Do you have enough batteries and flashlights on hand?"

"Yep. I'm fine. Don't worry about me. I keep telling you I'm fine. But I do have an idea that I want to talk to you about. I'm thinking of selling the house, buying a sailboat and living aboard ship. I want to travel up to Canada and down to the Carolinas. What do you think? "

Grace sighed. Her father was always cooking up new schemes. A few weeks ago, he was going to buy a farm in Maine and raise goats.

"I don't like that idea at all. A boat is a lot of work. And sailing up and down the coast is dangerous. I think the time has passed for that kind of adventure. But maybe when things settle down at the shop, we could take a cruise together. We could go wherever you want. Just the two of us. What do you say?"

"Being stuck on a big ship with a lot of fancy pants doesn't really interest me, but we can talk more about this later. But I do think that living on a small sailboat would simplify things. I don't need this big old house anymore."

"Right. We'll talk about this soon. See you on Saturday."

When Grace checked her cell phone, there was a message from Bruce, the bartender at Shifty's. It seemed he'd found out the name of the antique shop up in Brewster that Vernon Rugosa's new friend owned. The Blue Hyacinth. He was, he added, hopeful that Audrey might come and see him soon at the bar.

Grace leaned on the counter and peered in at Bella as she was rewiring an ornate art nouveau-style lamp. "That looks heavy."

"Indeed it is," Bella replied. She disconnected the old socket and was attaching wires to the new socket, matching the negative with the negative and the positive with the positive. The lamp was made of cast iron and reminded Grace all too vividly of the lamp lying on the carpet next to Danielle.

"Ever hear of the Blue Hyacinth Antique Shop in Brewster?"

Grace asked.

"Sure. Delores Fitch owns it. She's been a good source of old lamps for us. She sells some to us outright and has some cleaned up to sell in her shop. We should take a ride up there sometime. You'd like her. She's a lovely woman. A widow." She glanced at Grace. "Like us."

Of course it was true that Bella was a widow, but somehow Grace still had trouble thinking of herself in such a way. Weren't widows supposed to be old? Like Bella? After all, thirty-nine wasn't old. At least in the greater scheme of things.

"How many years were you married, Bella?"

"Forty-five wonderful, well, mostly wonderful, years. Alton was a good man."

"That's nice." Grace sighed.

"You'll fall in love again, Grace. You're young and beautiful."

"Someday, I hope." Grace said and then changed the subject. "I'd really like to meet Delores Fitch. How about we take a ride up to the Blue Hyacinth after we close up?"

"Today?"

"Yes, today. You see, I think Delores might be getting herself involved with a very unsavory character. She could even be in danger. I'll tell you about it on the ride out there. If all goes well I'll even treat you to dinner at the Scargo Cafe."

"Now you're talking. I'm ready when you are."

Chapter Thirty-Five

BY THE TIME Grace and Bella headed east on Old King's Highway, twilight was licking the snow, creating slick golden fields highlighted with deep cobalt shadows. The historical societies of the villages along the route had done a significant service by preserving the area in such a way that it was rare to see any building that might have been erected after the turn of the twentieth century. There was a congenial mix of styles: Colonial, Federal, Victorian, as well as Capes, half-Capes and three-quarter Capes.

They drove along in silence, murmuring their approval when they passed a home of exceptional beauty. The narrow, winding road surrounded by snowy, icy trees soothed their tired nerves. As they approached Brewster, a marker informed them that the town had been incorporated in 1803. They admired the lovely, graceful sea captain's homes painted in white or in Historical Society approved colonial colors, foot-long icicles hanging from the roofs.

Following Bella's directions, Grace drove along a narrow sandy lane lined with expensive homes and up a hill to a gray, shingled Cape that sat sturdily on a bluff overlooking Cape Cod Bay. The porch light was on, and there was a soft glow from a brass lamp in the bay window on the first floor of the rambling home. An older white Cadillac was parked in the driveway.

"Okay, Bella. You wait here. I'll go see if Delores is home. I'm not sure what kind of situation we might be walking into. You've got your cell phone, right?"

"Yes. I've got my cell phone, but I'm coming with you. You might need backup."

Grace looked at Bella, who was already scrambling out of the car. There was, Grace decided, noting the determined look on her face, no stopping her now.

They climbed the steep porch stairs, Bella gripping the railing and pulling herself along. For a moment, Grace wondered whether it had been fair of her to involve a woman so much older than she in this expedition. But her doubts were forgotten when, before knocking, they peered in the window next to the front door. Opposite the large foyer was a room with a roaring fireplace flanked by bookshelves. In front of the fire, relaxing in a dark leather chair, was a silver-haired man. He was smoking a cigarette and clasped a gimlet glass in his hand.

"Suppose that's Vernon Rugosa?" Grace asked.

"Could be. He sure looks right at home, doesn't he?"

Grace took out her cell and placed a call. "Hey Audrey, yes we're at Dolores Fitch's house now. Call them in about ten minutes. Great. See you later."

"Here goes," Grace said, pushing the doorbell. A few moments later the man, wearing a navy sport coat and carrying his half-empty glass, opened the door.

"Yes?" he said impatiently.

Bella spoke first. "Is Delores home? I'm a friend of hers."

"She'll be here shortly," he said, frowning. "Is she expecting you? She didn't mention that anyone would be coming by."

"She didn't know we were coming, Mr. Rugosa," Grace said and put her foot in the door as Vernon moved to close it. "And is that a cocktail that I see? I do believe that you have a no-alcohol condition as part of your probation for the DWI you had last summer."

For a moment, he looked flummoxed. "Now see here," he said, regaining his composure. "Who do you think you are, barging in here? I have a mind to call the authorities if you don't leave this house at once!"

"I don't think you'll want to do that, Vernon," Grace told him. "When the police see that you have an outstanding arrest warrant, it'll be you who will be leaving the house. It'll be jail for you, I'm afraid."

Vernon recoiled at the mention of incarceration. The color drained out of his face.

"And you look pretty comfy here, don't you?" she continued. "Is Delores your latest victim? Or is it the lady up in Boston?"

"I don't know what the hell you are talking about," he snapped. "I'm asking you once more to leave the premises."

"We didn't see you this morning at Danielle Whitney's funeral." Grace took a few steps forward, and after Bella stepped inside behind her, she shut the front door. "Was there some reason you couldn't make it? You and Danielle were such dear friends, I'm told." Grace couldn't keep the sarcasm out of her voice.

Vernon clenched his fists, hesitated and then pulled out an oversized handkerchief from his pocket and noisily blew his nose. He staggered backwards and sat on a Hepplewhite chair that was in the corner by a table with a gilded mirror hanging above it. "I couldn't bear to go," he muttered. "Poor Danielle. I was so in love with her. We were going to be married. I was so stricken with the news of her death that I wasn't physically up to attending the funeral." He looked imploringly from Bella to Grace. "I've been so devastated, you see, and I have a bad heart. The strain has been so great." He wiped away a tear from the corner of his eye and covered his face with his hands.

Grace and Bella glanced at each other. "Oh, brother," Bella said.

"When did you last see Danielle, Mr. Rugosa?" Grace asked as he blew his nose again. She wondered why it was her fate to be surrounded by dramatically demonstrative men. Her father, Clay, and now Vernon Rugosa. Actors. Princes of drama, all of them.

"Oh, my goodness. Let's see. I believe it was Saturday. Yes, Saturday afternoon. We were discussing our wedding plans. Oh, poor Danielle. Who could have wanted to hurt such a lovely lady?"

"That's funny," Grace said. "I heard from a good friend of Danielle's that she was breaking it off with you. And here you tell me about wedding plans. How odd. Grace said.

"Every couple has their little disagreements. I'm sure you ladies know that."

"Did your disagreement have to do with the fact that Danielle was calling it quits, and you weren't going to get married and get your hands on her estate?" Grace demanded. "Is that why you got angry and killed her?" Grace was now standing directly in front of Vernon.

Vernon's face paled to a greasy white, but he stood up and squared his shoulders. "Who are you? I don't have to answer your questions." With that, he grabbed a marble statue from a nearby table and swung it hard at Grace.

Grace ducked, and as he was coming at her again she grabbed his arm and pushed it backwards as far as she could. Vernon stumbled as Bella pulled a large flashlight out of her purse and held it firmly over his head.

"Let go of that right now before I knock you to Kingdom Come," she said.

Vernon, smart enough to know that he was no match for the two women, dropped the statue. He took a minute to regain his breath. "If you want answers, go talk to Danielle's neighbor. Maybe she had something going on with him."

Grace frowned. "Her neighbor?"

"Yeah. That spooky guy who lives next door. They were always flapping window shades at each other. If you ask me, that's who you should be talking to."

There was a crunch of tires on the gravel driveway. Bella looked out the window. "They're here."

"All right, Mr. Rugosa. The police are here. They're going to take you in on your warrant. I'm sure they will have lots of questions for you," Grace said as two rugged young men with brush cuts strode into the foyer.

"We got a call from a probation officer about a felon with an outstanding warrant," one of them said. "You Vernon Rugosa?"

"That's him," Grace said, pointing to the ashen-faced man who sat back down on the chair.

"Just in time too," Bella said as a tan Mercedes pulled in the driveway. "That's Delores. I'll go talk to her until you officers are ready. I think it's best if a friend breaks the news to her about the gentleman here." With that, Bella lumbered down the porch steps to the car where a short, stocky woman was struggling with the heavy car door.

After the arresting officers had driven away with Rugosa, Bella led her shaken friend Delores up the stairs. Grace ran down to the Mercedes and grabbed a couple of bags of groceries from the back seat and followed the two women into the house.

"I'm sorry, Delores," Grace said after Bella performed introductions. "It's hard now, but believe me, Vernon Rugosa was not who he appeared to be. And you're not the first woman to be taken in by him. He's what you would call a professional gigolo."

Bella helped Delores Fitch off with her coat, and she sat down on the same chair that was recently occupied by Mr. Rugosa. Now it was her turn to dab at her eyes with a handkerchief. "He seemed like such a nice gentleman. Well spoken and educated."

Bella put her hand on Delores's shoulder and spoke gently to her. "Is there someone I can call? You shouldn't be alone."

"I don't have any children, and my cousins are far away. I do have lots of friends, but I can't call them. I would be so humiliated!" She started crying again.

"Bella, what do you say we have dinner at the cafe another time? I can whip something up for us here and we can chat with Delores for a while." Grace suggested.

Delores waved her handkerchief in front of her face. "Oh, please! I'm fine. I'll be all right. You two run along to your dinner."

"Absolutely not. Like it or not, we're staying." Bella took Delores by the arm and steered her to a comfortable chair by the fire. "I'll fix us up some nice martinis, and we'll relax by your lovely fireplace. Shall we, Delores?" Bella asked.

Grace rummaged around in the kitchen while Bella and Delores drank cocktails in the living room. She found salad makings in one of the grocery bags and two T-bone steaks in another. Putting the steaks in the freezer for another day, she tossed the salad and heated up a quiche she found in the refrigerator. When it was all ready, she portioned it out on three white plates and carried them out to the living room on a tray. The fire was dying, so she put on another log and stabbed at it with the fireplace poker.

Bella and Delores were on their second or third drink by now, and both were looking a lot perkier. Delores finished off her quiche and asked if there was a smidgen more in the kitchen.

"No, don't get up," she told Grace, who was pulling herself out of her chair. "I'm much better now. I'll get it myself. And I've got some delightful Portuguese port in the pantry that I've been saving up for a special occasion." She gave a rueful laugh. "I'm sure glad I didn't waste it on that old con man."

"She certainly recovered quickly," Grace said to Bella when Delores left for the kitchen.

"Yes, she has." Bella nodded. "Apparently she had recently met him. She had her hopes dashed but nothing more serious. When I told her about Danielle Whitney, she just about fainted."

"I'm glad the cops have their hands on Vernon now. All that crying nonsense was such a con. I'll bet he killed Danielle."

She broke off as Delores returned with a bottle of port and three pink Depression-era glasses.

"When was that poor Whitney woman murdered?" Delores asked, pouring healthy measures of port into the glasses. "I shudder to think about it."

"Sunday morning," Grace replied.

Delores leaned back and plumped the pillow behind her. She took a sip of her port and looked first at Grace, then at Bella. "Well," she said, "that old goat might have been a gigolo, but he didn't murder that woman."

"What do you mean?" Grace asked.

"Because he was with me from Saturday night until half-past one on Sunday," Delores replied, blushing. "I'm afraid that I'm his alibi."

Chapter Thirty-Six

I T WAS NEARING ten when, after dropping Bella off at her house on Pine Street, Grace pulled her car into the old barn behind her cottage and secured the door. Another storm was due to roll in shortly, and swarms of snowflakes were drifting lazily in gentle gusts of wind. Grace looked across the frozen marsh at the little village where a few lights twinkled through the trees. From here she could see the courthouse and the back of the building that housed the Dolphin. Above the courthouse was the old jail, dark except for a single light above the front entrance. As she groped in the dark for her keys, she jumped as something furry rubbed against her leg.

"Clambake! What are you doing outside? You're an indoor cat!" Grace exclaimed, turning on the little flashlight that was attached to her key ring. The cat ran up the back porch steps and pressed his nose against the door.

Grace caught her breath and froze. There was no way that she left the house this morning without locking the doors and saying good-bye to Clambake. So that meant someone had been in her house. Or was still in there. Her heart skipped a beat or two as she aimed her little light around the door, now noticing that the window above the doorknob was broken. Flecks of splintered glass littered the porch.

She heard a loud bang coming from the front of the house. Picking up Clambake and holding him close, she tiptoed down the porch steps and started around the side of the cottage. Staying close to the wall, she crept up to a prickly evergreen tree and peered into the darkness. Someone was moving in the shadows across the road, but whether it was a man or a woman she couldn't be sure. Without thinking, she dashed out from behind the tree and ran toward the moving figure, but when she got to the street, she couldn't see anyone. She continued a few steps further, but it was futile to try to pursue whoever it was in the dark. And what would she do if she did catch them? She had no weapon. She turned around and headed back to her house. She dialed 911.

Several minutes passed as Grace stood with the squirming cat in the dark yard until she saw a patrol car pull up in front of her house. A flashlight beam blinded her.

"Over here!" she called out. "It's Grace Tolliver!"

"Oh, Ms. Tolliver." The voice was familiar. It was Officer Gelb, the first cop on the scene at Danielle's. He looked at her skeptically. "Got a call of a possible break-in."

"I think so, Officer," Grace said, her heart still pounding so hard that she felt short of breath. "I got home a little while ago and found my cat outside. I never leave him outside," she told him. "The window on the back door is broken too. I saw someone running away. Whoever it was ran across the street into the woods."

Gelb gazed skeptically at the dark woods. "All right. Let's have a look around," he grumbled. Grace imagined that he wasn't too keen about leaving the warm station for a cold trek in the dark around her house. She followed him around the back of her cottage as he waved his light back and forth around the yard and bushes. "Where's your vehicle?"

"In there." She pointed to the converted barn. Gelb's flashlight beam swept over the driveway and yard.

"There's no one around now," he said. "Let's see what things are like inside."

Glass crunched under their feet as they stepped into her kitchen. Gelb walked forward a few steps, his light illuminating the room. "You got a light switch here?'

Grace reached to her right and turned on the Pairpoint lamp with the inverted painted shade that rested on a table by the door. "Oh, no!" she exclaimed as she surveyed her kitchen. Cupboard doors hung open, dishes were broken, and drawers were dumped upside down.

"Wait here. I'll have a look around." Gelb said as he started for the dining room. "And don't touch anything!"

She listened as the officer rummaged around the house. After a few minutes, he descended the staircase and joined her in the kitchen. "Your front door is unlocked. That the way you left it?"

"No, of course not."

"Whoever it was came in through the back door and probably exited the front," he said. "What time did you last leave the premises?"

"About nine this morning."

"They must have run out the front door when you pulled into the barn. I'm going to call this in. Someone will be out to check for prints. In the meantime, look around and see what, if anything, is missing. But don't touch anything. Even papers."

Since she couldn't touch anything, it was difficult to tell at first glance what might have been taken. But one thing was clear: whoever had been here had gone through every room. There was disarray everywhere. Books strewn about and drawers dumped, their contents rifled. Even her couch pillows had been turned upside down. Gelb was on his radio. He reported the break-in and requested the crime services division. He hung up and turned to Grace. "Anyone else have a key to your house?"

"No."

"No ex-husbands or ex-boyfriends?"

Grace winced. "No one. Not even Father Murrey."

"What?"

"Never mind." Grace wondered why he was asking the question when it was pretty obvious that if someone had a key, the glass on the back door wouldn't have been smashed. He's young, she reminded herself. Must be on-the-job training.

Gelb frowned. "Let's have a look around the downstairs."

"I can't imagine why anyone would pick my house. It's the most modest house on the street," Grace said as she scanned the living room. "Can I take a look upstairs and see if my jewelry is still in my bureau?"

"Okay. Don't touch anything though," he repeated. "Could have been some local punks looking for some quick cash."

She gasped as she entered her bedroom. Whoever had broken in had been up here, too. Her favorite picture of Jack lounging on a sandy beach squinting at the camera was overturned on the dresser, the glass cracked. She wanted to pick up the velvet-lined case that her mother had given her when she turned fifteen, but remembering Gelb's admonition, she sank down on the bed. Up until now, the shock of finding that her house had been broken in to had taken the edge off of her emotions. Now, as she realized that the diamond and sapphire necklace, given to her by Jack on their first anniversary, her grandmother's cameo pin, and dozens of earrings, bracelets and necklaces that she accumulated throughout the years were all gone, she was overwhelmed with grief.

"Humph," Gelb cleared his throat. "Sorry, Miss. Can you make a list of what was in the jewelry box? We might as well start there." He handed her a notebook and a pen. "You can use this for now."

Grace took the paper and pen from him. "I think I'd like to go downstairs if you don't mind," Grace told him, brushing back the tears. "It's pretty creepy knowing someone was prowling around my bedroom."

"You got somewhere to spend the night?" Gelb asked as she seated herself at the kitchen table.

"I could go to my dad's or to a friend's house, but I think I'll stay here," Grace replied. It was late, and she didn't want to alarm anyone. She thought it was doubtful that whoever invaded her house would return.

"Suit yourself," he said. "I'll call you tomorrow morning. Write down everything that is missing, with a description. If you can, draw pictures of the jewelry. That'll help too." He scratched his head. "And if you know the value of the missing items, note that also."

As if she could place a value on her most precious memories. Thinking about her prized possessions recalled past experiences in her life that she now was forced to recollect. She remembered the old saying about life flashing before the eyes of one about to die.

Well, she wasn't about to die, but she now understood what the phrase meant. She remembered the flower earrings Jack bought for her at the Nantucket Daffodil Festival shortly after they met, the lobster pin she bought during a vacation to Sebago Lake in Maine when she was eight, the pin made out of pennies that she soldered together in summer camp. Monetary value of items, probably zero. Memories, priceless.

After the officers from the crime investigations unit had gone, Grace put on a kettle of water. When she felt stressed she liked to make a cup of strong tea. At this time of night it would have to be decaf, but the feeling of comfort would be the same. She fed Clambake his dinner and then, with cup in hand, she systematically went from room to room, checking drawers and cupboards and making a list. Cash from her hidden stash in the bedroom was gone, but change left in a turquoise Chinese bowl on her desk was still there. Apparently even thieves couldn't be bothered with coins. A fountain pen that Jack bought her in France on their honeymoon was gone too. But despite the considerable mess in her house, she couldn't find anything else that was missing. Whoever broke in was looking for a quick haul. They helped themselves to her money and jewelry. Things easily pawned. Maybe Gelb was right. It might have been some local kids needing extra cash.

A strong wind blasted the windows as Grace wandered around the spare room where she often worked on the lampshades she brought home. As she picked up papers and ribbons from the floor, she thought about the threatening note that Orange Hair left for her at the store. He could have found out where she lived. That was not hard to do in a small town. She shuddered to think of that creep in her home, rifling through her personal things.

Sleeping upstairs was not an option. And since the back door couldn't be locked, she propped a kitchen chair up against it so that she would at least hear if someone tried to get in. She stuffed the hole in the glass with a towel but frigid air still found a way to seep in. She left the heat on, bundled up in a pair of sweatpants and an old T-shirt of Jack's and wrapped herself in her chenille throw and her comforter. She remembered the fairy lamp called

Burglar's Horror. Now would be an appropriate time to have one nearby. As if a fairy lamp would scare her intruder away.

Chapter Thirty-Seven

"Hey, Grace. Come look at this." It was Thursday morning, and Michael was standing in front of the bay window. "Those awful television people are back. Don't they have anything better to report?"

Grace put down her paintbrush and joined Michael. Heavy snow was still falling, and the cars below were crawling down the street. A large white van with the letters of a local TV station was parked opposite the shop. The reporter who accosted her on Monday was frowning and earnestly speaking into her microphone. Her eyes were bright and she was sucking up to the camera that was inches from her face. Despite the brisk wind, her hair, which had a varnished look, didn't stir. Clay Davenport was behind her, doing his best to look nonchalant but obviously trying to get into the shot. The young waitress from the Beach Sparrow Inn stopped too and was listening intently. The reporter spoke a minute more, raised her arm and pointed dramatically toward the window where Michael and Grace were standing. Clay and the waitress followed the reporter's gaze as the cameraman aimed his lens up at Pearl's. Grace and Michael jumped back, Grace nearly knocking over one of her most valuable hurricane lamps.

"Danielle's murder and Duane's arrest are still big news, I see," she said, trying hard to sound nonchalant. "Well, there's nothing we can do about it. We'll just have to adjust to living in a fishbowl."

"Did you see Clay? He sure was taking his time crossing the street. He craves attention. He couldn't help preening in front of that camera."

"And here he is now," Grace whispered.

"Good morning friends!" Clay greeted them. Today, he was decked out in a long burgundy wool coat, black gloves and a black scarf embroidered with prancing red reindeer. His hair, which appeared to have been recently tinted, was dark and shiny. "I see we have our very own press corps out front. How exciting!" He clasped his hands together. "I'm sure all this publicity is wonderful for business!"

"Business is great," Michael assured him. "Looking for anything special today?"

"Well, yes." Clay said, sidling over to Grace's worktable. "How are you coming on that special order, the boudoir lamp we discussed on Monday? Almost done?"

"I haven't had time to even start that lamp, Clay. But, I promise you it will be ready by Christmas."

"Christmas?" Clay exclaimed. "I'm afraid that won't do. I assured my client that you would have it ready by Saturday. She's entertaining extensively during the holidays and she wants to have everything perfect when she shows off her newly decorated house to all of her friends. I thought I made that absolutely clear."

Grace leaned back in her chair and brushed her hair out of her eyes. "I don't remember setting a completion date," she said. "But I'll do my best."

"Doing your best doesn't sound very positive to me," he replied, stroking his long chin. "If you can't finish it on time, let me know now. Of course my client would be most disappointed. Perhaps the excitement of the past week is too much for you."

Michael was hovering nearby sifting through rolls of fabrics. "Grace has been having a very difficult week, Clay," he said. "Her house was broken into last night."

"Really?" Clay said, raising his right eyebrow several inches.

Grace looked up from an oval shade she was stippling. "Come in on Saturday morning and the shade will be ready." She vowed to herself that she would have the shade completed and Clay off her back, even if she had to stay up all night to do it.

"Delightful!" he replied, preparing to clamp a pair of fluffy black earmuffs on his head. "And now I must be on my way. I'm starting a new decorating job at Christine Sinclair's house. As I'm sure you know, Christine was a very dear friend of Danielle's. She's been so upset about the poor woman's death, I'm sure some fresh paint and fabrics will pick her right up."

"Is Grace Tolliver here?"

They both started as an attractive woman stepped into the room. Grace recognized Valerie Elkins from Danielle's funeral.

"Yes." Grace got up from her worktable and stretched out her hand in greeting.

"I'm Valerie Elkins," the woman responded, ignoring Grace's hand and taking in the shop with one dismissive glance. "I'm a real estate agent. I have a successful business here on the Cape and I've been hearing that you have taken it upon yourself to butt into my business affairs."

"Excuse me ... ?" Grace responded. Valerie, decked out in a pantsuit and a low-cut black lace top that revealed her copious cleavage, placed both hands on her full hips. Several holiday pins were scattered across her lapel. For an instant Grace remembered her own jewelry box lying open and empty on her dresser.

"Milo Sedgemore and Matt Taylor?" Valerie continued. "The previous owners of this establishment? You know them, of course?"

"Certainly." Grace responded. She glanced at Michael, who looked anxiously back at her from behind his big glasses.

Clay took a step toward Valerie. "Allow me to introduce myself, I'm Claiborne Davenport. I'm Cape Cod's most favorite designer. I'd love to work with you. You sell, I decorate!" He reached out with a manicured hand. "Here's my card."

Valerie gave Clay a withering glance and he stepped back, putting his card back in his pocket. "Why don't we go to my office? We can speak privately there," Grace said to Valerie as she frowned at Clay's maneuvering.

"I don't need to speak privately!" Valerie declared, pointing a finger that came remarkably close to Grace's face. "And I don't need anyone investigating my life! Matt and Milo have been speaking to my dear customers, whose house in Yarmouthport I have been entrusted to sell. Matt and Milo have told them that they are helping you investigate the murder of Danielle Whitney that sadly took place last Sunday morning."

Matt and Milo, Grace thought, were going to get her into more trouble, if that were possible, if they didn't keep their busy mouths closed.

"I also became aware of your investigation at Danielle's funeral when that scuffle broke out between that old man and Danielle's dear grieving brother Howard," Valerie continued. She stopped for a moment, glanced around the shop and pursed her lips. "Anyway, my clients had the nerve to ask me if I held my scheduled open house that morning. As if I wasn't the consummate professional that I am. As if my whereabouts on Sunday were significant. I want to assure you that I'm not a suspect in Danielle's death. She and I may have had some minor differences that we were in the process of coming to an agreement on, but it's preposterous that I should be dragged into gossip of this sort. Remember, Ms. Tolliver, it's your employee that's in jail. If anyone is responsible, it's you."

Grace had had about enough of Valerie and her rant. "If Duane committed the murder, then I take responsibility," she said. "But I don't believe he killed Danielle. So if you don't mind my asking, *were* you at the Claridge's open house on Sunday morning?"

"I don't have to tell you anything. Just stay out of my business. As far as I know, the police are in charge of this investigation. If they want to talk to me, they know where my office is." Whirling around, Valerie knocked over a display of light bulbs, sending many of them crashing to the floor. She didn't hesitate, but went stomping down the stairs. Grace, Michael and the abnormally quiet Clay all held their breaths until the downstairs door slammed.

"Ouch!" said Michael. "That hurt my ears!"

"My, my, my," said Clay. "She's certainly a charmer. I'm having second thoughts about blending my career with hers."

"What's going on in here?" Bella said, lumbering into the room, her cane at the ready. "I was on the phone and all of a sudden I heard a crash and yelling. I thought maybe that dreadful man with the orange hair had come back!"

"A man with orange hair?" Clay repeated.

"It's okay, Bella," Grace said. "It was the realtor, Valerie Elkins. It seems that Matt and Milo have been talking to their friends about Danielle's murder and have managed to upset her. However, she never did answer my question about where she was on Sunday morning."

"She certainly did overreact." Michael fretted as he began to sweep up glass. "She didn't have to knock over the bulb display. And she barely missed the stack of bobeches," he added, straightening the pile of glass rings used to catch melted candle wax.

"Maybe she didn't answer because she might implicate herself," Bella declared. "Well, folks, excitement's over. I'm going back to my work. Lots to do."

Clay crossed his scarf in front of his chest and threw both ends over his shoulders. "I must be on my way also," he said. "It's always such a pleasure coming to this shop. Lots of drama! I love it. See you!"

Grace followed Bella as she went behind the counter. Bella propped her cane next to the doorway and placed a pair of safety glasses on her nose. "I've been meaning to ask you about something Vernon Rugosa said last night. What do you think he meant when he referred to Danielle and her neighbor flapping shades at each other? He must mean that old man who lives next door. The one I've seen peering out of his window."

Bella smiled. "Watch out who you are calling old. That's Morris Bidlake. He's my age. Went to school together from kindergarten to high school graduation."

Grace blushed. "I'm sorry. I didn't mean you were old. Besides, he looks much older than you."

"Nice try." Bella chuckled. "I guess I am getting a bit creaky myself. Anyway, Morris and I have something else in common. Korea. Unfortunately, he was never the same after he returned. Shell shocked. I guess they call it post-traumatic stress disorder now. He's been in and out of hospitals pretty regularly through the years, but he doesn't seem to get any better. He stays inside of his house, rarely goes out. In fact, I can't remember the last time

I saw him anyplace other than his window. Sad case. As far as I know, his family has all passed away and he's alone now. He gets a disability pension, I suppose, and his family had some money. But it has to be a difficult life." Bella shook her head as she sat on her stool.

"It seems unlikely that he and Danielle would be friends," Grace said.

"Yes, it certainly is odd."

"Let's go pay Morris a visit," Grace proposed. "I know the police interviewed him, but maybe there is something to this shade-flapping stuff."

"Good idea. I do feel bad that I haven't made an effort to look in on Morris. But he doesn't make visiting easy. We'll be lucky if he will even talk to us."

Chapter Thirty-Eight

WHEN THERE WAS no answer to the doorbell, Bella stepped back and called up at the windows on the second floor. "Morris! It's me, Bella Benson. Can I talk to you, please? It's very important."

"It doesn't look like he wants to let us in," Grace said after a few minutes of silence passed.

"I guess you're right. We'll come back another time."

As they turned to go, the front door opened a crack. "That you, Bella?" a voice that sounded as if it hadn't been used in a long time croaked.

"Morris! Yes. Yes, it's me, and my friend, Grace Tolliver from Pearl's. She took over the shop from Matt and Milo a few months ago. They moved to Florida. Did you know that?"

The door slowly opened and Grace saw a man with stooped shoulders wearing a plaid shirt, the pockets overflowing with tissues. He looked suspiciously at her. "Wait a minute." He closed the door. A few minutes later he returned and stepped back to let them pass into the dark hallway. Indicating that they should follow him, Morris led the way up the stairs to his apartment. The dingy, dusty, fried meat smell of the apartment brought Grace back to her field visits in San Francisco when she would go into hotel rooms in the city's Tenderloin District, an area of pimps, addicts, thieves and lonely old men and women.

Morris scurried around the living room, removing books and items of clothing from the chairs, clearing a place so they could sit. Grace chose a straight-backed armchair with a woven cushion. Bella plopped down on the couch and put her purse on the coffee table while Morris hovered in the doorway, looking as if he had mistakenly found himself in the house of a stranger rather than his own home.

Bella tried her best to put Morris at ease. She talked about his health, his family and old friends. She asked if he needed anything. Morris responded with one word whenever possible. She was launching into a discussion of the recent week of storms when Grace noticed that the old man was staring at the floor and there were tears in his eyes.

"Morris," Grace said gently. "Were you a friend of Danielle Whitney?"

Morris nodded.

Grace continued. "Are you aware that she um ... passed away?"

Morris nodded again.

"Your window looks out on the side of her house, doesn't it?"

When he didn't respond, Grace got up and walked to the window that she had seen Morris sitting in. The row of trees that separated the two properties were spaced about five feet apart, and the house was close enough so that she could see Danielle's kitchen sink through the slatted wood blinds. The snow stopped about an hour ago and a strong wind, coupled with weak sunshine, threw blue shadows darting across the side of the house.

"Did you see anyone come to Danielle's house on Sunday morning, Mr. Bidlake?"

"It's all right, Morris, dear," Bella said when he did not respond. "Grace is a friend. She wants to help."

"I saw a man. Young. Blue jacket, blue hat, and blue jeans. I saw him leaving. He went up the street." At this point Morris started to breathe heavily. He sat down and started to cry. "Danielle was the only friend I had in the whole world." He gulped.

"Oh, dear!" Bella said. "I'll get you some water, Morris." She headed for the back of the apartment. A second later, the doorbell rang.

"It's the boys," Morris said, taking a wad of tissues out of his pants pocket and blowing his nose. "They've brought my groceries. Perhaps you'd be good enough to let them in."

Jose and Raphael went directly to the kitchen, where Grace could hear them chatting with Bella as they unloaded the groceries. Grace joined Morris in the living room. He had moved to the chair by the window and was gazing toward Danielle's house. "Morris, I don't want to upset you, but it's very important that I ask you one more question. Did you see anyone else go over there on Sunday morning?"

"I saw you," he answered. "And then lots of people." He started sobbing again as Bella, trailed by Jose and Rafael, came into the room. Jose's eyes widened at the sight of Morris's tears.

Morris got up and shuffled to a desk and pulled open a drawer. He reached in and pulled out a cloth wallet and extracted a roll of dollar bills. He handed the money to Rafael. "Thank you, boys," he said.

Jose put the dollars in his pocket. "Thanks, Mr. Bidlake," Rafael said. "We'll come back again on Monday. Come on, Jose. We've got work to do. Bye, Mrs. Tolliver. Bye, Mrs. Benson." Rafael and Jose ran down the stairs, slamming the door behind them. Bella handed Morris a glass of water. "Morris, do you have a cat?"

"No."

"I'm very worried about you," Bella said, reaching in her pocket and handing him a fresh tissue. "As you know, I work down the street at the lamp store. I can help you with groceries and . . ." Her gaze took in the room. "And other things. We've got to go now, but I'll come back in a day or two. Make a list for me of anything you need. Okay?" Morris sat on the edge of his chair by the window and wiped away a tear. He nodded but didn't speak.

Grace and Bella let themselves out of Morris's and started down the street to Pearl's. "I feel awful." Bella cried. "I had no idea how poorly Morris was getting on. I should have checked up on him long ago. There's no excuse for me. From now on, I'm going to help him any way I can."

"I guess we all get so caught up in our own lives we don't always notice the plight of others," Grace said, hustling to keep up with her friend who had broken into a determined stride. "I'll help you. That is, if Morris will let us."

"I always thought Morris had enough money to get by on," Bella said. "But it appears that he's in worse shape than I thought."

"He did look awfully thin." Grace said.

"That's because he's eating cat food!" Bella abruptly stopped and Grace almost bumped into her. "Cat food! That's what the boys brought. Bread, a little ham, milk and cat food! Oh! I'll never forgive myself," she said. "I've read about things like this. People so poor they eat cat food. To think that such a terrible thing is going on right here in our village. I must tell Michael. He'll help us too. But we should keep this to ourselves until we find out more. I don't want the busybody church ladies banging on his door until we've had a chance to find out what's what!"

What's what was about right, Grace mused, as she realized that they hadn't even asked Morris about the shade flapping.

Chapter Thirty-Nine

MICHAEL LOOKED DOWN on Grace and Bella from his perch on top of a stepladder. Although Michael was small in stature, it didn't keep him from getting things done around the shop. On his second day of work, he showed up with an aluminum ladder and hauled it up the back stairs. It was now leaning precariously against the Christmas tree. Strings of blinking bulbs were wrapped around his head and arms and he was festively dressed in a green sweater vest over a red shirt. A hat with a bell and curly-toed shoes was all he needed to be admitted to Santa's workshop, Grace thought.

"I brought some ornaments in," he said, holding on to the trunk with one hand and tottering slightly. "My tree is smaller this year so I had some left over. I thought I'd start with the lights. All white, like you said. Although, I prefer a bit more color myself. It's been quiet here since you left. Except for the phone. I put some messages on your desk."

"Please be careful up there," Grace cried. "God! You make me nervous."

"It's okay," he assured her. "I made sure the ladder was steady before I got up here. I'm really very nimble. I'll have this done in a jiffy." He draped a string of lights over the top of the tree. "And frankly, I'm getting tired of this sad tree. Not dressed properly. Not at all. It's time we got this place decorated."

Grace looked down at the pink slips of paper Michael used to write down her messages. She hadn't seen these pads in years until she took over the shop. It was strange to think that the evolution from paper and pen to computer had taken place during her professional career, and that here she was now, back to pink message pads. But, after all, this was a small shop and voicemail had no place here. Of course, she had her cell phone, so it wasn't like she had completely stepped back into the twentieth century.

There was a message from Andre Cruz to the effect that she should call him ASAP. Officer Gelb called to ask her if she had the list of items missing from her house ready. And then there was the handy man from Geezers, an odd jobs company that Grace called to fix her door. The employees were, for the most part, retired men who had wanted to work and keep up their skills while making a little money. Grace called them a couple of times before to help with a stuck window and to build some bookshelves. Not wanting to spend another night on the couch, she returned their call first.

Next, she checked in with Officer Gelb. No prints found. Everyone's wearing gloves in this cold weather. He'd be in touch with her.

She had better get back to Andre, she thought. Lunch yesterday had been kind of strange, and now that he had a motive for Duane to kill Danielle, to get money to help Gink, he might not be pursuing the case any further. She wondered if she should mention that Morris confirmed Duane's presence at Danielle's house. His confirmation wasn't anything new. After all, Duane never denied going to the house. Cruz told her that some officers already interviewed Morris on Sunday. The phone rang.

"Hey Grace."

"Oh, hi, Andre. I was about to call you." When did she start calling him Andre? she wondered.

"I heard about the break-in. Are you okay?"

"Yeah. But it was pretty creepy. I spent the night on the downstairs couch because I couldn't lock my door."

"You could have come here."

"Where? The police station?"

"Here. My house. You should have called me." Grace felt her

heart do a little flip before warning bells started ringing in her head. She turned the nearest pink message paper over and started doodling with a soft pencil, a habit she developed in grade school. It helped her think. More than that, it helped her stay calm.

"Oh, thanks," she said. "The guys from Geezers are going to repair it today. I should be fine tonight. Not that you said I could stay tonight. I just meant . . ." So much for staying calm.

There was a long silence on the other end of the line. He could have jumped in and said something to save her from further embarrassment, she thought. What was with those long silences anyway?

"Grace, hold on. There's another call coming through." Grace drew an entire rose complete with a long stem and spiky thorns by the time he came back on the line. "It's supposed to be my day off, but Emma called," he said. "Something's come up, and I've got to go in. But, I've been making Portuguese stew today. Why don't you come here, say around six and help me eat it? I've made a huge pot full. Unless you'd rather have dinner with a Geezer?"

Grace laughed. Throwing all caution to the wind, she heard herself reply, "Sounds great." Jotting down the directions, she obliterated the rose and began to think about what she would wear.

A few minutes later, Michael announced, "Mr. Twoberry over on Nantucket would like his buoy lamp delivered. It's all done," he enthused. "Bella took that waterlogged, barnacled chunk of wood and made such a unique piece. He's going to love it. The sea gull finial is perfect with the pale blue shade. I suppose I could deliver it."

"I can take the twelve-thirty ferry and be back in a couple of hours. I have a dentist appointment later this afternoon, but I'm sure I'll be back in time," Bella offered.

Grace looked up at Michael, still teetering on his ladder. "No, I need you both here. I'm the only one we can spare. A quick trip on the bay would be nice. I think I'll ask Jill if Sophie would like to come with me."

Michael let out an audible sigh. "I'm glad you don't mind going," he admitted as he clambered down the ladder and stood back to admire his handiwork. "I don't like boats all that much anyway. That's a nice idea to bring Sophie with you. I bet she would love to go."

"If Duane were here, I'd send him, of course. This is the kind of errand I hired him to do."

"If Duane were here, and you sent him on an errand to Nantucket, he'd probably end up on Martha's Vineyard."

Bella chuckled and Grace tried to hold back a grin. But he's right, she thought. She would have to go with him at least the first time. Thinking of Duane made her realize that she hadn't called his probation officer and his lawyer. She dialed his P.O. first, and when she got his message machine she left a brief message that she wanted to touch base with him and that he should call her if he needed any more information on Duane.

Duane's lawyer was Maria Glemming. She was bright, but she had a reputation around the courthouse for being more interested in attracting eligible men than anything else. She wasn't known as a go-getter, and that's what Duane needed now.

"Yes, Grace," Maria said. "I was going to contact you about Duane. I knew you'd be concerned. I think I can make a deal. A lesser sentence, given Duane's non-violent criminal history. He'll still be an old man when he gets out of prison, and he'll have to admit guilt, of course. Maybe you can talk to him. I don't seem to be able to get through ..."

"Don't you think it's premature to be discussing a deal? The investigation is still going on."

"I don't know who you've been talking to, but the D.A. is not budging on this."

"I don't believe that Duane is guilty, so I'm not going to try to talk him into any deal just so everyone can clear off their desks. What's the big hurry to hang Duane? I think Banks wants to make a quick name for herself after the last election. A man's life is at stake here. Doesn't anyone realize that? Doesn't anyone care?"

"Come on," Maria said. "You don't want to think Duane killed

Danielle Whitney because you're the one who sent him to her house. Which was a stupid thing to do, if you want my opinion."

"Just do your job, Maria, that's all," Grace said and slammed down the receiver. She put her head in her hands, telling herself to calm down and breathe deeply.

She thought about Duane sitting in his cell. She remembered that she meant to leave some money on the books for him. Jail was hard enough without cash to buy necessities or favors. Pinewood was probably helping. Sean wouldn't leave one of his program residents without funds. She called the jail and made the necessary arrangements. The deputy she spoke to told her that some of the other inmates were harassing Duane. But Duane was doing all right, the deputy assured her. At least, he was crying less each day.

Chapter Forty

GRACE AND SOPHIE settled into their comfortable seats on the *Grey Lady*, a high-speed passenger boat that would take them from Hyannis to Nantucket Island in one hour. Grace leaned back in her chair and was about to close her eyes and take a brief nap when she saw Christine Sinclair coming down the aisle. She was almost unrecognizable, dressed in a navy parka and blue jeans. Her hair was tucked underneath a wool hat that was pulled down low on her forehead. She didn't appear to be wearing any makeup, and she looked like she hadn't slept well in days. Her face was set in a grimace and she sank into her aisle seat and closed her eyes. She could have been asleep, but the rhythmic shaking of her crossed leg suggested otherwise.

The ferry chugged through the icy Nantucket Sound. The sea was navy blue, calm and looked deliciously cold. Grace and Sophie watched Nantucket Island gradually appear out of low fog that clung to the shore. As they came closer, they could make out the old whaling village, a collection of old clapboard houses, bare trees and church steeples. Smug-looking sea gulls balanced on pilings, facing into the weak sunlight, the wind ruffling their feathers.

As the boat nestled into its slip at the Straight Wharf, Grace grabbed Sophie's hand and hurried her along until they were standing behind Christine.

"Hello, Christine," Grace said.

Christine turned around to face her, and Grace took in the cold, startled look that swept across Christine's face.

"Oh, hello, Grace," Christine said. "Are you Christmas

shopping on the island too?"

Grace held up the green and gold Pearl's bag. "Delivering a lamp to a customer. Christine, do you know Sophie? Her parents run the Beach Sparrow Inn."

"Hello, Sophie," Christine said dismissively to the girl. "So here you are, Grace, the owner of Pearl's, and you're delivering lamps all the way out here on Nantucket. Such customer service. But I guess you don't have anyone else now that your young criminal is behind bars."

"Hi, Mrs. Sinclair. I'm going shopping," Sophie burst in with her usual loud enthusiasm. "After we deliver the lamp, we're going to buy presents for my mother and father. Who are you buying presents for?"

"Oh, lots of people, Sophie. Well, here we are. Good-bye," Christine said and set off down the dock toward Main Street with Grace and Sophie trailing behind.

Grace squeezed Sophie's hand buried in her thick mittens. "I didn't know we were going shopping," she kidded.

"Please, Grace. This way I can surprise Mom and Dad. I made them stuff in school, but I have some money saved up and I want to buy them real presents."

"How much have you got?" Grace asked.

"Thirty-two dollars."

"Okay. I know some shops we can check out. But let's take this lamp to Mr. Twoberry first. He lives on India Street. It's an easy walk. Sound good?"

"Very good!" Sophie exclaimed.

After they delivered the lamp, Grace and Sophie walked around the town enjoying the beautiful holiday decorations in the charming shops. Grace tried not to think about Pearl's and all the work waiting for her there. Sophie found a pair of shell earrings for Jill and a baking book for Tony.

After stopping at a cafe for some hot chocolate, they were heading back to the wharf when Grace saw Christine emerge from the basement of an old church. Several men and women straggled up the church steps after her. One of the women shouted something at Christine as she hurried down the street, her hands thrust in her pockets, her sunglasses obscuring her eyes.

Grace stopped in her tracks. Sophie, distracted by a window with a display of a miniature replica of a New England village, was pressing her nose up against the windowpane. Grace waited as two men from the church came toward them.

"Excuse me," Grace said as they approached. "Would you mind telling me what's going on in the church basement? A public meeting of some sort?"

The men, hatless and dressed similarly in tan overcoats, looked at each other and then back at Grace. One kept on walking but the other stopped. He pulled his collar up and leaned toward Grace. "Yeah, you could call it that. It's an AA/NA meeting. You know, drunks and addicts."

Grace looked down at Sophie who was still engrossed in the village scene. The man spat on the sidewalk and moved on. So Christine has a substance abuse problem. That might explain her strange behavior, Grace mused. She remembered the substantial cocktail Christine had been drinking when she had been at her house. And drugs couldn't be ruled out. There was a small but growing number of cocaine and methamphetamine users that defied the usual drug addict stereotype. Grace knew that addiction wore many faces. In fact, hadn't she seen a show on TV about housewives on methamphetamine? The news was probably a shock to much of Oprah's audience, but not to those working in the criminal justice system.

Grace was also aware that it wasn't unheard of for those with alcohol or drug problems to travel out of their own neighborhoods to seek treatment in order to protect their jobs and reputations. Poor Christine. She almost felt sorry for the woman. And there was a plus side. Perhaps if she got the help she needed today, she would give up on trying to run Grace out of town.

"Oh, my goodness!" Grace said, looking at her watch. "If we don't hustle we're going to miss the boat back to Hyannis. Come on, let's run." As they approached the ferry that would take them back to Hyannis, they saw Christine tramping up the gangplank.

"I guess she couldn't find any presents." Sophie said as she looked at the empty-handed Christine.

Chapter Forty-One

"HOW WAS YOUR trip?" Bella greeted Grace in front of Pearl's on her way back to the shop after her trip to the dentist. "I bet it was freezing out on Nantucket Sound."

"It sure was. But Sophie and I sat inside where it was warm. We had fun despite the cold. Sophie did some Christmas shopping, and we delivered the lamp to Mr. Twoberry." Grace stopped at the coat closet to hang up her coat and change out of her boots. Bella headed straight up the stairs, as was her custom. They both reached the landing and entered the main room of the shop together. Michael was nowhere in sight, but the Christmas tree was lit and decorated. The shop was eerily quiet and cold.

"That's strange," said Bella. "Michael always leaves a sign on the door if he has to go out."

Grace walked back to her office, peering into the fairy lamp alcove, the chandelier room and the kitchen on her way.

"And look, no wonder it's chilly in here," Grace said as she entered the kitchen. "The back door is wide open. It's so unlike Michael to be careless." She stepped out on the back porch and her attention was drawn to a patch of green on the white snow below. She paused for half a second. What was that? Had something blown out the door? A second or two later, she was running down the steps and yelling to Bella, "It's Michael! Hurry!"

Michael was sprawled at the bottom of the stairs, and he was very still. There was a bloody gash on his face and he was clutching an opaline glass table lamp, with its harp and finial still attached, in his outstretched hand.

Grace knelt down in the snow next to him. "Michael!" she

cried out. Bella came tromping down the stairs clutching the railing but moving faster than Grace had thought possible. Bella eased herself down on her knees on the other side of Michael. Unwinding her scarf, she folded it into a pillow and put it under his head and covered him up with her overcoat, gently tucking the sides in around him. Grace was on the phone dialing 911 when Michael's eyes opened. He looked at them with a dazed expression but didn't speak.

"Hold on, Michael, help's coming," Bella said. "Don't move. You're going to be all right, but you've had quite a tumble." Grace took the lamp from Michael's fist and Bella took Michael's hands in her own and started to rub them together. "It's so cold today I'm worried about hypothermia."

Michael's eyes closed again.

The EMTs arrived, bundled Michael up on a stretcher and carried him out to the ambulance with assurances that it looked like he was okay, although they added that a concussion couldn't be ruled out.

"Look," she said to Bella when they were gone. "The lamp is in perfect condition. Michael must have cradled it in his arms all the way down the stairs. Poor Michael. He should have let go of it and maybe he wouldn't be on his way to the hospital now."

As she cradled the lamp, she remembered Danielle's body lying on her living room rug, surrounded by lamp parts. She rolled the oval finial around in her hand. It was a brass sphere that matched the metalwork on the bottom of the lamp. There was something about the finial, a recollection that she couldn't quite capture.

"Come on, Grace. You're going to freeze out here," Bella said from where she stopped halfway up the stairs.

Grace followed Bella up the steps. She remembered worrying about Michael, teetering on top of his ladder when he was stringing lights on the tree. She would have to be more careful with Bella and Michael. They were wonderful employees, but they weren't young. Bella was having a hard time on the stairs, and Michael was always carrying heavy boxes and climbing up and down on the ladder. Bella would be retiring soon, but in the meantime Grace vowed to herself to keep a closer eye on the two of them.

Bella leaned against the porch railing and caught her breath. "Michael must have tripped on those sawed-off branches of the Christmas tree. It's all my fault. I kicked them down on to the stairs and then forgot about them. I'll never forgive myself. I don't know what is the matter with me. I've gotten careless in my old age. You'll be better off when I retire."

Grace tried to think of something reassuring to say as she reached the porch. Staring down at the steep steps and the snow angel depression left in the snow by Michael, she felt plenty of guilt herself. "It's no one's fault. It was an accident," she managed as a gust of wind whipped a tiny tornado of fine snow up the side of the stairs. And floating in the breeze was a piece of wire. Grace reached down to pick it up, but found it was attached to the bottom of the railing.

"Where did this come from?" she wondered out loud. She climbed down a few steps for a closer look.

Bella grabbed the railing and stood at the edge of the top step peering down on Grace.

"I don't remember ever seeing any wire out here. Do you think it was attached to the Christmas tree?"

"I suppose it could have been, but wait a minute. There's a metal loop attached to the side of the building." Grace extended the wire from the rail to the hook. It reached with several inches to spare.

"What would a loop be doing down there? Oh, my gosh! But, who would do such a thing?"

"I don't know for sure, but I don't think Michael's fall was an accident."

Grace and Bella closed up the shop and drove to the emergency room to see Michael. They had to sit in the crowded waiting room for almost an hour until their names were called and a young nurse escorted them to a cubicle where Michael was sitting up in bed and drinking orange juice. He was covered up to his chin with a white sheet. A blanket was rolled up at the bottom of the bed.

"I'm sorry," Michael said. A large bandage covered his nose. "What a nuisance I'm being."

"Oh, for goodness sakes, it's not your fault. It was an accident. You gave us such a fright." Bella patted him on the arm and plopped herself down in the nearest chair. Before leaving for the hospital, the two women decided that it wasn't necessary to alarm Michael with their discovery of a trip wire at the top of the stairs.

Grace leaned over and gave him a kiss on his cheek. Michael blushed. "How are you feeling?" she asked him. "What did the doctor say?"

"Oh, I'm fine. I've fractured my nose and I've got some cuts on it, so I guess I'll be wearing this bandage for a few days." He looked from Grace to Bella and back to Grace. "I'll be at work tomorrow."

"No way. You should stay at home and rest. I don't want you to even think about coming in. You've had a bad fall, and you need to take care of yourself. Aren't they going to keep you overnight?"

"I certainly hope not! They can't make me, can they? I've got to go home and feed Edith. I'm already late. She's probably starving. Where is that doctor? "

Grace patted him on the foot. "Take it easy. You remind me of my dad. He has no patience for hospitals either. I'll go by your house and feed Edith. She'll be fine."

"And I'll stay right here with you," Bella chimed in. "If they release you, I'll take you home. So you see, you have nothing to worry about. Now, tell us what you were doing out on the porch in the first place?"

"I got a call from Christine Sinclair. She remembered the opaline glass lamp from a previous visit to the store. She wanted to know if it was on sale now that Pearl's would be closing. She said she felt sorry for Bella and me, but it was time we were retired anyway. I told her in no uncertain terms that we were definitely not closing and, in fact, the price of the lamp had gone up since she had seen it. I hope you don't mind that I changed the price,

Grace, but she got my collar up!" Clearly not expecting a reply from Grace, Michael took a deep breath and continued. "To my surprise, she said she wanted to see it again anyway, and would I check it for any flaws before she wasted her time coming to the shop. I stepped outside to take a closer look in the natural light, not realizing how slippery the stairs were." Michael patted his nose, straightening his bandage. "Incidentally, the lamp is perfect. I'm sure we'll have a sale."

"Thanks to your heroics," Grace said. "Next time drop the lamp and save yourself. Agreed?"

Michael replied with a smile.

Grace excused herself and stepped outside the hospital. She had to call Andre and tell him she'd be late. That is, if he was still expecting her. It was about six-thirty now, and she hadn't called him yet.

When Andre answered the phone, Grace explained what happened. She assured him Michael was going to be all right, but she would be even later because she had to stop and feed Edith. He told her not to rush. The stew was hot and waiting for her.

The stew wasn't the only thing that was hot; Grace couldn't resist thinking.

Chapter Forty-Two

BRUCE SPRINGSTEEN WAS playing on her satellite radio when Grace left Michael's house and headed west on Route 6A. She punched in another station. Ah, Tchaikovsky. Much better. Springsteen was one of her favorites, but classical was more in keeping with the silent winter beauty illuminated by her headlights. Besides, she was feeling pretty jittery and she hoped the music might calm her down. So convinced of Duane's innocence, she had fought off feelings of responsibility in the death of Danielle, but what if Orange Hair installed a wire at the top of the back stairs? She had only herself to blame. She didn't have to make that 911 call and report his drug dealings to the police. She wasn't a probation officer anymore. She should have left them alone, and they would never have heard about her or Pearl's, and Michael wouldn't be in Cape Cod Hospital. God, she could be so stupid sometimes.

In this mood of self-recrimination, she entered Sandwich, the oldest town on Cape Cod, established in 1637. She drove past a row of tiny eighteenth-century cottages and then past the Daniel Webster Inn. Known as the Fessenden Tavern when it was first built, it had been a favorite of Webster's during the Revolutionary War. At the town center, she turned right at the Dexter Grist Mill and left on Grove Street. According to his directions, Andre's house was a short distance up the street, on the left, facing Shawme Pond.

Grace nosed her car down the short driveway. The house wasn't just facing the pond, Grace thought. It was almost in it. The conventional three-quarter Cape, which featured a window to the left of the front door and two on the right, appeared to be hovering on the very edge of the water. Her headlights played on the white shingles as she pulled into the driveway. Crushed clamshells mixed with snow and ice crunched under her wheels. Icicles two and three feet long hung from the roof, reminding Grace of frosty Christmas candles — or lethal weapons, she thought as the largest of the group fell to the ground with a crash.

Andre opened the door. He was wearing a chef's apron and juggling two wine glasses and a basket of crackers. God, I hate it when men wear aprons, Grace thought. A bottle of zinfandel, already opened, was on the coffee table.

She took a step into the hall and was almost knocked over by two big dogs. "That's Lola the Lab, and Frank is the German shepherd. They're big but friendly," Andre said.

He placed the glasses and crackers on the coffee table. "Probably too friendly," he said as Lola jumped up on her. "Sorry about that," he said. "She's been to training, but she gets excited when people come to the door. Some watch dog. She'd lick an intruder to death."

"Uh-huh," Grace said as she brushed a paw print off of her white sweater. She tentatively patted Lola on the head.

"Frank's another story. He flunked out of police canine school, but he's very obedient. He listens to me. But he's got a dark side." He ruffled the fur on Frank's neck.

A fire blazed in the living room, and there was a wonderful aroma of tomatoes and spices mixed with Christmassy pine scents. The room was furnished with beat-up leather chairs and chunky rugs.

"Wait a minute," Andre said, crouching behind a table near the fireplace, and before he stood up, the entire space was illuminated with hundreds of colored lights that were strung from one end of the room to another. A Christmas tree with sparkling multicolored lights stood near the entrance to the dining room, which she could see was decorated generously with strings of red chili pepper–shaped bulbs. There was an evergreen wreath hanging above the mantel, and it was haphazardly decorated with shiny tinsel and gold and silver bows. A wire cactus the size of a human flashed with lights the color of raspberries.

"Wow!" Grace exclaimed. "Incredible." She was hoping he wouldn't ask her what she thought of it, since what had come immediately to mind was a bar by the beach in Puerto Vallarta where she spent way too much time a number of Christmases ago.

"So, what do you think?" Andre asked.

Over the top and excessive were the first words she thought of, but Grace settled for, "Amazing. Did you do all of this yourself?"

"Emma helped me," he said.

"I see. I guess you and Emma are pretty close."

"Yeah, we're partners. You know how it is."

Of course she did. "Sure."

"It cheers me up. I like lots of color. I haven't had time to hang lights outside because I've been working overtime on the Whitney case. But I've still got a couple of weeks before Christmas. You'll love it when I'm done." He poured wine into the two glasses. "*Saude!*" he said. "A Portuguese toast, but a California wine. To your health!"

They sat around the fire for a while and made small talk. Grace surveyed the walls painted in strong primary colors. If lots of white brought her peace of mind, what did this noisy parade of colors do to Andre's psyche, she wondered? The colors screamed action, intensity, drama and decorating courage, at the very least.

The zin was going down really well, and Grace was beginning to feel its soothing effects, but she wasn't completely at ease with Andre. If he just wanted information from her, then why go to the trouble of inviting her to dinner? And she still hadn't forgotten the smile on his face when Emma joined them at the restaurant. She would have to be on her guard, she told herself, particularly since Andre, in spite of the apron, was looking incredible tonight in his black turtleneck and jeans. His dark hair, his olive complexion and that damned dimple that never went away were making her feel something she hadn't felt in a long time. That something, she was almost certain, was lust.

Andre's stew turned out to be more than decent. Mussels, clams, whitefish and chorizo sausage blended in a spicy tomato sauce. A green salad and Portuguese brown bread completed the meal.

"This is really, really good," she told him. "I'm impressed. Do you like to cook?"

"Love it. What about you?"

"Hate it." Grace wondered if that was a look of disappointment that flashed over his face. "This bread is incredible. Where did you get it?"

"My mother," he told her. "I'm Portuguese. My ancestors came from the Azores. A lot of the older women still bake bread at home. After I went to work this morning, I made a run up to Provincetown to see her and my dad. When I told her I was entertaining tonight, she insisted I take a couple of loaves, which, of course, didn't take much persuading."

"Did you grow up in Provincetown?" Grace asked.

"Yeah. I see you were up that way yourself last night." He put down his fork and gave her what she was beginning to think of as the Andre stare.

"Not as far as Provincetown. Brewster," she told him. "How did you know?"

"I got a copy of the police report today. Looks like you and Bella decided to pay a visit to Vernon Rugosa. Your names were on the report."

"Oh."

"I've got to hand it to you. We were looking for him up in Boston, but here he was right under our noses. How did you find him so fast?"

"Can I plead the fifth?" Grace didn't want to go into the specifics of how she'd located Rugosa or of her trip to Brewster with Bella. "It doesn't matter anyway. He's got an alibi for Sunday morning when Danielle Whitney was murdered. He was with another woman who said he was with her from Saturday night until Sunday afternoon."

"That would be Delores Fitch?"

"Yes. And she seemed credible to me." Grace placed her glass on the table. "It's still hard for me to figure out what women see in that man. He's such a disgusting creep. And Delores seemed liked such an attractive, smart lady. Women can be so stupid sometimes."

"Men too."

"Of course." He certainly is being agreeable tonight, she thought. Must be the wine.

"Any idea who might have broken into your house?"

"No. They took cash and most of my jewelry. Nothing of great value, except to me. But they went through all of my drawers and closets. The place is a mess. I don't know when I'm going to get around to cleaning up." Grace sighed. "I got a call from the repairman. The door's been fixed."

"The Geezers? Those old retired guys?"

"Mostly old and retired," Grace said, remembering the hunky, youngish retiree who unstuck a jammed window last summer.

"I'm glad it's fixed. There's always the possibility that you were the victim of a random burglary, but it's kind of strange, don't you think?"

Strange didn't begin to describe her feelings about everything that was going on. The murder, the break-in, and the way Andre's green eyes were staring deeply into hers. "I guess I didn't tell you about the man who stopped by the shop yesterday after we had lunch. I think it was the dope dealer from the Sandman apartments. I guess he figured out that I made the 911 call. He left a note with Bella and Michael that I'd better watch myself."

"Why didn't you tell me about this before?'

"I don't know. I've been so busy. I didn't think too much about it. I've been threatened before. Nothing ever happened." she sighed. "But something happened today that's got me scared. It looks like someone might have put a trip wire on the top of the back stairs. That wire might be what caused Michael to fall. I've got to be more careful. I've got Michael and Bella to think about too."

Andre frowned. "I'm going to call that in. I'll get someone to go and take a look. The wire still there?"

"Yes."

"There seems to be an increase in narcotics trafficking lately. Guys coming from off Cape have always been a problem, but there's a lot more methamphetamine coming in lately. Did anyone from Narcotics get in touch with you?"

"No."

"They will soon. They'll want a description of the third man who was at the apartment that day. In any case, you better be extra careful. These guys in the methamphetamine and cocaine trafficking business don't like anyone messing with their business. There's often a lot of money involved, and they can be very dangerous when it comes to protecting their turf."

"You're right," Grace conceded. "I'll be careful. I hope they catch up with him soon. Anything new with the Danielle Whitney case?"

"I have to admit that this investigation is turning up some interesting possibilities."

"Like what?"

"We interviewed the priest, Gavin Murrey. He was very defensive and not exactly forthcoming. If Danielle was threatening to expose their affair, his fear might have been enough to push him over the edge. After all, he's got a reputation to uphold and, although unlikely, he's worried the church could revoke his retirement income. And he lived right around the corner from her. He knew Danielle, so presumably, she would have opened the door for him. Motive, means and opportunity. The holy trinity of murder."

"Did he tell you he has a key to her house?"

"He didn't volunteer that information, but he produced the key when we asked. He said his mother could vouch for him."

"Did you meet his mother? I don't think she would know Sunday from Thursday."

"I agree."

"What about a diary?"

"Diary?"

"My dad said that Danielle kept some kind of journal or diary and was planning on writing her memoirs," Grace explained. "Dad's a photographer. He helped her and her friend Christine Sinclair with their modeling portfolios. They were both intending on getting back in the business. He doesn't do that much work anymore, but he's known them for years. Especially Danielle. I think he rather liked her."

"The priest mentioned the memoir she planned to write. He admitted he took some letters, which we now have, but he didn't say anything about a diary. Why didn't you tell me about the diary before we interviewed him?"

"It slipped my mind," Grace fibbed, remembering their lunch at the wharf that was interrupted by Emma. "If there is a diary somewhere, it could be very revealing."

"We're doing another search of Danielle's house tomorrow. We're bringing in a whole crew. We're going to turn that place upside down. Whether her brother Howard likes it or not." Andre stood up. "He's been rather difficult, to put it mildly. I don't think he likes cops."

"Maybe he doesn't like anybody." Grace said. "I suppose you've checked him out?"

"He's obnoxious all right, and he is the principal beneficiary. He lives in Providence. It doesn't look like he was hurting for money. He was home Sunday morning making pancakes for the wife and kids."

"Sounds like a good alibi, although family members have been known to cover up for their loved ones. What about Christine Sinclair?" Grace asked.

"What about her?"

"I took a trip to Nantucket to deliver a lamp this afternoon, and I saw her come out of an AA/NA meeting in a church basement. I guess she has some kind of problem. She sure is an unpleasant person. Bella heard that she's circulating a petition to get the city council to close Pearl's. She called the shop today and suggested to Michael that we would be closing soon."

"She is an odd one. Frazzled, irritable. Angry too. Sometimes, in an investigation like this, the whole town seems grumpy. Anyway, she didn't offer us much new information, although she expressed concern about Danielle's involvement with Vernon. He's got a pretty lengthy record. His alibi sounds good. But I hope Delores Fitch isn't covering up for him. He's very manipulative with women."

"Delores seemed relieved to be rid of him. But I guess you have to take his persuasiveness into account," Grace said. "Is he still a suspect then?"

"Let's say he's a person of interest. I'm not ready to clear him yet. We'll see what turns up. He's not going anywhere for a while because of his probation hold, so we've got some time."

"I had a visit at the shop today from a real estate agent named Valerie Elkins." Grace told him as they cleared dishes from the table and deposited them in the sink. "She and Danielle were feuding over a commission that Valerie said Danielle owed her from when Danielle's house was on the market. She was in the process of beginning a lawsuit when Danielle was killed. Rumor has it that she may have financial problems. In any case, she was supposed to be at an open house on Sunday morning but she never showed up. At Danielle's funeral she heard my dad say that I was looking into the case, so she came by to tell me to mind my own business. Do you know anything about her?"

Andre wiped his hands on a kitchen towel, walked to a closet and took out two dog leashes. Lola and Frank left their spot by the fireplace and put in an appearance in the kitchen. "Emma interviewed her. We heard from a number of people about the real estate deal that fell through and Valerie's plan to sue Danielle. Valerie was bad-mouthing Danielle all over town, from what we hear. She's definitely in some financial difficulties; she's living way above her means and she may have to file bankruptcy. Emma said Valerie initially lied about being at the open house, but we knew she hadn't been there. She finally admitted that she decided not to have the open house because of the storm. She didn't want her clients to know because she couldn't afford to lose their business. She claims she was home the entire morning."

"Can anyone vouch for her?"

"No. She said she slept in and didn't see or talk to anyone."

"It does make sense. I don't think too many agents would have held an open house in that storm. But no alibi and she was angry with Danielle," Grace mused. "I hear that she lives near town in a condominium. She could have walked to Danielle's to confront or pressure her, and she could have hit her in a fit of rage."

"Okay, Detective Tolliver." Andre didn't smile, but Grace picked up on the amusement in his eyes. She wondered if he was being condescending. She felt confused again and decided it was time she was getting back to her house.

"I'd better go. It's late and I've got a bunch of stuff to do and..."

"I like talking to you." Andre interrupted. "I couldn't talk to my ex-wife at all. She knew next to nothing about the criminal justice system and had no interest in it. You're smart, and you get it." He wrapped a gray scarf around his neck. "Want to take a ride to Sandy Neck? I've got to take the dogs for a run. I've been so busy they haven't been getting enough exercise. It's not the closest beach, but it's on the way to your house."

"Isn't it freezing out on the beach?" Grace asked. "And dark?"

"Yes, both."

"Okay." Grace smiled as she put on her coat and hat. "I'll take my car and follow you. I've got to go home from there and work on a shade for a client of Clay Davenport. Do you know him?"

"Oh, sure. I know Clay. I arrested him for a drug offense several years ago. We got an anonymous call of drug activity at a party in Falmouth. Clay was there. He had some cocaine on him, but it was a small amount so the DA dismissed the case. There were lots of bigger fish to fry that night. I think he has a record for petty theft too."

Grace couldn't hide her surprise. "Incredible," she exclaimed. "I had no idea. Clay always acts as if he's so much better than anyone else around here."

"Yeah, that sounds right. He was very difficult when we arrested him, but he calmed down as soon as he figured out he had a chance of being released. Ready?" Andre opened the front door and the dogs bounded out into the snow. "You know your way to Sandy Neck?"

"Sure. But I'll follow you. I don't think I've ever been there at night." Grace said.

"It's beautiful. Hell, it's always beautiful at Sandy Neck. If you haven't seen it on a winter night you're in for a treat. You'll thank me for taking you there." He smiled at her as she got in her car. "I promise."

Chapter Forty-Three

ON A CLEAR day, from her kitchen window, Grace could see a slice of Sandy Neck, the six-mile-long barrier beach that protects Barnstable Harbor. But now, as she followed Andre's truck along the winding road, she could see nothing but the snow-covered sand dunes illuminated by the headlights of their vehicles. At the parking lot Grace pulled her car next to Andre's truck. She could hear the thunder of the surf as it pounded the shore before she even opened her car door. When Andre handed her Lola's leash, she felt the pressure of Andre's fingers through her thick gloves.

"Got her?" Andre asked.

"Oh!" Grace exclaimed as Lola hauled off down the steps leading from the parking lot to the beach below, where the sea was black and deafening as it battered the shore. The snow was deep, and walking was difficult. Andre held a lantern, and it gave off just enough light if they stayed close together. When Lola tugged on her leash, causing Grace to stumble, Andre took her arm and didn't let go even when Lola stopped to take a long smell of seaweed. After playfully pulling her hat down over her ears and tucking her scarf into her collar, he pulled her close to him and she felt the warmth from his body through his heavy parka. She looked up into his eyes and saw laughter in them. He bent his head and his lips grazed hers. The dogs, in their excitement, pulled them away from each other.

Andre stepped back and reached into the pocket of his windbreaker. He pulled out a rubber ball and threw it far down the beach. It was propelled by the wind blowing from the northwest and seemed to fly forever into the darkness beyond the lantern's rim of light. They both let go of the leashes and the dogs bounded away from them, barking and jumping until they were no longer in sight.

Grace and Andre ran after them, Andre waving his arms and calling out to Frank and Lola. The dogs were racing along the water's edge, and they struggled to keep up with them. Andre ran ahead and Grace slowed down to a brisk walk. The salty sea air was stinging cold, but she was warm from the short run and the heat generated by Andre's embrace. She watched as Andre's lantern bobbed up and down as he hurried to catch up to Lola and Frank. Taking a deep breath of the cold night air, she felt relaxed and happy.

"Grace! Where are you? I can't see you."

"I'm here," she yelled as she ran toward the glow of his lantern.

"Oof! Oh, my God!" Grace said as she tripped and fell over a large spongy mass. "Oh, God, I'm such a klutz," she muttered, as she lay sprawled in the sand. She could hear Andre and the dogs approaching and started to laugh. She sat up and brushed sand out of her face and placed her hat back on her head. Andre snapped the leashes back on the dogs and they were pulling him hard and fast across the sand toward her. Andre held the lantern low and she couldn't see his face.

Lola was barking, but Frank was quiet until they were a few yards away. Then Grace heard a low growl followed by furious barking from Frank. Andre stopped in his tracks but the dogs were straining on their leashes.

"Grace, come over here," Andre said in a commanding voice she hadn't heard before. Her heart sank. She was embarrassed. Caught up in the moment, the dinner, the wine, she had allowed herself to let go of long pent-up emotions. She was such a fool.

The dogs were barking as she got up and wiped the sand from her face. "Just some seaweed. Tripped me up." She walked the few steps to Andre but he didn't speak. He pushed the leashes into her hand. "Take these. Hold tight."

She grabbed on to the dogs and planted her feet in the ground as they lunged forward. Andre was standing by the dark mound she had fallen over. He held the lantern high and in its glow, she caught a glimpse of orange tangled in seaweed. Orange Hair.

Chapter Forty-Four

AT SEVEN A.M. Friday morning, Grace was slumped over her worktable, wearing flannel pajamas and gluing pink feathers on the rim of the shade she promised Clay. She stayed up all night, unable to get the image of Orange Hair out of her mind. He was on his stomach, his arms at his side. There was a gash of red on the snow. And to think she had, literally, stumbled over him. She felt sick, but concentrated instead on holding on to the dogs while Andre called in his location and gave instructions.

First Danielle, and now Orange Hair. She hoped she learned his name soon. Now that he was dead, her nickname for him seemed rude, to say the least. She had met hundreds of drug dealers during her career as a probation officer. They were often ruthless, selfish and deadly, but they were someone's son or daughter. It was important to remember that. And his death was violent, disturbing. Her notion of safety in the little village had now completely dissolved. Feeling more lonely and vulnerable than she had in a long time, Grace went into the kitchen, returning a minute later with a cup of coffee. Inhaling the smoky aroma of French roast, she turned on the radio and listened to the weather report. More snow predicted.

Feeling foggy from lack of sleep, Grace forced herself to sit down and finish off the lamp for Clay. After installing the wire harp in the lamp base, she topped it with a shade and a flamingo finial, plugged it in and spun it around. The fabric she had chosen was semi-transparent, and the light was soft and feminine. She thought it looked amazing. She hoped that Clay's client would love it too. The flamingo was an inspired choice, giving the lamp a tropical, kitschy look.

As she tightened the finial, she remembered how Michael held onto the opaline glass lamp when he had fallen down the back stairs of the shop yesterday afternoon, and she flinched involuntarily. He held on to it so tightly that it hadn't suffered even a scratch, and the harp and finial were still attached. Poor Michael. And poor Danielle. Killed by someone wielding a lamp. She remembered the bronze base without its shade, the harp still attached. Blood all over. Grace shuddered. But where had the finial at Danielle's been? Had it rolled under a piece of furniture or something? It's not as if she searched the room or anything. And what had Danielle said about the lamp? Something about it being a gift. Had it been a gift for a friend or a relative? Danielle had specifically mentioned the finial. She had said that Grace would get an idea for the shade from it. Her curiosity piqued, Grace decided to ask Andre about the murder weapon. It must be in the police evidence room. She would ask if a finial was found.

At quarter past seven, the phone rang. Picking it up on the first ring, Grace cradled it in her neck as she made an adjustment to the shade where the feathers met the fabric.

"Did I wake you?" Andre asked.

"No, not much chance of sleep after last night. Actually, I'm gluing feathers on to a shade," she told him. "How's it going?"

"Tired," he confessed. "But I wanted to thank you for taking the dogs home for me. I really appreciate that."

"Oh, that's okay. "

"We got an I.D. on the guy on the beach. Justin Aloysius Blake. Long rap. On parole in California. He's a long way from home."

"Interesting. Where in California?"

"San Francisco. I took a quick look at his criminal history. He's got pages and pages of arrests for narcotics offenses, among other things. Probation revocations, prison, parole. Your basic career criminal. He must have finally met up with someone tougher than himself out on the beach. He was shot twice, in the back of the head."

"Nice."

"Sorry, Grace. I'm up to my neck here, what with two murder investigations, so I better go. I just wanted to check up on you. Make sure you're okay."

"I'm fine. But a quick question."

"What?"

"It's about Danielle's murder."

"Grace, I'm really busy. Can it wait?"

Grace ignored his question and proceeded with her own. "Do you have a description of the lamp that killed Danielle? I saw it, but I don't remember exactly what it looked like."

"Yeah, the report is right in front of me. Hold on. Okay. Bronze, twenty-nine inches tall, weighed about twelve pounds and was made in France. Anything else?"

"Was a finial recovered?"

"A what?"

"A finial. The small decorative piece at the top that holds everything in place."

"Let's see." Grace heard the rustle of papers as Cruz scanned the report. "No, nothing like that. But it says here that there was a harp, whatever that is, attached to the lamp. Does that mean anything to you?"

"I'm not sure ... I need to think a few things through."

"Grace, I don't have time for this. If you know something I need to know, just tell me."

"I was thinking that there should have been a finial attached to the lamp. That's all. Maybe if the finial were located, it would lead to the killer. You know, a clue."

"Okay. Whatever. I've got to go, Grace, but I want you to promise me something."

"What?"

"That you'll concentrate on your shop, work on your lamps and not get yourself involved in Danielle's murder case. This Blake was a really bad guy. He might even be the person who broke into your house. He may have some associates that are not going to want anyone poking around in their business."

"I know," she said, aware of a heightened sense of exasperation.

"But Duane is having a hard time in jail, and you don't seem to be making any progress in getting him out. Anyway, Blake didn't have anything to do with Danielle's death. Or did he?"

"Maybe. I can't tell you any more. But thanks for the vote of confidence," Andre said and hung up.

She'd blown it again, Grace thought as she went into the kitchen to get another cup of coffee. When was she going to think before she spoke to Andre? Or, maybe he was just too touchy. She made a mental note to increase her dwindling supply of French roast. It was going to take a lot of caffeine to get through the next few days.

As she smothered a cinnamon raisin muffin with blueberry jam, she started to feel sorry for what she had said to Andre about the investigation. She realized he had his hands full with two murder investigations, And he hadn't had any sleep either. But it was discouraging. Almost a week had gone by, and Duane was still sitting in jail. The District Attorney was still pushing forward with the prosecution, and even Duane's defense attorney wanted to deal.

Grace picked up her dishes, rinsed them off and put them in the dishwasher. She looked outside at her thermometer and discovered that it was fourteen degrees. No wonder very little snow had melted. Staring out her window at the white, frozen yard, she could barely make out the outline of Sandy Neck. The low strip of land across the marsh was shrouded with mist and low-hanging clouds. A few hours ago she had been running and laughing on the beach, feeling warm despite the chill and glad to have Andre's arm around her shoulder. Now she was exhausted. Cold and fog. What an awful combination. But today it suited her mood.

So, Orange Hair had a name and was from San Francisco. Justin Blake. The name didn't mean anything, of course. But she might have stumbled across him — no pun intended — during her years working in probation. From her experience, it was unusual for drug dealers to travel away from their home areas. Despite the fact that the local police knew them, they usually went back to the streets they knew best as soon as they got out of custody.

There were always exceptions, of course, and some of the bigger suppliers moved about. She wondered what had brought him to Cape Cod.

Finished with her breakfast, she fed the hungry Clambake, who was doing his little cat dance on the kitchen floor, and headed upstairs for a shower and some fresh clothes. She let the water run until it was steaming, and she stayed under the spray for a long time, until she started to relax. After her shower, she liberally applied lotion to her skin and dried her hair with a towel and dug around in her closet to find her tan cords and a black sweater. The bedroom closets, bureau, and floors were still in a chaotic state from the burglary. She looked hopefully around the room for her gold twisted loop earrings, but no such luck. If it was Orange Hair, a.k.a. Justin Blake, who had broken into her house, it was unlikely that she'd ever see any of her stolen items again. But there might be a way she could find out more about him.

Grace looked at the clock on her bedside table. It was five after nine, and six in the morning on the West Coast. She knew that there would be some probation officers in San Francisco already at their desks. She used to be one of them, arriving at work at five forty-five. She liked getting a jump on the day, but the best part was getting out early and beating the heavy rush hour traffic home.

Going downstairs again, she dialed Clive Sutter, a friend and former co-worker of hers.

"Probation." Grace heard the familiar voice and smiled.

"Clive. It's Grace Tolliver. How are you?"

"Grace! Wow. How you doin'? Haven't heard from you in months. How are things at Barnstable Probation?"

"Great." Clive didn't know that Grace didn't work for the probation department anymore. It didn't seem the time to tell him about Pearl's. "I'm sorry I haven't been in touch lately," she said. "I've been really busy. Everything okay with you?"

"Oh, yeah. Usual stuff. You know."

"Listen, Clive. I don't have much time to talk, but could you do a favor for me? Can you look up a guy by the name of Justin Aloysius Blake? He's got a lot of arrests in San Francisco." She could hear him tapping on his computer.

"I got him. There's a couple of Justin Blakes but only one with the middle name Aloysius. He's got at least ten arrests here. Most of them for drugs. What do you need?'

"If it's not too much trouble, can you get me copies of the old San Francisco police reports and fax them to me?"

"Okay. Give me your fax number."

"Thanks, Clive. And don't mention this to anyone. Okay? It's kind of a sensitive investigation."

Grace was almost ready to leave for the shop when she heard the clicking of her fax machine. Sitting down at her desk, she started with the oldest police incident report first. The offense date was more than twenty years ago.

The first report was an assault charge, after Blake had been involved in an altercation with another man in one of the city's rundown hotels. However, according to his rap, the charges had been dismissed. He also had a number of lesser offenses involving marijuana possession and drinking in public. She scanned about a half dozen more reports before she struck gold. In 1989 Blake had been arrested for drug possession and sales. There were at least two pages detailing the large amount of contraband and par-aphernalia found at the scene of the arrest. He'd been sentenced to state prison, fouled up his parole, was returned to prison and again released. He'd gone on to bigger things: armed robbery, assault with a deadly weapon, and domestic violence. But what caught Grace's attention were the names of his two co-defendants from the 1989 arrest: Sean Anderson and Terry Struthers.

Grace grabbed for her phone. Andre wasn't answering. She left a message. It was unlikely that Andre would have this information yet. He would be so busy tracking Blake's last few days on earth, he might not even think of looking at Blake's co-defendants from twenty years ago.

Chapter Forty-Five

HOPING THAT THE fresh air would revive her, Grace decided to walk to work. After checking on Clambake and locking up, she put on her leather jacket, her head spinning with this new information about Blake, Sean and Terry. Could they possibly be back in business together? She couldn't believe it. Sean had been running Pinewood for such a long time, and he had a great reputation, particularly as a successful fundraiser for the rehab center. In the process, his criminal history had been pretty much forgotten. As for Terry, he had been Sean's assistant for almost as long as Sean had been executive director. Grace had always thought he was a bit of a flake, but he seemed harmless enough. But now that she thought about it, hadn't Gink mentioned something about things being awry at Pinewood? It wasn't unusual for rehab places to have recurrent drug problems. But until this past week, she'd never heard about anything even being remotely amiss at Pinewood. And she had to remind herself that just because Sean, Terry and Blake had known each other years ago, that didn't mean they had a connection now.

As Grace passed the cemetery, she saw Jose and Rafael up on the hill, hiking along the familiar path among the graves, their shovels over their shoulders. There had been so much snow the past several days that the school district shut down the schools until next Monday. Grace could see the tip of the roof of Christine Sinclair's house through the bare trees. Smoke was fluttering out of one of her two chimneys.

A figure clad in black crested the top of the hill and started down the path toward Grace. It was Father Murrey with his beagle tagging along behind him on a retractable leash. His shoulders were hunched to shield his face from the wind. Seeing Grace waiting for him at the foot of the slope, he abruptly changed course and headed back up the hill. Out of the corner of her eye, she saw Bella scuttle across the street, dodging cars, and carrying two brown grocery bags.

"Hi, Grace," she called. "I'm going up to Morris's with some groceries.

"I'll go with you," Grace said, taking the larger of the two bags. "I just saw Father Murrey, and he completely ignored me."

"What do you expect?" Bella asked. "You and I know his deepest secret. He's not ready to face us yet. Goodness! If you don't mind my saying so, you look like you've been up all night."

"Oh, Bella, I have so much to tell you. Let's take these things up to Morris, and then I'll fill you in," Grace said. "Have you heard from Michael?"

"They released him from the hospital last night, and I took him home," Bella told her. "He was so anxious about Edith that he convinced the doctor he was good to go. He says he's going to come to work today about noon."

"He should have spent the night in the hospital," Grace said, frowning. "He needs to rest up after his fall. Gosh, I fed Edith last night like we agreed.

"I know," said Bella. "But Michael is so devoted to Edith. He couldn't bear her being alone in the house the whole night."

The door at Morris's house opened about half an inch in response to Bella's insistent knocking. "Morris. It's me, Bella. I'm here again with Grace," Bella said. "We've brought you some groceries."

Morris was still wearing the black and gray plaid shirt from the other day. He didn't speak but moved his hand in the direction of the stairs, indicating that they could come in.

Bella marched right into Morris's kitchen. Grace followed her and put her bag on the counter. The kitchen was in a state of disarray but didn't appear unclean. There were a few pots in the sink, and a stack of newspapers was piled on the linoleum floor near the back door. Bella and Grace emptied the bags, and Grace folded them flat. Morris looked at the array of food. His hands shook as he picked up a bottle of freshly squeezed orange juice.

"You have to take better care of yourself, Morris," Bella scolded. "I'm going to bring you groceries from time to time, and after the holidays, when I retire, I'll come spend some time with you. Then we can see about organizing things around here. I don't want to embarrass you, but I was awfully upset when I saw you were reduced to eating cat food."

"Eating cat food!" Morris exclaimed, steadying himself against the counter. "I don't eat cat food."

Bella put her hands on her hips. "Morris, I saw what was in the bags that those boys brought you the other day. Cat food! I asked you if you had a cat, and you said no. So, if you don't have a cat, who is eating cat food around here?"

Morris looked sheepish. "I'm afraid I lied about the cat, Bella. I do have a cat."

"Well, I want to see it. Why would you lie about a thing like that?" Bella asked indignantly. "Honestly, Morris, what's going on here?"

Morris slowly walked to a door on the far side of the kitchen and opened it. He stepped into the dark room and turned on the light. Grace and Bella followed him. It was a storage room of some sort, Grace thought. More piles of newspapers, chairs piled on top of one another and a lumpy blue and green striped couch. On top of a stack of red felt cushions, curved in to a tight ball was a gray cat with white whiskers.

Grace and Bella looked at each other. Bella let out a low whistle as Grace stepped over a plastic milk crate, reached down and stroked the cat's head. "How long have you had this cat?"

"Not long."

"Does it have a name?"

"I call it Chester."

"I see," said Grace. She fumbled in her purse and brought out one of Sophie's flyers. Holding it up in front of Morris she said, "Look, doesn't Chester look like Stanley? He's been missing since last Saturday, and a little girl has been looking all over for him."

Morris took the paper from Grace and scanned the picture. He was silent.

"Now see here." Bella said. "You've got to admit that the two cats are identical. Look at the front feet. They're white on both cats."

Morris crumpled the flyer up and threw it on the floor. "Chester is my little buddy," he muttered, and Grace could see that there were tears forming in his eyes.

Bella wrapped her arm around Morris's frail shoulder. "I understand. But a little girl named Sophie has been so worried about that cat. She's put these flyers all over town. I know she will be so happy when she sees what good care you've taken of him."

"I don't think I can give him up, Bella."

"Of course you can. You've got to, Morris. He doesn't belong to you. Sophie's a sweet girl. She misses her cat so much."

Morris turned and abruptly left the room. Grace and Bella followed him out to the living room where he deposited himself in his favorite chair by the window. "First I lose Danielle and now Chester." He rubbed his nose with the back of his hand and gazed at Danielle's house. "Danielle used to keep an eye on me. Now, no one knows if I'm alive or dead. For twenty years I'd raise my shade at nine in the morning and nine at night. She'd do the same. We'd wave. Once I overslept and she called the police. They woke me up banging on my door."

Grace shot a glance at Bella. "Morris, last Sunday, the day that Danielle died, did she raise her shade at nine?" Grace asked.

"Yes, she did." Morris started to cry. "Right after the young man left. Well, the first time he left."

Grace gripped the back of the chair she was standing next to. Bella's mouth dropped open. The old man continued to stare out the window at Danielle's house. "Sunday morning. She was wearing a gray sweater. She waved at me and I waved back. That was the last time I saw her."

"Are you sure you saw her after the young man left?" Grace asked.

"Yes. He went up on the porch. I can't see the front door from here on account of the trees. Then I saw the same young man about half an hour later. He went up on the porch, and then I saw him running down the porch steps and down the street. Looked like he'd seen a ghost." Morris straightened up a bit.

"How long was he at the house? The second time?"

"Oh, a couple of seconds."

"Did the detectives come and talk to you? Did you tell them this?" Grace asked. Her heart was beating fast.

"Yes. Yes, a policeman came here. It was Officer Gelb. He asked me if I saw anything. I told him I saw the young man go up on the porch."

"Did you mention that you had seen Danielle after that, when she opened her shade and waved to you?"

"No, I don't believe I did." Morris stroked his chin.

"Why not?"

"I don't believe he asked me."

Chapter Forty-Six

GRACE TURNED ON the thermostat, and Bella got the espresso and coffee machine going, but the shop seemed dreary without Michael. As they stood shivering around the pot with their coats and gloves on, Grace told Bella about the murder on Sandy Neck.

"I've been up all night. First Danielle, then Michael's fall, and now this."

"And the break-in at your house as well." Bella replied. "I admit I'm struggling with all this too. I'm not sure if I'm shivering from the cold or from fear. Everything is so unexpected. I've taken to locking my doors again."

"Yes. We've got to keep our wits about us and be careful, above all else. I'm going to tell Michael about the wire on the stairs. I hate to upset his cheerful little self, but he deserves to know. I feel terrible that I've created such a dangerous situation for both of you."

Bella put her arm around Grace. "We'll work through it, my dear. How about some coffee?"

"Sounds good." It was midmorning now, and the temperature was a chilly twenty degrees. To Grace it felt about the same inside the shop as outside on the street.

"Next week, I'll call the heater repair people and have someone take a look at this whole system," Grace said. "And that's a promise."

"I've been working and freezing here for thirty years, so don't do it for me. A new system will be very expensive."

Bella grabbed the pot by the plastic handle and poured the

thick brew into their cups. She took a sip. "Ugh! I guess there is a knack to this fancy coffee thing. I'll have to ask Michael to explain it to me."

Grace took a sip and rolled her eyes as the hot liquid rolled down her throat. "Ah, caffeine."

"I hope you thought it was all right that I told Morris that he could keep Chester, a.k.a. Stanley, to use your law enforcement jargon, until this evening. I know Sophie is desperately trying to find him, but I think Morris needs a little time to adjust before giving him back to her."

"It's a difficult situation," Grace replied. "No doubt about it. He's attached to that little cat, but he does belong to Sophie, and she loves him too. I think we should let Sophie know that Stanley's been found, he's safe, and we're working on getting him back to her as soon as we can."

"You're right, of course, I'll give Jill a call. I feel like King Solomon must have felt," Bella said. "Did you call Detective Cruz?"

"Yes. I left him a message about Morris and Danielle and the shades. He already thinks I'm critical about the progress of his investigation into Danielle's death. He's not going to be happy. He told me to stay out of the investigation."

"It's not like you were interrogating Morris or anything. His story came tumbling out. And I think it's very significant. He saw Danielle alive after Duane went into the house the first time. Duane wouldn't have had time to kill her if he was inside just for a few seconds the second time. At least it seems unlikely."

The phone rang. Her cell. Grace put it to her ear but before she could say "Hello," she heard Audrey's voice.

"Ohmigod!" she said. "There's been another murder. Out on Sandy Neck. And you were there with Andre Cruz!"

"Hi, Audrey," Grace said.

"Everyone here is buzzing. Once again you're the talk of the probation department. Actually, the talk of the whole courthouse. Even that security guy. Remember him? He was asking me about you and Andre. And I don't know anything! Spill it, Grace. What's going on?"

Grace smiled. The security officer was the single most effective news-passer in the building.

"I have so much to tell you," she said. "I'm going to be working here at the shop late tonight. Why don't you come by after work? We can talk while I paint shades and get ready for the Village Stroll, which I can't believe is tomorrow. Thank God for Michael and Bella. They've been fantastic this past week."

"That sounds great. I can hardly wait to hear everything. I might not get there until after six. I'm going on a field trip to Nantucket."

"You got probationers out there?"

"Yeah. A guy who likes his booze and a woman who likes to help herself to some pricey items in some of the finer shops."

"Say, did your guy ever mention an AA/NA meeting at the church near downtown?"

"Yes. Funny you should ask," Audrey said. "I was talking to him this morning to arrange for my visit, and he said that a woman, who came to the meeting on Wednesday, was asking people where she could buy some methamphetamine. Can you imagine having the nerve to show up at a meeting and try to buy drugs? He said he'd never seen her before, but that she looked like some rich bitch, to use his phrase. I swear, every day around here is a wonder."

Grace didn't speak. She took a big swallow of coffee.

"You okay?" Audrey asked.

"I've got to go. Michael won't be here until twelve, and I hear a customer coming in. Bella doesn't like dealing with them unless she has to. I'll see you tonight." Grace hung up.

Was Christine at the meeting in the church basement to get help or was she trying to buy methamphetamine? Her addiction and need could explain her bizarre behavior. The idea appeared absurd, but Grace had been surprised before by the odd behaviors and deceptions of ordinary people.

She walked with her phone to the back door, where she looked out the window at the rooftop of the one-story building next door. A lone gull was strutting up and down, pecking for crumbs in the deep snow. She punched in her father's number. No answer.

Bella was standing with her hands on her hips while two women circled around the shop. "It's okay, I've got it," Grace said.

"I'm looking for something to hang over my dining room table," one of the women said.

Grace led her to the chandelier room.

"Wow, these hanging fixtures are gorgeous. I love the silver one with the five arms. Is it real silver?"

"It's silver plate. Quite formal. Would it work in your home?" Grace asked, wishing Michael were here. He'd know all about this piece. Probably sell her one for her bathroom while he was at it.

"It might. If you'll write down the dimensions, I'll do some measuring when I get home."

Grace picked up one of the many measuring sticks that were handily placed around the shop and wrote the measurements down on one of Pearl's new green and gold business cards.

"We saw you on the news," the younger looking of the two women said. "Weren't you afraid, having a dangerous criminal working here with you?"

Before Grace could answer her, the older woman blurted out, "And sending him on an errand to a customer's house is so preposterous. We had to stop by and see for ourselves just what kind of an operation you're running here."

Grace slapped the business card down on the table. It didn't take but a minute of her silence and her steely gaze for them to get her message and scurry away.

Although she was physically exhausted from her lack of sleep, the encounter with the two bothersome busybodies energized her, and she found herself going over the week's events again. Two murders. Two victims whose lives appeared, on the surface anyway, to be poles apart, now needed further examination. Could there have been something in their very dissimilar worlds that connected them, however unlikely? Or was it an odd and unlucky coincidence that two lives ended within a few days and a few miles apart from each other? Grace thought about Danielle, the elegant and beautiful French woman, looking forward to igniting a lost career, and Justin Blake, a drug dealer and career criminal from San Francisco. She shook her head. No, not a chance that they could be even remotely connected.

"Oh, that's my cell," she said, responding to the chimes coming from her office. "I'd better get it. It might be Andre. Watch the front for me for a minute, will you?"

"Andre?" Bella grinned. "Are you referring to Detective Cruz?"

Grace felt herself flush as she walked back to her office. When Andre came on the line she tried to sound as businesslike as possible when she began by asking him if he'd received her message about Blake and his old friends, Sean and Terry, and Morris's revelation about the shades.

Andre let out a low whistle. "I've got to hand it to you. That was real good information. I would have gotten around to it eventually, but you were on top of it."

Grace felt some of the tension she had been carrying around with her since this morning ease a little. At least she'd taken the first step and he hadn't hung up on her again. For a moment she was tempted to tell him about Christine. But, she warned herself, that was only speculation. For the time being, it was wise to stick with what she could prove.

"In fact," Andre continued, "we've been having a little chat with Sean Anderson and Terry Struthers. Separately, of course."

"I can't believe Sean could be involved with Blake," Grace said. "And murdering him. That seems like a long shot to me."

"We'll see. Emma's been talking to Sean. She said his alibi for last night is pretty solid. Now Terry. He's another story. I'm letting him sit and sweat for a while. We've got people still going over the crime scene out on the beach.

"As for the Whitney case, we'll be talking to Morris Bidlake again, too," Andre continued. "That's interesting, what he said about seeing Danielle after Duane left her house. Gelb interviewed him for us, but he's young and inexperienced, and Emma and I haven't had time to get back to Bidlake ourselves."

"Do you think Terry's good for Blake's murder?"

"I'm not sure. He admits that he not only knows Blake, but that he's seen him recently. He also admits to some recent drug dealing."

"Wow. That's so incredible. He's been at Pinewood for years. He's got a good job there. Why would he do something so stupid?"

"I'm tempted to say once a criminal always a criminal. But I won't."

"You're not getting all social-worky on me now, are you?"

Andre laughed. "Don't get your hopes up."

"I won't," Grace told him. "Believe me, I won't."

"Oh, my. I missed this place so much," Michael enthused. "It's good to be back."

"It's eleven-thirty. You've only been away from the shop for half a day," Bella protested.

Michael patted down his silky brown hair and straightened the Santa Claus tie he wore over a green and white checked shirt. A large bandage, secured by adhesive, covered his nose and extended from one elfin cheek to another. Grace opened up her arms and gave him a big hug.

"Are you sure you wouldn't rather be home resting?" she asked.

"I'm right where I want to be," he assured her. "I've got a lot to do today. I'm going to finish trimming some of those shades you completed, and then I'm going to spiff up the shop and finish decorating. You ladies haven't even plugged in the tree. It's obvious that you can't get along without me."

"That's for sure," Bella said. "But before you start your other tasks, I'm sure Grace would appreciate it if you would dump out that sludge I made and make her a decent cup of coffee."

Michael looked worried. "You didn't mess with my coffee machine did you, Bella?"

"Take a look for yourself," Bella told him gruffly. "I'm going to make myself some sweet tea and then solder some lamp fittings together. And I've got lots of polishing and wiring to finish up today." Bella walked back to the counter that separated her area from the main room. "There's a couple of lamps ready for delivery too. As if we don't have enough to do. Remind me why we're doing deliveries, Grace?"

"Customer service," Grace said. "That's the best way we can compete with the big guys." She joined Bella at the counter. "Isn't that porcelain lamp the one that Christine Sinclair wanted rewired?"

"Yes, it's done. And it's a pretty piece."

Grace picked up the lamp and examined the tiny fleur-de-lis stamped into the base that matched the one on the finial. The shade was showing significant signs of wear and should be replaced, but Christine had only asked that the wiring be updated

"Yes, it's nice. French, probably."

"Christine is a Francophile." Michael whispered *Francophile* as if he were saying *serial killer*. "She's got French stuff all over her house. I know, because it was open during the Historical Society house tour last October. You should see it, Grace," Michael said. "Although it's a bit overdone for my taste," he added.

"I've been in her house. I was there a couple of days ago. But I wouldn't mind seeing it again. I'll take the lamp to her. I won't be gone long."

"But what about your coffee?"

"Save it for me, Michael. I'll be right back."

Chapter Forty-Seven

ONCE OUTSIDE, GRACE felt tiny flakes of snow fall on her face, becoming enmeshed in her eyelashes. The sky had darkened and a northeast wind was blowing strong. The village was quiet. There had been so much snow this week that everyone had stocked up on supplies and were hunkering down as best they could. Smoke circled from several chimneys, and as she passed by the cemetery, Grace noticed that even the crows that usually peppered the hillside were tucked away in the barren bushes and trees.

As she trudged along, she pulled out her phone and dialed her father again. Still no answer. Now she started to worry. Usually he was home this time of day. It certainly was difficult having an elderly father who had more energy and more dreams than just about anyone else she knew. He was fighting aging with everything he had. Which, to a point, was a good thing. But if he would cooperate with her a little and get some help, she'd be able to sleep better at night. As she was mulling over her options, her cell rang.

"Gracie! Don't worry," her father told her. "I'm all right. It was just a little fire. Nothing to worry about."

"Dad? What do you mean fire? Where are you?"

"I'm at Irene's. Uh-oh. I have to talk to the nice fireman here. I'll call you later."

"Dad! Put Irene on the phone," Grace told him before he could hang up on her. A minute later she heard Irene's cheery voice on the line.

"He's okay," she said reassuringly. "He was setting up a barbecue grill on his back porch when he must have added too much liquid starter to the coals and the porch railing caught on fire. He tried to put it out with an extinguisher. That's when I saw him and called 911. But I'm afraid the porch is lost."

"Setting up a barbeque? It's December! It's snowing! Has he lost his mind?"

"Don't know, but he said he was craving a grilled steak. You want me to have him call you back?"

"No. I've got a quick errand to run, and then I'll be over. Thanks, Irene. You're a lifesaver."

Grace hung up. Fear, anger and exasperation flooded over her in one tidal wave of emotion. No doubt now. Her father needed some help. She'd have a showdown with him after she delivered Christine's lamp.

A few minutes later she was standing in front of Christine's house. For the first time she noticed the fleur-de-lis pattern in the black wrought iron fence that surrounded the property. She was curious about Christine. Could she have been the woman trying to score methamphetamine at the AA/NA meeting on Nantucket? Grace remembered the look that passed between the participants as they came up the church's basement stairs. If, in fact, it had been Christine, who was she trying to buy it for? Herself? A friend? Grace had assumed that Christine had an alcohol problem, but her erratic behavior could just as well be attributed to drugs.

The latch on the gate creaked as she opened it and stepped inside the yard. Tall firs cast long shadows that criss-crossed the front yard. Grace picked her way up the uneven brick walk. There were hollows filled with ice and snow, and her feet slid on the slippery surface. She reached the front porch when the door opened and Christine, who was dressed in black pants tucked into black suede boots and a pine green sweater, confronted her. Her hair was loose and she had on makeup. Coral lipstick, green eye shadow. She looked better than she did on the Nantucket ferry, Grace thought, but she still had that raw, unhappy edge about her.

"You've got my lamp?" she said by way of greeting.

"Bella finished it this morning," Grace told her. "It's a very lovely lamp. If you ever want to replace the shade, I'd be glad to do it for you. A row of hand-painted fleur-de-lis along the edge would complement the base."

"Maybe some time. I'll think about it. Why don't you come in and I'll get my checkbook."

Grace followed her down the hall to the library where they had sat a few nights ago. Or rather, she had sat while Christine paced.

"Looks like we're in for another storm," Grace said, trying to ease the tension in the room.

"Wait here a minute," Christine said.

Christine was gone for about five minutes, which seemed to Grace more like an hour, probably because the room was dark and cold, the fireplace unlit. There was a glass of amber liquid on a round table next to the blue velvet chair. Grace picked it up and sniffed. Rum. No rocks, no Coca Cola. Whew. Grace set the glass back down when Christine came back from the other room, a suede checkbook in her hand.

"How's your investigation of Danielle's murder going? Found the killer yet?"

"The police are checking out lots of leads," Grace told her. "The case isn't solved yet. They're looking deeper into Danielle's background."

"They're wasting their time," Christine snapped. "They've got their killer behind bars. All they need to do now is get on with the prosecution. D.A. Banks better get her act together soon, or I'll make sure she isn't reelected. I might even start a recall campaign. The safety and reputation of our village is at stake." Christine picked up her glass and then put it back down on the table without taking a sip. "I understand that you used to be a probation officer."

Grace found herself wondering how Christine had found out this information. It wasn't a secret, of course, but it appeared that Christine had been doing some investigating of her own.

Christine twisted the ring on her right hand. She looked at Grace a full thirty seconds without blinking. "There isn't much crime around here," she continued. "Maybe shoplifting once in a while. I don't suppose that we have any kind of a drug problem, although I've seen on the news that there are drugs everywhere these days. I don't expect there are any drug dealers around here for instance, are there?" She gave the ring another twist and looked out the window.

"I don't know. Why do you ask?"

"Just curious," Christine responded. "It's always good to know what's going on in one's own neighborhood. If there were a house where people were selling drugs, I'd want to know where it was so I could stay away from it. Are there any houses like that near here?"

Now that Grace had a chance to study Christine, she noticed that despite the makeup, her face was pallid. She looked like she hadn't slept for days. She was very thin.

"I saw you come out of the AA/NA meeting on Nantucket the other day," she said. "And I know you tried to score some drugs while you were there."

"That's preposterous! What would I be doing at a meeting of that sort? And buying drugs? Are you insane?"

"I think you need help. I can turn you on to the right people. Being an addict isn't a crime, Christine. What do you use? Cocaine? Meth?" Grace was pretty sure it was one of those.

Christine shook her head. "You're wrong."

"Look at yourself. You're not sleeping. You've lost weight. You're trying to find out from me where there are people who sell drugs. It's so obvious that I can't believe I didn't put it all together before now."

"It's that obvious?" Christine said, sinking down on the chair. Placing her elbows on her knees, she rubbed her face with her hands.

"Yes."

Christine sighed. "What do you think I should do? Can you help me?"

"I can help you get help. The rest is up to you. If you're sincere about wanting to get yourself together."

"You're right. I've let things get out of control. I can't sleep, can't eat. All I think about night and day is getting my hands on some meth."

"What happened to your supplier? You seem to be going to

great lengths to make a connection."

Christine ran her hand through her hair. "I don't think I should tell you that."

"Was it a man with orange hair named Justin Blake?"

"I don't know. Please don't ask me that," Christine cried. "Excuse me for a minute. I need a glass of water.

There was, Grace knew, nothing to do but wait and hope that she returned. For the second time, she felt a surge of sympathy for the woman who was so clearly in need of help.

In the meantime, she also knew that she had to get things straight in her mind. Blake had likely been selling drugs in the area. And according to Andre, Terry had been, too. And now Christine had admitted using methamphetamine, a drug with which more violent crime was associated than any other. And there had been two murders in a week. Grace wondered how far the tentacles of Blake's enterprise might have reached.

A clock on the mantel struck the hour. Grace noticed that it was a beautiful French carriage clock, which, if authentic, was probably from the early nineteenth century. Christine did have some lovely things. The living room was spacious and luxurious, but it looked like it needed a good cleaning. She peered inside a deep mahogany cabinet with a set of glass-enclosed shelves. It was dusty. Christine was probably too strung out lately to worry about cleaning her collections.

The cabinet shelves were busy with tiny collectibles. A shelf for fleur-de-lis, a shelf for lovely Limoges boxes and another, which was dedicated to Eiffel Tower–themed miniatures. Grace spotted a pencil sharpener, a paperweight, a rhinestone pin, coasters, and a lamp finial.

Grace took a step closer and peered through the glass at the bronze finial shaped like the Eiffel Tower. Her hand flew to her chest. Danielle's lamp had been made in France. She had said that the finial would indicate the kind of shade she wanted Grace to paint. But there wasn't a finial at the murder scene. Grace reached down and grasped the cabinet's key and turned it clockwise until the door gave and she pulled it open. Everything on the shelf was dusty. Except, that is, the Eiffel Tower finial.

For a second the room seemed to tilt. The thoughts that had been spinning in her head the last few days suddenly came together. Could this be the finial that was missing from the crime scene at Danielle's house? Danielle had said it was going to be a gift for a friend. Perhaps a friend who loved all things French? She didn't have all the answers, but she now knew without a doubt, that Christine killed Danielle and taken the finial as a souvenir. She shuddered. She'd make an excuse to get the hell out of here and then she'd call Andre. She was closing the glass door when she heard Christine's voice behind her.

"Don't move," she said. "I've got a knife."

Grace froze as she felt the cold, hard steel of the blade against her neck.

"That's good," Christine said. "Now I'm going to have to figure out what to do with you. I thought I could play along with you and get you out of here. I'd accept your gracious offer to help me with my drug problem and make a show of going to a few meetings and all would be fine. But I see you've found my finial. It did occur to me that you might know Danielle's lamp had one, and I knew from your father's outburst at the funeral that you were investigating the murder, to free that dope fiend that you hired from Pinewood. But until now, I thought the chance of you putting two and two together would be a long shot. No one would connect me with Danielle's murder, and your employee or this orange-haired guy, whoever he is, would get blamed."

"He's dead."

"Oh. Well. No matter. Now turn around slowly."

Grace did as she was told and faced Christine, who was holding a large serrated kitchen knife up to her throat. "I wanted you to see that I'm not bluffing," she said. "Turn around again and put your hands behind you."

Christine wrapped a few feet of twine around Grace's wrists. She meant business, all right. The twine was already cutting into her flesh. "You killed Danielle?" Grace tried to make her voice sound stronger than she felt. "I thought she was your friend."

"She was no friend," Christine hissed. "Not that arrogant witch. Just because she quit doing meth and I couldn't."

"Danielle used meth too?" Grace asked doubtfully.

"Of course she did. Who do you think I got it from? A man with orange hair? Give me a break." She turned Grace around again. "Danielle would get some stuff and we'd party. I don't know where she got it. But it was always good. I was hooked. It was cheap and I liked being thin."

"But I don't understand. Why did you kill her?"

Christine sighed theatrically. "She quit a few weeks ago. She wouldn't tell me where she got the stuff because she wanted me to quit too." She laughed. "Why should I quit just because she does? Danielle was like that. She always thought she was better than anyone else. Parisian born, high society and all that. So she cut me off. I was desperate for a fix, so I went over to her house early on Sunday, begged her to give me the name of her connection and she refused."

Grace saw Christine's fist tighten on the knife, and knew that she was deadly serious. It was a terrifying thought.

"I used up the last of my supply. I was desperate," she went on, almost as if she were talking to herself. "Tweaking, I guess it's called. We had an argument, and she said she was going to call the police. I couldn't let her do that, could I? It was easier than I would have thought to kill her. When she got up to use the phone, I grabbed a heavy lamp and hit her with it. I hadn't set out to kill her, but all she had to do was help me out. After that, I searched around to see if she had any drugs in the house. I found a small stash in the armoire. That's been keeping me going all week. I would have looked around for more, but I heard those kids outside shoveling snow. I did manage to sneak back in later Sunday night, but I couldn't find anything. She must have hidden it good. So anyway, I took off my coat — there was blood on it — and went out the side door. I crossed the street and went through the cemetery. I thought the boys might have seen me, but I guess they were busy in the front. I stashed my coat and gloves in my barn and was back inside my house in a matter of minutes," Christine rasped. "That Danielle. Holding out on me. It's her own fault that she's dead. She liked her party time just as much as I did. Who did she think she was? I have no regrets."

She wasn't rational, of course. Grace knew this reaction all too well. The best she could do now was to keep Christine talking.

"I think she was having the lamp fixed up for you as a Christmas present."

"Really? Who cares?"

"And you couldn't resist taking the finial."

"You got that right. It rolled across the carpet and I scooped it up. A lovely addition to my collection. I've washed it so no one will find blood on it."

"Ever hear of luminol?"

"Luminol? No."

"Detectives use it at crime scenes. It's a chemical that glows when it comes into contact with blood. Even though the finial was washed, blood probably seeped into the crevices."

"That's interesting. But I'm sure I won't have to worry about anyone coming here and checking out my Eiffel Tower collection." Christine opened a drawer in a round table near the blue velvet chair. She pulled out a roll of packing tape.

"What are you going to do?" Grace cried out. "Don't make things worse for yourself. You can get help. It's not too late. I know people who can give you the help you need. We can work this out."

"It is too late, Grace," Christine said grimly, taping her mouth. "Too late for you, anyway. Come on. You can sit in my nice cold barn while I figure out what to do with you. Now walk!" she commanded.

Chapter Forty-Eight

THE BARN WAS a cavernous space, dark and damp. Christine guided Grace past a couple of vehicles and shoved her into a small room that had once been a horse stall. The floor was dirt. There were no windows. It was empty.

"Hold still." Christine said, wrapping twine tightly around Grace's ankles. "The temperature is supposed to drop below zero tonight. I don't think it will take too long for you to freeze out here. Then I'll figure out a way to dump your body in the ocean or a pond. There are hundreds of ponds on Cape Cod. No one will ever find you."

When Christine slid the bolt back into place, Grace knew real fear. She'd only been in the barn a few minutes and she was already starting to shiver. Beads of cold sweat broke out on her temples. At least she had on her jacket. That might buy her a little time.

She was comforted by the thought that surely Bella and Michael would come looking for her when she didn't return to the shop. After all, they knew where she had gone and that she intended to come right back. She told Michael to save some coffee. She'd have to stay as warm as she could until help arrived.

Grace tried hopping around the room. The pain in her wrists was intensifying. She wiggled her fingers as much as she could and performed every Pilates, yoga and stretch exercise that she could remember and that was possible with tied hands and feet. She did this for a long time, until she sank, tired, back onto the ground.

She had begun to shake harder now, and her teeth were chattering. She realized, during her shamble around the perimeter of the old stall, that even if Bella and Michael came looking for her,

Christine would simply tell them that she had been there and left. At some point in their search, they'd go by her house and then back to the shop. They'd try her cell phone, but it would ring unanswered in her purse, which she'd left on Christine's library floor. Maybe they'd call her father or Audrey. All this would take a lot of time. Furthermore, they probably wouldn't call anyone right away, assuming that she was off doing other errands.

Her heart aching, Grace knew that she had to save herself. Spotting a small hole in the wall near the bare floor, she noticed that one of the planks surrounding it had a jagged edge. She hopped over, turned around, eased herself to the floor and began to work her arms up and down. She cut her hands on the rough board, managing to loosen the knot about an inch, but giving her hands slightly more range of motion. Blood was running down her fingers and her whole body was aching. She felt exhausted and the tape was stinging her face and lips. Her eyes filled up with water. She closed them as tears slid down her face, then froze on her cheeks. She was beginning to lose hope.

Chapter Forty-Nine

THERE DIDN'T APPEAR to be any chance that Christine would come to her senses. She'd killed once. And she was right about one thing. With Grace out of the way, who would suspect her, a nice, middle-class woman who was grieving for her lost friend? Grace rested her head on her knees and felt fear course through her body. And then she heard Sophie's voice calling "Stanley!"

Grace bolted upright. There was no way she could scream, given the tape across her mouth. But then, as she pressed herself against the shed wall, she felt something in her pocket. The bell! The bell she had taken from the door of the shop and forgotten.

She stretched her arms out behind her back as far as she could, and then groped around until she could reach her pocket. Extending her fingers as far as possible she maneuvered them into her pocket and grasped the bell. She carefully pulled it out. There was only one way to ring it. With energy Grace never knew she possessed, she began to jump up and down.

She heard the bolt slide back on the door and in a minute, Sophie was inside the stall. "Oh, gosh!" she heard Sophie gasp. "I'll go and get Mrs. Sinclair. She'll help you."

Grace shook her head vigorously. "Mmmmmph!" she said.

Sophie reached up to Grace's face and grabbed hold of the tape. She still had her mittens on and couldn't get a good grip. Crying in frustration she pulled off the right one, and with shaking hands tugged on the tape until it came off.

"Sophie!" Grace gasped. "Thank God you found me. Do you think you can get my hands lose?"

"I think so," she said in a loud whisper. Grace felt the twine loosen around her sore wrists. "Thanks," she exhaled. Sophie was staring at her bloodied hands.

"We've got to get out of here," Grace said. "Christine might come back." She flopped down on the ground and began untying the rope from around her ankles. She pulled her legs free as she heard a door slam. Someone was coming from the house toward the barn. Too late to run. Not with Sophie. Too dangerous. Christine was armed with a knife. There was no place to hide in the empty stall.

"Do as I say," she told Sophie, shoving her through the stall door and into the main section of the barn. "Secure the bolt and hide behind the car. Hurry! And be quiet!"

As soon as she heard the bolt slide back in place, Grace sat down and looped the twine around her ankles. She leaned back against the wall with her hands behind her. She put her head down and hoped that Christine wouldn't notice that the tape was no longer covering her mouth.

Her heart was pounding so fast she was sure that it would burst through her chest. She heard a shuffling noise, and then Christine was standing in the doorway. The blade of her knife flashed in the beam of her flashlight.

"Good thing I came to check on you," Christine said, "I thought I heard a noise out here. The wind blew the front door of the barn open. Can't have the neighbors noticing, now can we? This time I'll be sure to padlock the big doors. I must say you're looking pretty cold, Grace. I checked the thermostat on the way out here. It's ten degrees and dropping! Good night! Sleep tight!"

Christine closed the door. Grace heard the bolt slide back again. She held her breath as Christine walked back to the outer barn door, listening for the door to close. And when she did, she called Sophie.

The wooden bolt slipped back again and Sophie rushed in. Her cheeks were flushed and her eyes were bright and shiny. Grace put her finger up to her lips to sign for Sophie to be quiet. She whispered, "We're going to look around here and see if there is a way we can get out. Stay close to me." Grace stepped into the large central barn area. She walked around the edges of the large space with Sophie gripping the hem of her jacket. They stumbled over piles of boxes and old furniture in the dim light. The back wall was full of farm implements, a clamming rake, ladders, old harnesses and even a saddle. Faint light poured through the rafters and through some cracks in the wall but it was getting dark fast. There was little time to find a way out. She heard Sophie start to cry.

"Sophie, I'm going to get you out of here. There doesn't seem to be a back door, and the front is padlocked. We're going to go back to the stall and you're going to crawl through the hole in the corner."

Pulling Sophie along, Grace ran back into the stall and kneeled down in front of the hole. "This is our only chance. You've got to squeeze through the opening."

"I'm too fat! I can't do it!" Sophie whispered.

Grace grabbed Sophie by her puffy pink sleeves. "You can do this, Sophie. You are not too fat. Now, take off your coat."

Sophie did as she was told.

"Now your sweater. Okay. Lie down and try to inch your way through the hole."

Sophie squatted down and looked doubtfully at the hole. "I don't think I can."

"Of course you can. Put your mittens on. When you get outside I'll pass your jacket out to you. Put it on and follow the path behind the barn that goes into town. Be sure to stay out of sight of Christine's house. You've been on that path before, haven't you?"

Sophie nodded. "I think so."

"You'll find it. Straight back behind the barn, then turn left. You know your left, don't you?" Sophie held up a blue knitted mitten with snowflakes. "Good," Grace said. The mitten reminded Grace of how young and vulnerable Sophie was. She hated to send her out alone, but she had to get her out of the barn, and fast. "The path will bring you to the Dolphin. Go in the back door and straight to the bar. Tell the bartender to call the police. Tell them I'm locked in Christine's barn. Tell them that Christine is a bad person. Okay?"

When Grace gave her a hug, she felt the girl trembling through her blouse. "Run fast. Don't stop until you get to the Dolphin. You'll be there in a few minutes."

Here's your jacket," Grace shoved the pink garment through the hole. "Be careful as you run by the marsh, and don't talk to anyone until you get to the Dolphin. We can't trust anyone now, Sophie."

Chapter Fifty

G RACE'S HANDS WERE stiff. She wondered if the stiffness was a sign of hypothermia. She took Sophie's sweater and wrapped it around her head. She had read somewhere that covering your head would slow down heat trying to escape from your body. She got up and started out toward the main part of the barn again. Christine could come back any time; she couldn't wait for help to arrive. She closed the bolt to the stall. If Christine did return, she wouldn't notice right away that Grace managed to get out.

Hoping to find some clothes or blankets, Grace stumbled around the barn, almost falling over a pile of bricks. As she steadied herself, she observed what appeared to be a workshop. She rushed over. There was a large flannel shirt and a pair of garden gloves. She put them on. She was pulling on a pair of baggy soiled khakis when she thought she heard the back door of the house open and then shut.

She dove behind one of the cars. Her heart pounded wildly again. She heard the crunch of someone walking on the snow. Then a shuffling, knocking sound and the barn door scraped open. She saw Christine's thin frame backlit by the falling snow. The knife was in her outstretched hand.

"Where the hell are you?" Christine's voice was shrill. "I heard a noise out here! You better not be up to something, Grace Tolliver!" she said.

Grace crouched down. She saw Christine pull back the bolt and step into the empty stall. Holding her breath, she turned around and searched the rough wall behind her with her fingers. Her hands shook as she reached up and gripped a long, heavy handle.

"What the hell!" Christine turned back to the door as Grace ran up and shoved the clamming rake against her neck, making sure that Christine felt the cold steel prongs against her fair skin.

"Back up Christine! And drop the knife!"

Christine hesitated.

"I said drop it!" Grace said in her most commanding voice. "And back up all the way to the wall! And don't think I won't run this right through you if you so much as move a muscle."

"What are you going to do?" Christine wailed. "You can't leave me in here! I'll freeze!"

"That would be the idea," Grace said as she closed the door and slid the bolt across.

"Help! Help me, someone!" Christine shouted.

"Yell all you want, Christine. The cops are here," Grace called back over her shoulder.

Radios crackled and red lights flashed as Grace stepped out in front of the barn and held her hands in the air. It was a precaution she would have taken even if she hadn't had Sophie's sweater tied around her head and wasn't wearing the enormous flannel shirt, gardening gloves and baggy pants.

"Grace!" Andre's voice was clear as a bell above the din.

She smiled into the headlights that flooded Christine's driveway.

Chapter Fifty-One

"PHEW!" AUDREY SAID, as she flopped down on the Martha Washington chair, her flute in her lap. "I had no idea so many folks would turn out for the Village Stroll. I'm exhausted. I must have packaged and wrapped twenty lamps and a dozen shades. In between musical numbers, of course."

"You were a big help," Grace told her. "We couldn't have survived without you. And your music was beautiful. Dad, you were great too. I love that you wore a tuxedo to greet the customers."

"Thank you, Gracie, I thought it would add a touch of class to the event. I think I've got some good photographs too."

"Hey, I just remembered," Audrey said. "I brought some salads and sandwiches last night but we didn't eat them because we were too worried about you. I put them in the refrigerator. We can add them to the leftover cookies and brownies that Michael brought in this morning. Anybody hungry?" She pulled herself to the edge of her chair.

"Now that you mention it, Audrey, I am feeling a bit peckish," Michael said.

"I could do with some sustenance," Bella joined in. She removed her red and white Santa Claus hat from her head and fluffed up her hair.

"Sandwiches coming up!" Audrey announced, leaping out of her chair and heading off to the kitchen.

"The tree lighting ceremony starts in about an hour," Michael said. "I think we can clean up by then." Despite a long, busy day, Michael's voice was chipper.

"Leave everything where it is," Grace told him. "Shop's closed tomorrow and Monday. You and Bella have both been amazing. And the shop looks so beautiful." She looked around the room at the tasteful white lights and evergreens, her eyes filling with tears.

When the phone rang, Michael answered it and mouthed, *It's Matt and Milo.* "Yes, The Stroll was absolutely wonderful," he told them cheerfully. "We sold a lot of lamps. But wait until I tell you what happened yesterday! You won't believe it!" He took the phone to the other end of the room, sat down and appeared to relish telling M and M all about Christine and Blake, Sophie and Grace.

"Bella filled me in on most of what happened yesterday, but I have a question," Grace's father said as he parked himself down in the chair that had been vacated by Audrey. "How did the little girl find you in Christine's barn?"

Grace reached in her pocket and pulled out the bell that had hung on the shop's front door for more than a quarter of a century. She gave it a ring. "Ta-da!" she said. "I took this off the door earlier in the week because I found it annoying."

"I bet it wasn't so annoying when you found it in your pocket last night," Audrey observed as she joined them, looking around for a place to set down a large platter.

"I'm going to get a new bell for the door. Michael was right. It's a good security feature. But I'm going to keep this one with me as a lucky charm," Grace said, shoving the bell back into her pocket. "But it was Sophie who saved the day. She was so brave. She ran all the way to the Dolphin and stormed right up to the bar. She told the bartender to call the police and he did. After that, he called Sophie's parents, and by the time they got there, Sophie was wrapped in a blanket and sipping hot chocolate. When I saw her later at the police station, she was remarkably calm. She was able to tell the officers everything that happened and in great detail. She's a strong little girl."

"That she is," echoed Bella. "And she was thrilled with the fairy lamp you gave her this morning. I thought for sure she'd choose the owl with the red eyes but when she saw that new wee-sized gray and white cat she had to have it. Two and a half inches high and an amazing look-alike for Stanley. Perfect for her."

"Matt and Milo said they knew Christine was the killer all along," Michael said, returning the phone to its stand. "They said they always thought she was odd."

"Wait a minute," Grace said. "What happened to their theory that Valerie Elkins was the murderer?"

"Oh, that was on Monday," Michael said with a dismissive wave of his hand. "On Tuesday, they told me they thought it was Danielle's new boyfriend. On Wednesday, they thought it was a snowplow driver. On Thursday, I believe they thought it was a florist. And yesterday, they were convinced it was someone connected with her New York days. Now that Christine has been arrested, well …" Michael paused. "They always knew it was her." He chuckled. "They've made up with Valerie too. She told them that Howard is listing Danielle's home with her. She's pretty sure the people who wanted it before when Danielle changed her mind are still interested. And, you know …"

He broke off at the sound of heavy boots pounding up the stairs. Duane Kerbey burst in, punched his arms in the air in a Rocky salute and yelled, "Yes! Yes! I'm free! Free at last!" He took off his blue ski cap and tossed it in the air. "Thank you, Miss Tolliver!" His cap went flying out of his reach and as he went to catch it, he knocked over the display of finials. Small elephants, frogs, baseballs, sailboats, horses, shells and spheres scattered everywhere. "Oops!" he said. "Gosh, Miss Tolliver. I'm sorry. I'm so excited to be back here with all of my friends!" He got down on his knees and crawled around the floor.

Michael let out an audible sigh. He raised his eyebrows at Bella as he went to get the broom from behind the door.

"I'm going to have me a sandwich," Bella said as she grabbed a croissant stuffed with chicken salad.

"Come on, Thomas, help yourself before Duane gets to them." Audrey said to Grace's father.

"It's okay, Duane," Grace said, getting down on her knees beside him. "I don't think much of anything is broken and if it is, I am not going to worry about it." She picked up a finial with a feather design. "Are you ready to come back to work?"

"Really? Can I?" Duane exclaimed.

"Absolutely. Check with Sean to see if Tuesday would be good."

"I will, Miss Tolliver."

"And Duane. Please call me Grace. Okay? That's what my other employees call me."

"Will do, Miss Tolliver."

Grace sighed and stood up. In the commotion caused by Duane's arrival, she hadn't noticed that his friend Gink was standing quietly by the top of the stairs. Dressed in black jeans, boots and jacket, with her tattoos and piercings, she looked uncomfortable among the antique lamps.

"Hey, Gink. It's good to see you again. Come on in and join us for some sandwiches."

"Thanks," Gink said.

Grace's father gestured toward the table of food. "Yes, young lady, there's plenty left."

"Is someone having a party?" Clay Davenport said, appearing at the top of the stairs. He strode vigorously into the room and went directly to the table of food, a Pearl's shopping bag dangling from the crook of his left elbow. "What have we here? Michael's brownies? I can't resist." He daintily picked up a brownie with his leather-clad fingers, closed his eyes, took a sniff and then popped it into his mouth. "Heavenly," he said. "I've been to every shop in town and you have the best spread. Although I must say that the free hot dogs down the street are of exceptional quality this year. Oh, goodness," he added, catching sight of Duane, who was shoving finials back into their case. "Are you back?"

"Yes, sir!" Duane said.

"And you're working here?"

"Yup!"

Clay looked him up and down. "Then get me a cup of coffee." He held up an empty pot. "This needs refilling."

"There's another pot in the kitchen, Clay. Go and get it yourself," Grace said. "Duane's not working until Tuesday."

Clay looked stunned. He lowered the pot and appeared to

weigh his options. Thirst or humiliation.

"I can get it," Duane said, taking the pot from Clay and sprinting off to the kitchen with a surprising show of initiative.

"Well, Grace," Clay gushed, comfortable again. "Everyone in town is abuzz with your misadventures."

"Adventures," Bella corrected him.

"Whatever. Who would have thought that Danielle and Christine were using drugs? Shocking really, that activities of that sort were going on in the village."

It was, Grace thought, a remarkable display of hypocrisy, but she held her tongue. There wasn't any point in exposing her knowledge of Clay's arrest for cocaine. Clay was Clay. She couldn't change him. There was good change, bad change, unfortunate change and no change. Clay was of the no-change variety.

Brushing the crumbs from his hands onto the just-swept floor, Clay walked to Bella's counter and opened the Pearl's bag. With great deliberation he pulled out the pink feather tropical lamp. "I'm afraid my customer doesn't want this lamp." He sniffed, propping it up on the ledge. "She's changed her mind. In fact, she wants her money back."

"But I stayed up all night finishing that lamp!" Grace protested. "What doesn't your client like about it?"

"She's decided to go with a southwest design and of course, this simply won't do. You must agree."

"But you assured me that there wouldn't be a problem," Grace persisted. "This was a very special order. It might be hard for me to sell it."

"I'll buy it."

All conversation in the room stopped. Andre Cruz appeared at the top of the stairs, walked to Clay and took the frilly lamp out of his hand. "How much, Grace?"

"Andre! I didn't hear you come in," Grace said. "Really, you don't have to. I mean, I can't see this lamp in your house. But it was nice of you to offer."

"No. I want it." He looked at Clay as if he was a spider in need of a stomping. "I like it."

Clay shrugged his shoulders and seemed to wither under Andre's gaze. He started to say something, but instead retreated to the plate of brownies.

Andre looked at Grace. "Can I talk to you for a minute?" He put the lamp down on Bella's counter. "Alone, please."

When the door had closed behind them, Grace offered Andre the folding chair, but he shook his head and leaned against the doorframe. His hands were in the pockets of the same long overcoat he had worn when she saw him almost a week ago striding through the gates at Danielle's house. He looked at her with solemn intensity.

"You okay?"

"Sure. Sore wrists and ankles, that's all." She smiled, but she felt her eyes tear up. Andre stepped forward, closing the gap between them, and took her in his arms.

"Oh, darn, I didn't mean to get emotional," she said into his shoulder. They stood still for a moment, Grace breathing in the crisp, outdoorsy, warm wool smell of Andre.

"You've been through a lot. It might take a while for you to feel normal again," he said.

"Normal? I've never felt normal in my life." That was certainly true, she thought, but if this — hugging Andre — was normal, she was pretty sure she could get used to it.

"I've got some good news for you," Andre said as they awkwardly pulled away from one another. "When we searched Blake's motel room we found some things you reported missing from your house after the burglary. You'll have to come to the station and go through it. He didn't have much time to pawn anything, so maybe it's all there. He probably burgled your house to scare you off. Not that it worked."

They both started at a loud crash coming from the kitchen, followed a few seconds later by "Damn! I mean darn!" and then Duane opened her door and stuck his head in Grace's office. He looked warily at Andre. "You're not going to arrest me, are you?" he asked.

"I don't know, Duane. Is there any reason I should?"

"Nope. But I broke your coffee pot, Miss Tolliver. It flew out of my hand. I'll buy you another one," he said

"The coffee pot was Michael's," Grace said. "I'm afraid you'll have to answer to him."

"You were right about Duane all along." Andre said as Duane disappeared, muttering something about how Michael was going to kill him. "We interviewed Morris Bidlake again. It's clear from his statement that Duane didn't have time to kill Danielle. And Duane was right about one thing. Danielle probably was busy in the bathroom the first time he came by.

"Christine may have entered Danielle's house through the back entrance," he continued. "Her footprints would have been shoveled away by the boys. And they had reported seeing her come out of her barn a short time later. And that business with the missing finial. We might never have figured out that the most important clue and piece of evidence wasn't even at the crime scene."

"Do you have the tests on the finial back yet?" Grace asked him, although if she were honest with herself, she would have admitted that finials were the last thing on her mind right now.

"Yeah. The blood type matches Danielle's. No surprise there. We'll have to wait for further tests for confirmation, of course. Christine told us you planted the finial in her cabinet to frame her and to cover up for Duane."

"She's not lacking in creativity, is she?"

"No, but we found a bloody coat and gloves buried in the barn," Andre said. "Not likely you buried them there."

"Especially with my hands tied behind my back."

"I suspect she'll be talking soon," Andre mused. "Her lawyer will want to make some kind of deal. Right now she's not saying a whole lot. That meth. It's bad stuff. It can make your heart turn to stone. During our investigation, several folks commented on Danielle's recent mood changes too."

"Yes, it's sad," Grace agreed. "Secret addictions. A lot of pain." She hesitated. "Did you ever find her diary during the search of her house?"

"No. I bet the priest has it stashed somewhere."

"Yes. And another thing I've been wondering about. How come there wasn't evidence of Danielle's drug use in the initial toxicology report?"

"Actually, there was."

"You mean you knew all along that Danielle was using drugs? And you didn't tell me?"

"Couldn't tell you everything," Andre said. "You know that."

"I guess," Grace admitted. "Did D.A. Banks know?"

"Sure. It didn't keep her from thinking that Duane was the killer, though she knew we were investigating further. There was always the problem of motive. We even played with the idea that Duane was Danielle's drug connection. The idea that he might have wanted to rob Danielle to help Gink was a possibility, but it always seemed like a long shot. The real break on our side came when you gave us that information about Blake's prior arrest with Terry and Sean. Terry admitted that he had sold drugs to Danielle. He said he knew she shared them with Christine. At first he denied murdering anyone, of course, but we found cartridges on the ground near Blake's body that matched a gun found in Terry's room at Pinewood."

"Wow. I guess they better start searching everyone's room over there. Not just the residents."

"I think Sean got that message loud and clear. In the future there will be checks of everyone's living quarters. Staff included."

"I remember Gink telling me that she left Pinewood because she was being harassed. Do you think Terry was trying to involve her in his dealing activities?"

"Don't know for sure, but it's a possibility. We haven't had time to talk to her again. But she told us she was in the program for alcohol problems. Terry would have looked for a non–drug user to work for him. They make the best dealers."

"She probably wouldn't have told Duane either. She knew he was doing well, and she didn't want to mess up his probation if he left Pinewood too." Grace knew she was just speculating, but this scenario made sense to her. She hesitated. Something was on her mind, and she had to come forward with it. Now seemed as good a time as any.

"About that information on Sean, Terry and Blake. I got it from San Francisco Probation," Grace said. "The probation officer I talked to didn't know that I'm no longer a P.O. He assumed I was. If he knew, he never would have faxed me that information. I don't want him to get into any trouble over this."

"Don't worry. If it comes up at trial, I'm sure the prosecutor will be able to handle it. He's not going to get into any trouble."

"What about me?"

"Did you misrepresent yourself as law enforcement?"

"No. I evaded the whole issue."

"Really, Grace. Don't worry about it. It's done. Two murders have been solved."

"Okay." Grace said and relaxed a bit. "But why did Terry kill Blake?"

"We're still putting the pieces together, but according to Terry's story, Blake was his drug connection. He looked Terry up at Pinewood and convinced him to work for him. Blake was moving large amounts of drugs into Cape Cod. We found a cache of methamphetamine manufacturing supplies in his motel room. After Danielle was murdered, Terry told Blake he was going to get out of the drug-dealing business. That was when Blake tried to blackmail him. Threatened to expose him." Andre paused. "Terry was supposed to make his first payment on Thursday night out on Sandy Neck. He brought a gun along because he knew Blake was a tough customer and he didn't trust him. He says he paid Blake but that Blake wanted more. They got into a fight and Terry shot him. He says it was self-defense."

"He shot him in the back of the head, didn't he?"

"Yeah."

Grace shook her head. "How did Terry ever hook up with Danielle in the first place?"

"He claims that she approached him at a fundraiser and told him what she was looking for. According to him, Danielle told him she used diet pills and cocaine years ago in New York. She told him she was planning on reigniting her modeling career and was hoping to lose some extra pounds."

"Do you believe him?"

"No reason not to." Andre's phone rang. "That was Emma. They want us at the lighting ceremony."

"Oh, sure," Grace said. She felt a slight stab of uneasiness. She hated to feel jealous. After all, she and Andre had shared nothing more than a brief kiss and a hug. But, there it was, rearing its ugly green head.

"Are you going to be there?" he asked.

"Absolutely," she assured him. "I wouldn't miss it for the world."

"How much do I owe you for the lamp?"

"You don't want that lamp. But thanks."

"No, I do want it, and I'm taking it with me. Unless I could come by your house later and pick it up?"

Grace smiled at him.

"I'll see you later then, Gracie," He kissed her on her lips and strode out of the office.

And all she could think of was that he had called her Gracie. Not Grace.

But Gracie.

Chapter Fifty-Two

MICHAEL WAS TURNING off the lights, and everyone was piling on hats, coats and gloves getting ready for the short chilly walk to the lighting ceremony. Grace peered out the front window. Main Street was full of people milling around enjoying themselves. It was early evening and the streetlights had come on. The wind from the bay had picked up, and snow was falling rapidly, adding another layer to the three feet already on the ground. Kids were throwing snowballs at each other as their parents gazed into glowing shop windows, sipping steaming cups of hot chocolate and coffee drinks. Grace spotted Clay in the free hot dog line behind Rafael and Jose. Father Murrey, bundled up in a plaid wool coat, was helping out behind the grill, turning hot dogs, and chatting with the hungry crowd.

Sophie and Jill were standing in front of Morris's door. Jill held a large box. She watched as Morris opened the door and Jill handed him the carrier. She couldn't see his expression but she knew a new cat would go a long way to help Morris cope with his demons.

"Congratulations, honey," Grace's father said, coming up behind her and giving her a warm hug. "Your first holiday event in your own shop was a huge success. I'm so proud of you. But most importantly, I'm so thankful you're all right. You know I worry about you all the time."

"You worry about me?" Grace said with surprise. "I'm okay. I can take care of myself. It's you I worry about."

"Well, then, you're going to love this new idea I have," he told her.

Grace groaned. "Trekking to the North Pole? Scaling Mount Everest?"

"Those are good ideas, but maybe next year. For now, I've decided that you're right. I could use some help around the house. You know, cooking, cleaning, driving." He looked across the room. "Gink has agreed to come and work for me."

"Oh!" Grace exclaimed. Maybe Gink was very capable, but she would need to find out more about the girl. She had, after all, been living at Pinewood because of an alcohol problem. And what kind of a name was Gink, anyway? Gink was an unknown at this point, but Grace didn't want to ruin her father's plan. At least he was now open to the idea of getting help. And he'd clearly made a connection with Gink. She'd just have to see.

"Hello?" Beau Henderson's lean frame appeared above the stair railing.

"Hey, Beau, come on in," Grace said, welcoming her down-stairs neighbor. "Michael, could you flip the lights back on? Beau's here."

"Hello, everybody," Beau said. "I don't want to keep you all from the festivities. I'm on my way there myself. But Grace, if you don't mind, may I have a quick word with you?"

"Sure, what's on your mind, Beau?"

"I have an idea that I want to run by you," he got right to the point as soon as they were alone together. "My business is pretty slow these days, but I'm not ready to quit yet. The competition from the big stores is fierce, but I think if I specialize in books about Cape Cod and the Islands — you know, the history, the painters, writers, sailors, architecture, food and everything — maybe I could turn Beau's Books into a destination."

Beau spoke rapidly with increasing enthusiasm. "I want to carry old and new books. Everything Cape Cod." He paused to catch his breath. "The reason I'm telling you this is that I wondered if you would be interested in trading places? I could move up here. The space is smaller, and I'd be willing to give up my street-side location. Presumably, the rent would be less, and it would take some pressure off of me while I get established."

It was, Grace thought, an interesting proposal, particularly since, thanks to an addition, the downstairs had an extra room. Also, she could display her lamps and shades in the two bay windows. And her customers wouldn't have to trudge up and down her steep stairs.

"That sounds like a great idea, Beau," she said. "Let's go and see what the others have to say about it."

As they walked down the hallway to the main room, Beau turned to Grace. "I just wanted to say you did a good thing, helping Duane get out of jail. He's a good kid. I have a sense about people. He's okay."

Grace nodded. She wanted to ask him what his sense told him about Gink but decided it could wait for another time.

"Hey, Beau's got the most interesting idea," Grace said, rejoining the others. "What would you all think if I moved the shop downstairs and Beau came up here?"

Michael spoke up immediately. "It's a wonderful idea. Street level is so much better for a shop like this. And I wouldn't have to escort old ladies up and down the stairs with their bundles. Not that I mind, of course."

"I'll help with the moving," her father said. "If Grace won't let me buy a boat or raise goats, I might as well be helpful around here."

Bella cleared her throat noisily and took a deep breath. "Grace, if you move downstairs, I'll stay on. Those stairs are getting steeper and steeper every day. But the last week has been so stimulating, I couldn't possibly retire. I feel positively rejuvenated! Retirement would bore me to death"

"Beau, how do you feel about sharing space with mice?"

"Mice don't bother me," he said.

"Well, then, it's settled. If Bella is going to stay on, I don't need to think about it for another minute." Up until that moment, she hadn't realized how important it was to her to keep their threesome intact.

There was a round of applause as everyone congratulated each other on the day's efforts and the new plan for the future. Duane rushed downstairs and held the door as Grace, Audrey, Gink, Bella,

Michael and Beau piled out of the warm shop and joined the knots of people moving down the street. Bella started to sing "Deck the Halls" in her proudest moose-like voice; Thomas, Michael and Beau were engaged in a conversation about winter weather patterns on Cape Cod and Duane was whispering in Gink's ear, causing her to laugh. Grace caught a glimpse of Andre and Emma a block or so ahead of them. The jealousy was there, but it was only a pale green now. She could still feel Andre's cheek against hers.

In a few minutes, they had reached Danielle's house. Grace said. "I'll catch up with you all. I'll just be a minute."

She reached in her pocket and wrapped her fingers around the bell that had saved her life. "I wish you could have had something to save you too, Danielle," she said softly. She took the bell out of her pocket and hung it on the gate. Grace stood there a moment and watched as a thin layer of snow formed on its curved edge. Then, pulling up the collar of her jacket, she wrapped her scarf tighter around her neck and headed down the street.

About the Author

Patricia Driscoll was born in Westport, Connecticut. She spent many summer vacations on Cape Cod and her family relocated there in 1970. After graduating from the University of San Francisco, she worked for many years as a probation officer for the San Francisco Probation Department. *Shedding Light on Murder* is her first novel.

Patricia lives in northern California with her husband, a retired police inspector. Visit her website at www.PatriciaDriscoll.com.